ALSO BY KEVIN ROBERT ALDRICH

Mysteries & Thrillers

CAMERON HAUK MYSTERIES

Eyes in the Dark

Key Witness

Scale of Justice

Tête A Tête

Burden of Proof

Romance

Flames of Freedom

Bare Trap

Spellbound

Racing Hearts

Alli & Ollie

BURDEN OF PROOF

KEVIN ROBERT ALDRICH

Burden of Proof

Copyright © 2024 by Kevin Robert Aldrich
Published by Aldys Books
Cover and layout © 2024 by Aldys Books
Cover design by Payton Shay/Aldys Books
Front cover art © Vacclav | Depositphotos
Back cover art © sepavone | Depositphotos

ISBN: 978-1-965387-99-3 (Hardcover)
ISBN: 979-8-9870927-9-8 (Trade paperback)

This book is licensed for your personal enjoyment only. All rights reserved.

Burden of Proof is a work of fiction. Names, characters, places, and incidents either are the product of the author's imagination or are used fictitiously. Any resemblance to actual persons, living or dead, events, or locales is purely coincidental.

No part of this book may be reproduced in any form or by any electronic or mechanical means, including information storage and retrieval systems, without written permission from the author, except for the use of brief quotations in a book review.

WARNING TO SENSITIVE READERS

This novel contains the following elements, which may be disturbing to some readers:

- Swearing
- Sexual situations and innuendo (mildly graphic)

BURDEN OF PROOF

For Holly, Jayda, and Taegon

PART I

1

It was the first Christmas Celina Maxwell had spent with her boyfriend, Cameron Hauk.

Boyfriend. She still got stuck on that word.

Twenty-eight years old and Cam was the first boyfriend Celina had ever had.

Not for lack of offers. There was an endless line of men trying to get into Celina's pants, and every one would have killed the guy in front of them to be her boyfriend. And why not? She was a hot piece of ass. And rich, on top of that. A fucking hot, rich piece of ass.

But she didn't give a fuck about men. She was a fuck 'em and chuck 'em kind of gal. Men were needy and insecure and generally stupid. And they were the worst kind of stupid, the kind that was too stupid to know they were stupid. As soon as they realized you were smarter than them, as soon as they saw they weren't the center of your world, they would try to dominate you by force of will or force of fist. They'd insult you, overtly or subtly. They'd bully you. They'd gaslight you and try to make you doubt yourself or feel inferior. Or they'd resort to straight up physical intimidation.

Celina had learned a long time ago how to take care of herself. And she'd learned a long time ago not to trust men for shit.

She'd also learned that when a woman who knew what she was doing actually stood up to a man, the man would crumble nine times out of ten. Nine times out of ten, they'd immediately flip from a puffed-up dickhead to the sniveling shitstain they were.

So, no. Celina had never had a boyfriend. She'd had lovers. Lots of them. Some of them more than once. But never a boyfriend.

Until Cam.

Cam was so unlike any man Celina had ever met that she often wondered if he was the same species. Maybe Celina had discovered the next evolution of the male Homo Sapiens. Cam might be the first. Since she'd discovered him, Celina had the right to name his species. Homo Celina. Cam was the very first Homo Celina on record, and Celina had decided to keep him all to herself.

They'd spent that Christmas in Celina's San Francisco beach house. No snow, but plenty of sea spray. Instead of sleigh bells, they heard crashing waves outside the window. When the tree tops glistened, it was from the fog that had rolled in overnight. It wasn't a white Christmas, but it wasn't too shabby, either.

Truth be told, they'd spent most of the day in bed, exchanging gifts. Over and over again. Cam's broken ribs had finally healed from the rifle shot he'd taken in his Kevlar vest two months earlier. The bruise had faded completely, and Cam could finally laugh or take a deep breath without wincing.

Which was a damn good thing, because Celina was starting to go nuts from sitting around the house. They'd been sequestered there for the duration of Cam's recovery. Make no mistake, it was a big house, and there was plenty to do there. A theater room, an art gallery, the lab where she worked on her latest tech projects. There was plenty of tech to play with, a beach out back, a view of the Golden Gate Bridge from the deck. The basement had a full weight room, a training room, and a gun range. There was no reason to be bored, but Celina still found herself antsy after so long in one place. She liked to move, to be engaged in something. A job, a project, anything.

Which is what drew her to her laptop on the morning after Christmas. In the cool, quiet air of the empty house, their tiny three-foot Christmas tree on a table in the corner by the hearth, ornaments winking in the morning sun, she put an empty coffee cup on the tray of the machine and started it brewing. She stood at the counter in the kitchen, bent over the keyboard.

Something had been stolen from Cam. A pair of glasses. Very special glasses. Augmented reality was technically correct, but too narrow a term for what these glasses could do. They could show you any people in your vicinity. They could help you see in the pitch dark. They could magnify text from across the room, let you read over the shoulder of someone a hundred yards ahead of you. They would let you communicate clearly with less than a whisper, and they would identify any weapons or potential weapons that might be around you. That's in addition to the usual things, like face recognition, information overlays, internet searches, and the like. And that was only scratching the surface.

They were very special glasses, and very valuable ones.

Someone had stolen them, and Celina had a pretty good idea who it was.

The glasses had GPS tracking on them, of course. And, of course, the idiots who had stolen them either didn't realize that or hadn't been able to figure out how to turn it off. Which confirmed that they were men.

One man, in particular. Attorney General William Jenkins. Soon to be President William Jenkins, if the election next November played out the way it looked like it would.

Shortly after they'd been stolen, Celina had traced the glasses to Jenkins' office in the Department of Justice building in Washington, D.C. She'd hacked into the security system there and confirmed it with the camera feeds from the office. The glasses had sat there for a little while until Jenkins had finally found someone smart enough to tell him what the glasses were.

Once they started to move again, Celina tracked them to a wealthy town in Westchester County, outside of New York City. To the home of an old acquaintance of Celina's, in fact. Kat Nestrom. A woman.

Which is why the GPS tracking signal stopped shortly after the glasses arrived.

Kat was no fool. She and Celina had led remarkably similar lives. Both the daughters of tech innovators who had changed the world, cashed out when the world got its grubby mitts on their hardware, then changed the world again. Kat's father, Christopher Nestrom, had designed the first PC an actual human would want to use, then essentially perfected the mobile phone. Celina's father had worked on the back-end, pioneering the way information moved through the internet, then developed the cryptographic techniques that were now ubiquitous for information security around the world.

And both, coincidentally, had been working on a pair of augmented reality glasses when they died in sudden, unexpected ways.

When Cam's glasses arrived, Kat did the first thing that Celina would have done. She figured out what signals the glasses were sending and shut them down. From what Celina understood, Christopher Nestrom had turned his workshop into a Faraday cage of sorts. Kat might have brought the glasses down there and got lucky, or she might have actually disabled the GPS. Either way, she'd done the smart thing and switched off Celina's ability to track the glasses.

So, Celina would do the next best thing. She'd contact Kat directly.

Cam came into the kitchen in pajama bottoms and a t-shirt, his bare feet padding over the tile, his shaggy hair still mussed from sleep and sex. He stretched like a cat, his arms reaching up toward the ceiling, lifting the bottom of his shirt to expose the ridged muscles of his belly, the sharp V that led below the waistline of his bottoms. By force of habit and irresistible attraction, Celina's eyes traced the line of that V. Her body instantly heated.

She was addicted to that man. She had no idea why, but she'd given up fighting it a long time ago. It was instinctive. Chemical. She couldn't keep her hands off of him. Couldn't keep her legs off of him. Couldn't keep anything off of him. She wanted to ravage his body every fucking time she saw him, smelled him, heard the low tones of his voice, the heat of his whisper against her ear, the soft touch of his hands on her.

She groaned involuntarily.

Cam came out of his stretch and looked at her, then smiled that sly smile that also drove Celina wild, and walked around the counter to stand behind her. He nuzzled her neck, slipped his hands under her shirt and ran them slowly down the sides of her breasts, across the flat of her belly, under the band of her loose sweatpants and over her bare thighs. Celina let her head loll back, giving Cam more access to her neck. She reached behind and put her hands on his ass, pulled him against her from behind, felt him stiffen.

She was addicted, hopelessly and irrecoverably addicted. There was no point in resisting.

By the time they finished, Celina's bare ass was on the counter, Cam standing naked between her legs. Her coffee was cold on the tray of the coffee maker, the laptop shoved against the backsplash of the counter.

"Good morning," said Cam with a smile once he'd caught his breath.

Celina kissed him deep, sucking hard on his lower lip. "Fucking great morning, I'd say."

"Didn't mean to interrupt you," Cam said, turning to the coffee machine. Celina admired his muscular ass and his long, lithe, wide-shouldered back. He dumped out Celina's cold cup and started another one, then pulled a cup from the cabinet for himself.

"No need to apologize," said Celina, hopping off the counter and collecting her clothes. She grabbed Cam's pants and t-shirt and threw them at him, then dressed herself.

"What were you up to?"

"Working on your glasses," she said.

"Yeah?" He handed her the cup of coffee, then turned back to the machine and started his own. "What did you find out?"

"Jenkins finally pulled his head out of his ass, took them to someone who knows what they're doing."

"Well, he is a busy man. You know, keeping crime off the streets, taking bribes, running for president." He drummed his fingers on the counter while he waited for his coffee. "Who'd he take them to?"

"An old friend of mine," Celina said, leaning against the counter and sipping her drink.

Cam had interrupted her before she'd had her first sip. Sex was always a good thing to wake up to, but the rich, heady scent of the coffee, the smooth bite of it as it hit her tongue, was what Celina's body always craved in the morning.

"The daughter of a friend of my father's," Celina continued. "You met him, actually. You probably met her, too."

"What's her name?" asked Cam, turning and bringing his steaming cup to his lips.

"Her dad was Christopher Nestrom," Celina said, watching those lips slip around the rim of his glass cup. Fucking addicted. "Her name is Kat."

Cam choked a bit on his coffee, and Celina felt a stab of jealousy at the look on his face. She figured he and Kat might have a history. Cam had told her the story of his time with the Nestroms. Two or three Christmases ago, now. It was a good story, full of mystery and intrigue, greed and lies, and a murderous family. And, she had always assumed, a fair amount of sex. Kat and Celina had similar attitudes toward men, and toward sex. And Cam was hard to pass up.

Celina had assumed as much. But seeing it confirmed by the stricken look on Cam's face sent a jolt of jealousy through her that she'd never felt before. Cam was hers. She wasn't about to share. Not even with Cam's past.

It was ridiculous. She had a past riddled with lovers. Cam was entitled to his own. It was unfair of Celina to be jealous of someone Cam had been with years before. Celina was smarter than that. She was bigger than that. Jealousy was something that weak people felt, people who didn't believe in their own worth.

She kept her eyes on Cam's face as he wiped the spilled coffee from his face. She brought her cup to her lips, took another rich, biting sip, and tried to pretend the jealousy she felt wasn't real.

2

CAM NEARLY CHOKED on his coffee when Celina said the name.

Kat Nestrom.

He should have guessed. Perry Maxwell and Christopher Nestrom were the only two people on the planet who could have invented augmented reality glasses that actually worked. And Celina and Kat were the only two people smart enough to continue what their fathers had started.

According to the tech news sites, Perry and Christopher had once been rivals, then had become friends once they'd both become unfathomably wealthy and disillusioned with the tech world. And, according to Celina, William Jenkins had been Perry's political protégé for a time, so it made sense that he would have met the Nestrom family at one point or another. Given the circumstances the last time Celina and Jenkins had met, Jenkins couldn't come to Celina for advice on the glasses. His only recourse would be Kat Nestrom.

The same Kat Nestrom Cam had spent a wild

Christmas with two years earlier. The same Kat Nestrom Cam had slept with, and who hadn't wanted Cam to leave.

The same Kat Nestrom who had helped her family kill their father.

"He took the glasses to Kat?" said Cam.

Celina nodded as she sipped her coffee, her eyes watching Cam closely.

He didn't know why he felt so nervous all of a sudden. Kat was in his past. He'd been with her for three wild days. He'd met her on a train, had never seen her before, and hadn't talked to her since. She didn't even know Cam's real name. He'd been using his Sam Davis alias that whole time. What they had was a fling, an intense, crazy fling. What he had with Celina was real. There was no comparison.

He knew that. And Celina did, too. Didn't she?

"So what do you think we should do?" asked Cam. "Do you want to steal them back?"

Celina shook her head. "That would be fun," she said, "but I don't think it'll be necessary." She took another sip of coffee. "Kat and I go way back. I'll just give her a call."

"And what? Ask her to give the glasses back?"

Celina frowned and nodded slowly.

"You're right," she said. "It probably won't be that easy." She frowned for a moment longer, then snapped her fingers and looked up at Cam, her face bright. "I know." She smiled broadly. "I'll invite her out here."

Cam could feel the blood drain from his face.

"What?" His voice came out in a weak croak. He cleared his throat. "Why would you do that?"

"It's always easier to talk to someone in person," Celina said. She drained her cup and set it in the sink, then came over to Cam, put her hands on his hips, and pulled them hard against hers. "I can be very persuasive in person."

Cam laughed nervously and threw back the rest of his own coffee. Kat Nestrom and Celina Maxwell were two of the strongest, most brilliant people he'd ever met. If the two of them got together, they could reinvent the entire world.

And if the two of them got together with him in the room and things went sideways, they could burn the whole world down.

Cam put his arms around Celina and kissed her deep. The feel of her in his arms, of her pressed against him, of her soft lips on his, it calmed him. He loved Celina. He knew that in his core. He'd never loved anyone like he loved Celina. And she knew that, too. Cam had nothing to worry about.

Celina smiled at him, then turned away. She picked up her phone from the counter to look up Kat's number.

There was no reason for Cam to be nervous. Kat was in his past, and she would stay there. They were all adults. They could work together productively and let the past be the past.

He rinsed his cup and set it back in the machine. He definitely needed another coffee.

Celina spent fifteen minutes on the phone with Kat, but that was enough for them to arrange for Kat to come out to Celina's house in just two days. Celina offered to send her jet to pick Kat up, but Kat demurred. She had some business to attend to in Silicon Valley, she said, so she'd come on her own jet.

Rich people.

Unlike a lot of people in her financial circumstances, Celina didn't have staff beyond what her father had employed before his untimely death. A housekeeper came in once a week to tidy things. A chef came in twice a week to prep meals. Celina made sure to call them both and let them know there would be a house guest coming in. They asked how long the guest would be saying. Cam gulped when Celina said she didn't know.

Things were weird for the next two days between Cam and Celina. They did the same things and said the same things, but there was a frenetic tension behind it all that wasn't usually there. Cam didn't know if the tension was coming from Celina or if he was projecting his own nervousness. Cam kept reminding himself that there was nothing wrong, that the problem was all in his head. But the tension remained, all the same. They both pretended not to notice it, but by the time the day of Kat's arrival came, they were bouncing off of each other like super-heated atoms in a pressurized chamber.

Celina could have ordered a car to pick Kat up from the airport, but she decided to do it herself, instead. From Celina's home on the ocean side of the Golden Gate Bridge, they drove down Route 1 toward Half Moon Bay, where Celina had instructed Kat to land. It was a cool, sunny day, so they took Celina's four-seater Aston Martin DB12 convertible. She took the corners like a Formula 1 driver and the Aston responded in kind, the twelve-cylinder engine roaring along with the sound of the sea to Cam's left.

The day could not have been more beautiful. The sun sparkled off the blue-grey water, spreading out to the horizon in every direction. Dark rocks jutting from the curves of the land formed a stark, scenic contrast to the white foam crashing against them. Lines of pelicans, massive wings spread wide, glided over the water, searching behind the waves for schools of fish to dive-bomb and eat.

The two-lane road wound like a serpent through the green and yellow scrub that clung to the steep hillside above them to Cam's left, and the cliffs to his right were steep enough and stark enough to give just a bit more thrill to the high-speed turns that Celina pushed the Aston through. As if Cam's stomach needed more to churn about. The closer they got to the airport, the more he felt like he would just hang his head over the side of the car and let his barf spray all over the road behind them.

Celina wore large black sunglasses and a scarf over her head to keep her hair from flying. She looked like Audrey Hepburn, if Audrey Hepburn were a bit more beautiful and a hell of a lot more bad-ass. Celina turned to Cam, saw him watching her, and grinned back as she took a fifty-degree curve at seventy miles per hour without even looking.

Cam's seat belt was already securely buckled. His hands were so tight around the oh-shit handles he'd lost feeling in them. He trusted Celina, but centrifugal force was centrifugal force, so he hung on as best he could and tried to enjoy the ride.

He'd enjoy it more if knew what to expect at the end of it. Despite the unspoken tension, Celina had acted oddly breezy about the whole thing for the last two days. He wasn't surprised that she would be totally fine with meeting an ex-lover of Cam's, but her overly-casual attitude felt somehow off to him.

Cam and Celina had only been together for a little while. Their one-year anniversary would be on March 4, just over two months away. But they'd spent more time together in ten months than some married couples spend in ten years. He knew her pretty well by now. Celina was not the kind of woman that anyone could ever know completely, but Cam had developed some reliable instincts over the last ten months, and his instincts were telling him that all was not as it seemed with Celina right now.

Kat Nestrom was the opposite. He'd only known her for three days or so, and that was two years ago. In those three days, Kat had met him on a train, whisked him to her house for the holiday, introduced him to her family, fucked his brains out over and over, killed her father, and tried to talk him into staying after he'd gained enough leverage to convince her family to let him leave with his life. She was gorgeous, impulsive, headstrong, and unbelievably smart. Before Celina, Kat was the most formidable person Cam had ever met.

Celina had taken that title from her. And now the two of them were going to meet. Head-to-head. Two great champions battling for the title of the Greatest of All Time.

And yet somehow Cam felt like he might end up feeling like the goat in the end.

3

It wasn't a test. Celina didn't test her boyfriends.

To be fair, she'd never had a boyfriend. No one had ever passed her tests before.

But this wasn't a test. She would never test Cam. Tests were for those needy, insecure girls who spent half their day doing their hair and makeup, the other half of the day picking out their outfit, then spent all night clinging to the arm of some boring loser who was only using them for sex. They would test their loser boyfriends to assure themselves that their instincts were wrong, that he wasn't leering at that carbon-copy tit balloon across the bar, that he wasn't cheating on her every time she turned her back.

Tests were for fucking idiots. And Celina was the furthest thing from an idiot.

Which made the churning in her gut all the more inexplicable. It had started the moment she saw where the tracking dot on her laptop was headed. Cam had told her all about that crazy Christmas at the Nestrom's. It read straight out of an Agatha Christie novel. Locked in by a winter storm. A murder whodunit. Cam bargaining for his life at the end, promising not to tell the authorities what he knew.

And a torrid love affair with Kat Nestrom. The beautiful, beguiling Kat Nestrom.

Good for Cam. Kat was smoking hot. Hell, Celina would fuck her. She almost had, one wild night when they were younger.

But Celina was just as hot, just as smart. There was no reason for Cam to choose Kat over her. He'd never mentioned any regret about leaving her. She'd killed her father, for fuck's sake. Cam was anti-violence, said he had terrible luck with women because every woman he fell for turned out to be a murderer.

Celina thanked whatever higher power did or did not exist in the universe that she hadn't pulled any triggers herself. Lord knows she would have, given the chance. Cam himself had talked her out of wringing fucking Vernon Stratham's neck when she'd had the chance.

But Cam could change his mind. He could bend his own rules. Love could do that. Love worked in mysterious ways. Or maybe that was God. Whatever. Love made people do stupid shit.

Was she actually insecure? Celina Maxwell, insecure about a man?

Fuck.

She gunned the engine on the DB12, the tires screeching as she drifted around one of California Route 1's iconic curves. She grinned over at Cam. He looked like he was about to blow chunks.

Good.

Celina couldn't help the thought. It just popped into her head. It wasn't fair. Cam hadn't done anything wrong. So he'd fucked Celina's biggest rival. So what? He hadn't cheated on her. She knew that because she was looking at his head on his shoulders, not mounted on the fucking wall in her game room.

Now she was thinking vindictive thoughts. Jesus, what was wrong with her? If this was what having a boyfriend was like, she didn't want any part of it. She was behaving like all those idiot women she hated. Next thing you knew, she'd be looking at herself in the mirror, wondering if her ass was too flat and her tits too small.

She had to pull her shit together.

She pushed away the jealous thoughts and focused on the feel of the road. Through the leather steering wheel of the Aston, she could feel the texture of the asphalt, every groove and nook. She tuned into the rhythmic feel of the weight of the car shifting from the right tires to the left tires and back as she took the curves at speed, using the width of the road, letting the car drift where the curves were particularly sharp. She'd installed a sensor on all of her cars that would look a quarter mile down the road for oncoming traffic. A small green light on her console screen let her know the road ahead was clear.

The way Celina drove, the airport at Half Moon Bay was only ten minutes down the road. Just a few miles north of Half Moon Bay itself, the tiny airport was Celina's destination of choice. It was close, it usually wasn't crowded, and the airstrip was just long enough to handle all but the most ostentatious of private jets.

She glanced at the console screen again. She'd hacked the system long ago, of course, so she could display whatever she wanted. At the moment, the screen showed a real-time view of the location of Kat's plane. It was on final approach, just as Celina came through Moss Beach, the last curve before the airport. Perfect timing.

She thought through the plan. Meet Kat on the strip, introduce her to Cam, watch them both for any sign of latent attraction, watch Cam for any hint of deception.

Fuck. She was doing it again.

Well, what the hell. Never hurt to be cautious, right?

Since when was that a motto she believed in? That sounded more like something Cam and his mother, Paulie, would say. They were the ones who liked to research a job to death before going to work. Celina had to admit that it was smarter that way, but a lot less exciting. And it took way too long for her. Patience was not one of her strengths. Probably something she should try to work on.

She started over. Get Kat, introduce Cam, go back to the house, and eat some food on the deck. It would be late afternoon by then, nearly dark. They'd eat, drink, talk, catch up, watch for signs of Cam's duplicity.

Fuck.

And then Celina would talk to Kat about the glasses.

Celina figured one of two things was going on. Jenkins might have told Kat nothing, said he'd come across these odd glasses and was interested in learning more about them. Or he could have cut her in on a deal and promised to give Nestech, Inc. favorable treatment in his administration if she helped him out. He could have told her exactly how he'd found the glasses and told her his intentions.

The problem was, Celina couldn't be sure what those intentions were. She and Cam had already struck their own deal with Jenkins. As far as Jenkins knew, the incriminating evidence they had about him—his dirty donors, his connections to organized crime, the hits his head of campaign finance had ordered on various individuals, including Celina's father—had been destroyed in exchange for Paulie's release from prison and a complete pardon for her past crimes. Jenkins had held up his end of the deal and, as far as he knew, Celina and Cam had held up theirs.

It was bullshit, of course. Digital files were ubiquitous. Jenkins had to take Celina's word that there were no other copies. And Jenkins was no idiot. He'd be looking for more certainty.

But what was his involvement, really? Celina had come away from their meeting feeling like Jenkins was in the dark about Stratham's dirty dealings, especially the murders. And Celina's bullshit detector was top of the line.

Jenkins was a master politician, though. Her father had taught him everything he knew about managing people, navigating competing interests, dealing with large-scale issues and even larger-scale egos. But Jenkins had come into that training with a set of natural skills that were remarkable. His ability to control his emotions, to act on command, would have earned him a shelf full of Oscars if he'd gone to Hollywood instead of Washington. It was possible that he was good enough to fool even Celina's bullshit detector.

Celina had to assume the worst. She had to assume that Jenkins knew all about the murders, that he'd even approved them. That would explain why, as far as Celina could tell, Vernon Stratham was still working in Jenkins' campaign, still in the same position of authority. She certainly hadn't seen any news stories about a scandal in the ranks of the leading contender for the presidency. And this would absolutely be a scandal, if the news broke.

Which was all the more reason why Jenkins was unlikely to let it go.

The question was Kat Nestrom. Was she a pawn in Jenkins' political chess game, or was she the queen about to make a key move to protect the king?

Celina was about to find out.

Kat's jet taxied to a stop outside the main hangar at the airport as Celina pulled the Aston onto the tarmac.

"Do you mind waiting here for a minute?" Celina said to Cam. "I want to say hi myself before I blow her mind by introducing you."

"She doesn't know I'm here?" asked Cam.

"She knows I'm bringing my boyfriend, Cameron Hauk." Cam beamed at her. They didn't use the boyfriend/girlfriend words very often. Celina felt a little thrill herself when she said it. "But as far as she knows, you're Sam Davis."

"Right." Cam nodded. "I'll wait here."

Celina leaned over and gave him a long, deep, lingering kiss, running one hand up the inside of his thigh as she did. She felt Cam harden under her finger, gave the outline of his cock a quick, playful stroke with one finger.

Gotta give the man something to think about when he sees Kat again.

Celina got out of the car and stood by the front bumper as the ground crew chocked the jet's wheels and the engines whined down to a low idle, then stopped altogether, the swirly pattern in the front of the turbines slowly spinning to a halt. The jetway door popped open, then swung down, the gangway stairs unfolding gracefully as it did.

Celina strolled toward the stairs, her arms folded, watching the dark doorway. Waiting.

Kat would probably keep her waiting, anticipating, for a few moments longer. That was her style.

Kinda bitchy. Kinda cool.

Mostly bitchy.

Fuck.

4

From inside the convertible, Cam watched Celina wait near the jetway stairs. His knee bounced uncontrollably in front of him. He chewed on his thumbnail.

Why was he so nervous? He had zero interest in Kat Nestrom. Yes, she was gorgeous. So was Celina. Yes, she was stupid smart. So was Celina. There was nothing Kat could offer that Celina didn't already give him, and he and Celina had so much more. A deep connection, a boundless passion, a real love.

It was real love, wasn't it? It felt like it to Cam. Did it feel that way to Celina, too?

The wind kicked up, coming off the ocean in a stiff blast. The Half Moon Bay airport was right next to the water. Cam could literally walk a few hundred yards straight off the runway and off the cliff into the Pacific Ocean.

In that moment, waiting for Kat to come out of the plane, the idea didn't sound half bad.

He watched through the windshield as the wind streamed Celina's hair around her face, pressed her loose shirt against her back and her flowing high-waisted pants against her legs. It outlined her slim figure. Cam let his eye trace the curve of her ass, the line of her leg.

Kat Nestrom had nothing on Celina Maxwell. Nothing.

Celina took three slow steps forward toward the bottom of the stairs, and Cam's eyes traveled up them to the door of the plane. Kat Nestrom stood there.

And his heart flipped three times.

Or was it his stomach?

It had to be his stomach. He felt like he might throw up.

Kat stood at the top of the steps in a trim black business suit and large, dark sunglasses. Even from a distance, the suit commanded professional respect with its perfect cut and its obviously expensive material. With Kat's regal bearing, the look was intimidating as hell.

Adding to the intimidation were a few extra touches. The high-heeled jet-black shoes, the low cut white blouse that revealed a deep wedge of chest and just a hint of the inside edges of Kat's breasts, the way the blazer and the pants accentuated every one of Kat's many curves. Where Celina exuded power, razor-sharp intelligence, and passion, Kat projected wealth, sex, and unassailable sovereignty. That was Kat in a nutshell. That image oozed from every one of her pores.

Cam shrank down a little in the leather car seat and shifted so that most of his face, from Kat's angle, was hidden behind the post of the windshield. He watched through one unobstructed eye as Kat stepped down the stairs, her long, dark hair shimmering in the bright sunlight, streaming behind her like a silken sheet.

The two women hugged—briefly, but warmly—and stood chatting for a moment before Celina gestured toward the Aston with one arm.

Showtime.

Cam took a deep breath and climbed out of the car, keeping his head down and his back turned toward the approaching women.

"Kat Nestrom," said Celina, "I'd like you to meet Cam Hauk." She paused for a moment. Cam thought he heard a little steel in her voice when she added, "My boyfriend."

Kat said, "It's a pleasure to meet the man who finally tamed—"

As Cam straightened and turned to face her, Kat's voice caught in her throat and her eyes went wide. She'd been holding her arm out to shake Cam's hand, but after a moment of surprise, she threw herself at him instead, wrapping her arms around his neck and burying her face against his skin.

Instinctively, Cam's arms came up around her. He held her lightly, staring shocked and wide-eyed at Celina. She looked very annoyed.

Kat ran one hand along the back of Cam's neck. The touch of her fingers and the floral scent of her perfume, warmed by her skin, brought back a flood of memories. Pleasant ones. Very pleasant ones.

Uncomfortably pleasant ones.

Kat pulled out of her hug, slid her hands to Cam's cheeks, and kissed him, full and long, on the lips, not giving Cam a moment to react, to step back, to break the embrace.

The kiss held all the passion Cam remembered. He didn't return the passion—he no longer felt it for her—but his body remembered those lips. It remembered every curve and angle of the figure pressed against him. How could it forget?

"Jesus, Kat," muttered Celina.

Kat broke the kiss. She took a step back, running her

tongue slowly over her lips, slid her hands down Cam's arms to his hands, held them as she scanned his body from head to foot and back again. She looked at him, her dark eyes shadowed with lust.

He remembered that look, too.

"You look good, Sam," she said, her voice a low growl.

"Um..."

Celina stood beside Cam, slid her arm around his waist and pulled him hard against her side.

"He does look good, doesn't he?" she said with a smile that said *I will eat your guts raw and grin while I do it.* Cam wasn't quite sure if that smile was for Kat or for him. Probably both.

"And his name is Cam," Celina continued, "not Sam."

Kat's brow furrowed as she glanced from Celina back to Cam. Cam nodded.

Kat's expression shifted to one of amused intrigue. She gave his body another quick scan.

"Well, well," she said, her tone sultry. "What other surprises do you have for me?"

Celina pulled open the car door and flicked the lever to flip the passenger seat forward.

"You can sit in the back, Cam," she said, then glared at Kat. "Behind me."

Cam cleared his throat and got into the car.

This was going to be a lovely visit.

The drive home was uneventful. The wind was so loud that Cam could barely hear what they were saying in front, and they weren't turning to talk to him, anyway, so he just sat back and tuned out, closing his eyes and letting the whipping wind and the crashing waves ease the nausea he felt from the twists and turns in the road and the tension in the air.

When they arrived, Celina's chef had put out a beautiful spread on the deck and pushed back the sliding wall so that the living room flowed unbroken to the outside air. They all dug in with relish, sitting at one end of a long outdoor table. Celina and Kat chatted about friends and colleagues they had in common, catching up and making small talk.

The tension from the airport seemed to have drifted away on the wind during the car ride. Cam mostly sat and listened and watched the two friends reunite, marveling at the subtle shifts in Celina's energy as she slid back into old habits, old ways of being around this woman she'd known since she was a child. In many ways, they were very similar, with their backgrounds, their wealth, their beauty, their personal tragedy.

But in a few ways—a few very important ways—they couldn't be more different.

The sun dropped to the horizon while they ate and treated them to a gorgeous sunset at the end of the meal. Celina pressed a button on a remote control and ignited both the fire pit on the deck and the fireplace inside the house.

When they had all eaten their fill, they moved to the lounge chairs around the fire pit, glasses of white wine in hand.

Between the food, the wine, and the tension that was still palpable, Cam felt sleepy when his head hit the back cushion of the lounge chair. Kat excused herself to change out of her business suit. Celina offered to show her to her room, but Kat waved her off. She was going to snoop around the house at some point anyway, she said. Might as well get it done now.

Celina took the chair beside Cam, already slid close enough for them to touch each other easily.

"Kat seems to remember you," she said lightly.

Cam sighed. "I noticed that."

Celina put her hand on Cam's thigh, stroked the inside lightly.

"How much did you notice?"

Cam turned his head toward her on the cushion. She turned hers to him.

Cam gazed at the line of her cheekbone, gilded in the glow of the fire pit. He reached out and ran the back of his hand over it, across her cheek. He touched the back of one finger to her full, soft lips. She pursed them, kissing his finger lightly. She caught it between her teeth and bit down lightly. Her gorgeous, beguiling green eyes watched him, glittering in the firelight.

"There's nothing between us anymore," Cam said softly.

She stared at him for a long moment. He let himself fall into her stare.

"I think she'd disagree."

Cam set his wine glass on the deck, took Celina's hand in his, and rolled onto one shoulder to face her. He kissed the back of her hand, then her fingers, then rolled it and kissed her palm. He held her hand warm against his cheek.

"She can think what she wants," he said. "She can do what she wants."

"She can be very convincing."

"True," Cam nodded. "But I know what I want."

"Mmm," Celina smiled slyly. "Do you?"

The sky had darkened, and the shadows of the fire cast her face in a gorgeous, golden light. Cam felt a swelling in his chest. It took him a moment to realize what it was.

It was love.

"I do," said Cam, and he'd never meant it more. He wanted to spend every day with Celina Maxwell, every day for the rest of his life. Nothing would make him happier.

"That's good," said Celina, her smile spreading. Then the smile faltered. "But I know Kat. She's not going to give up easily."

"She can try," said Cam, though he hoped she wouldn't. "But it takes two people to make a relationship."

"Three works, too," said Kat, her voice distant, "if they're naughty."

Cam and Celina sat up and turned to look behind them. Kat sauntered through the open doors from the living room, dressed in flowing white pajama pants, a white camisole, and a long, fuzzy white cardigan sweater. From a distance, it looked like a normal set of pajamas, but as she came closer, into the light of the fire, Cam could see that the pants and the camisole were made of some kind of sheer fabric. In most light, they looked silky. But when the light caught them just right—and the firelight seemed to be just right quite often as Kat sauntered toward them—Cam could clearly see the dark areolae of her nipples, the swell and curve of her breasts, and a thin, tidy strip of her dark pubic hair below her waistband. In the right light, the outfit left nothing to the imagination. Kat might as well have been naked.

Which, Cam was sure, was exactly what she wanted him to imagine.

She slowed her walk as she approached, being sure to give them both plenty of time to watch, then slid a third chair up on the other side of Cam, even closer than Celina's chair, and lay down, stretching her arms above her head and arching her back before settling down.

"Jesus fuck, Kat," muttered Celina.

Kat turned her head toward them both, her expression as open and innocent as freshly fallen snow.

"What?" she said lightly. "Did I interrupt something? What are we talking about?" Her eyes glittered in the firelight as she gave a wicked grin.

"Okay," said Celina, standing from her chair and draining the last swallow of her wine. "I think I'll put on my pajamas, too." She turned to Kat. "My *real* pajamas."

"You don't like them?" asked Kat, looking down at her outfit and pulling the shirt down as if she were inspecting it. Instead, all she did was pull the fabric tight enough that Cam could clearly see the curve of her breasts and the peak of her nipples, hard in the cool night air, even without the right lighting.

"I'll bring you a blanket," said Celina, "before those giant nipples of yours freeze off."

Cam listened to them spar. Some men would be overjoyed to have two beautiful women fighting over him, but Cam just felt sick to his stomach.

He was a thief, and a damn good one. When it came to a job, he could boldly break into a secure facility or play a role and fool someone to get information or distract them. He did his homework, came prepared, and had the skills to handle anything. He feared nothing and no one.

But, like most people, when it came to real life he preferred to avoid confrontation. And when it came to women, he'd always been fairly passive. He'd been lucky enough that women had always approached him.

And now he had Celina. That was all he needed, all he wanted. The last thing he wanted was Kat Nestrom trying to steal him away.

Celina disappeared through the open wall into the living room. Kat tossed her long hair back and turned to her side on the lounge chair, facing Cam and propping her head on her elbow against the back of the chair.

She was a beautiful woman, and she knew it, knew how to use every bit of her sexuality to get what she wanted. The firelight limbed the curves of her body. It reflected in her dark eyes, like the fire was burning inside her instead of the fire pit.

She set her free hand on the curve of her hip and arched one eyebrow at Cam.

"It's good to see you"—she frowned for a moment—"Cam."

She laughed, a light, entrancing sound. She moved the hand from her hip and set it on Cam's hand in a friendly, playful way that Cam knew was anything but.

"It's going to take me a minute to get used to that," she said.

She ran her hand lightly, casually, up Cam's forearm.

"Looks like it's just you and me," she said, watched her hand trace over his skin. She flicked her gaze up to his eyes from under her lashes. "What should we do?"

Cam gulped.

"Cam." Celina stepped out of the darkness back onto the deck. "Why don't you come upstairs with me and get changed?"

"Coming," he said gratefully, springing up from the lounge chair and rushing inside with Celina. She glared at Kat, took Cam by the elbow, and led him inside.

Yep, he was right. This was going to be a lovely visit.

5

CELINA DID her best to control her fury.

Her best, in this case, was not great.

She wanted to smash Kat in her beautiful face with the sharp end of a moving bullet. She wanted to rip those gorgeous tits off her fucking body.

And she wasn't any happier with Cam, either. He'd just sat there, gaping, while Kat lay there basically naked and threw herself at him. Celina wanted to scream at Cam, punch him in the face, and kick his ass. And then fuck his brains out, just to show Kat that she could. Or scream and punch and kick while she was fucking him.

That wasn't too far off of reality, some nights.

Fucking hell, Celina. She shook her head. Get your shit together.

She pushed Cam up the stairs to their bedroom, pushed him a little faster, a little rougher than necessary, all of these thoughts spinning through her mind.

Fucking Kat Nestrom.

Celina loved that bitch. They'd been peas in a gold-lined pod when they were growing up. They had the same attitude toward men and toward life. They took the world by storm, drinking and fucking and throwing their money around like sailors on shore leave at night, then leading parts of their fathers' business like bad-ass bosses during the day, effortlessly making decisions middle-aged middle managers had sweated over for weeks, and minting money while they did it. They were both gifted with the same attitudes, the same acumen, the same assets.

And the same taste in men, it seemed.

Celina loved Kat, and she fucking hated that bitch.

They'd fought over men in the past, competed with each other. But that was always for a one-night stand or a quickie against the bathroom wall. It was just a game, and men were easy targets. There weren't many men out there who would say no to a woman asking for a quick fuck, let alone a fuckbomb like her or Kat. It was quick and easy and the men were just betting tickets at a horse track, important for the moment, but ripped up and thrown on the floor without a second thought once the race was over.

But Cam was different. He was no one-night stand. Cam was the real deal.

And Celina was pretty sure Kat felt the same way.

Same taste in men, right?

Fucking bitch.

They got upstairs to their bedroom and Celina pushed Cam through the door. He turned around, expecting her to say something, but she just stalked past him into the changing area instead.

The changing area was a large, square room with doors on all four sides. One door led to the bedroom, where Celina had come from. In the center of the room was a low tufted bench flanked by two valet stands. The stands had a wide tray for jewelry, a low shelf for shoes, fixed hangers for shirts and pants, and a tall hook for dresses or suit coats. Along the walls were dressers holding their jewelry, t-shirts, underwear, and pajamas. The doors on either side of the room led to large walk-in closets that held the rest of their clothes, one for Cam and one for Celina. The fourth door led to their large bathroom, with a soaking tub with plenty of room for two and a massive doorless shower, as well as vanities and the usual bathroom fixtures.

Everywhere Celina looked, she saw a place that she and Cam had made love. The tufted bench, the floor of the changing area, bent over the dressers, pressed against the racks of clothes in the walk-in closets, in the shower, in the tub, on the tub, even on the fucking toilet.

And everywhere she looked, Celina couldn't help but see images of Cam fucking Kat in all those same places.

She swore softly, yanked off her rings and earrings and threw them onto the changing stand, and practically broke the buttons from her blouse as she undid them. She still hadn't gotten control of herself, and the last thing she wanted to do was unleash some lame-ass tirade on Cam. If he saw her crazy jealous side—the one she didn't even know she had until a few days ago—she'd push him away. By the end of the night, he'd be begging Kat to take him away from his fucked-up girlfriend. And Kat would be more than happy to oblige.

Celina removed her blouse and bra and shimmied out of her pants, standing naked except for her thong. She pulled her pajamas out of the drawer, set them on the valet stand, and walked into her closet to hang up her clothes.

Celina had never been in this position before. She'd never cared enough about a man to give a shit if he went to someone else, though no man had ever been stupid enough to even try. Celina was always the one leaving. It was the opposite of the movies. In Celina's experience, the men were the ones whining and begging to stay. But once she'd gotten what she wanted from them, she usually couldn't wait to get out of there. Even the rich, confident ones, the ones who could get any woman they wanted, still begged like she was their fucking mommy and they wanted her to buy them a toy at the fucking supermarket.

But Cam was different. She didn't know why, but he was.

And Celina felt different about him. Again, she didn't know why. She wished to fuck she did, but she'd felt different about him almost from the very start. When he stood in her doorway asking for Reggie Moon, assuming it was some guy living in her apartment instead of the false identity she'd chosen for herself, something had stirred inside Celina.

At the time, she had assumed it was lust. Cam was smoking hot, but in an unassuming kind of way—which made him even hotter—and she hadn't had a good fuck in a few weeks at that point.

She did feel lust for him. But it turned out to be a hell of a lot more than just that.

Cam came into the closet as she was hanging her pants. He stood behind her, skimmed his hands along the back of her bare shoulders and down her arms, standing the pale, thin hairs on end. He kissed her gently from her shoulder to her neck. She tilted her head, and he continued the kisses up to her ear. He slid his hands to her midriff and pulled her against him.

"You okay?" he said softly into her ear.

Celina didn't know how to respond, so she just leaned her head back onto his shoulder and closed her eyes, feeling Cam's hot breath against her ear, his soft hands roving across the tight skin of her belly, up to the curve of her breasts, down again to the jut of her pelvic bones, hinting, teasing, enticing, exciting.

She put her hand over his and led him down lower, pushed down her thong and used his hand to pleasure herself. He let her guide him, pulled her tight against him. She felt him grow hard against her lower back. That made her gasp even more, come even harder, all the tension she'd been feeling releasing in moments with a scream that Celina did not hold back.

She spun in his arms, had his pants down in a fraction of a second, pushed him back against the wall and climbed him, rode him as he held her by her thighs until they were both gasping and screaming with release.

Celina locked her ankles in the small of Cam's back, wrapped her arms around his neck, and draped her head over his shoulder as he sagged against the wall. She could feel his legs quivering as she hugged him tight. They leaned like that, chests heaving, until their breath slowly returned to normal.

That helped. Sex always helped clear Celina's mind. She could see things with fresher eyes now.

Kat was here.

Celina needed her here.

And Kat wanted Cam.

Fine. Bring it the fuck on.

They were three full-grown adults. They could take their own actions, and they could make their own decisions. If Kat wanted to try for Cam, let the fucking bitch come.

And Cam could make his own decisions. If he decided he wanted Kat, he could have her.

Though Celina doubted Kat would want him as much after Celina cut his cheating dick off.

But that was up to Cam.

Game on. And may the best woman win.

"I hope you saved some for me," said Kat when they came back downstairs.

Celina could hear the irritation in her voice. Kat was bundled up tight in her sweater coat, and Celina noticed that she'd opened a new bottle of wine. Good. Let the bitch pass out drunk and freeze her cooter off. It didn't snow in California, but that didn't mean you could wear tissue paper pants outside at night.

Celina picked up the empty wine bottle. "Looks like you didn't," she said.

Kat glanced up at her, then out to the dark ocean, clearly annoyed.

Celina smiled to herself.

"Sit down, Cam," said Kat, patting the lounge chair beside her. "We've got some catching up to do."

Kat was still looking into the darkness, but Celina noticed the purse of Cam's lips and the clench of his jaw as he dutifully lowered himself into the seat beside Kat.

Again, Celina smiled to herself.

Cam was hers. If Kat wanted to steal him, she had some work to do.

And she was going to have to get past Celina to do it.

When it came to Cam, this wasn't a test.

This was a fucking war.

6

WHEN HE SAT down on the deck chair again, Cam steeled himself for more come-ons from Kat. Surprisingly, she didn't come on to him at all. No more double entendres, no more innuendos, no more stretching or exposing her body to him through her gauzy pajamas.

Instead, Kat kept her sweater tightly closed around her, filled his wineglass and Celina's, and started telling Cam stories about her and Celina when they were younger.

At first, he was relieved at the shift. Soon he realized it was just another tactic.

The stories Kat told painted Celina in the most unflattering light possible. Drinking and drugs and sex with countless men and women. Throwing her money around, using her sexuality for power, lording her wealth over people in business and in life. To hear Kat tell it, Celina was a self-centered, insecure monster whose carnal appetites were only matched by the unfillable emptiness inside her.

The tactic was just as ridiculous as throwing herself at him had been before. Cam started to wonder what he had ever seen in Kat in the first place. When they'd met, he'd been sketching on a train, on his way to see his mother in prison just before Christmas. Kat hadn't been like this back then. She'd been funny and perceptive and... well, kind might be too strong a word for it, in retrospect, but she'd at least been considerate. When a massive blizzard closed the tracks at her stop, she'd brought Cam to her family home with her for Christmas.

The reality hadn't turned out to be as sweet as the intent; that was the Christmas that Kat had helped her family murder their father. But Cam did still believe that the intention was well-meant.

And she'd been kind enough, smart enough, sane enough for him to think he was in love with her. Sure, he'd only known her for a day or two when he started thinking that way, but when Cam fell, he fell hard. It had always been like that for him.

And he usually ended up broken from the fall. That was how it had been with Kat.

She was a murderer. She'd killed someone.

But could Cam say he was any better? He'd killed someone, too. Just a few months earlier. Bashed a man's brains against a stairway.

But it wasn't the same. Cam had been trying to save Celina. He hadn't meant to kill the man, just neutralize a threat.

Kat, on the other hand, had murdered her own father in cold blood. First-degree. Premeditated.

But death was death. Murder was murder. Did the circumstances really matter, in the end?

Cam took a long pull of his wine and leaned his head back against the lounge chair. Kat was prattling on about

Celina giving some sheikh a shake in a back room in Abu Dhabi. If half of what she said was true—and that might be a stretch—Celina had lived a colorful life. But if Kat thought she was putting Cam off, she didn't know Cam.

And how could she? They'd only been together for three days. Three. Days. He and Celina had been together for ten months, and they were still going strong. There was no comparison.

Maybe Kat thought Cam was like any other guy, willing to jump from one woman to another with the shake of an ass cheek and a flash of side boob. Cam just wasn't wired that way. Never had been.

And for Kat to tell these stories, she had to have been right there beside Celina in that Abu Dhabi back room. She was giving Cam plenty to tease Celina about, but no reason to leave her. Celina liked sex. Cam liked it, too. He especially liked sex with Celina. As long as Celina didn't cheat on Cam, her past was past, as far as he was concerned.

And unlike Kat—and Cam—Celina's hands had no blood on them.

During a lull in the conversation, Cam drained his wine glass and stood.

"I think I'll turn in," he said.

"I'll join you," said Kat.

Celina gave a cold laugh. "You and I have a few things to discuss, Kat," she said.

Cam bent and kissed Celina, a long, lingering good-night kiss. Let Kat know that her see-through pajamas and her sordid tales hadn't changed his mind one bit.

Celina smiled sleepily up at him as he disengaged. God, she was gorgeous. Her green eyes flared orange and yellow with the reflections of the firelight. Cam wanted to lift her in his arms and carry her to bed with him.

Kat sighed heavily.

"Fine," she said. "But let's go inside. I'm freezing my ass off out here."

Celina glanced over at her, then back up at Cam, and grinned.

He grinned back. Score one for Team Celina.

Not that it was much of a contest.

Cam fell asleep quickly, only stirring when Celina slid into bed and snugged up to him, burrowing her ice-cold bare feet between his toasty warm legs. He woke like that, entwined with her, the morning sun streaming through the windows.

When put on a robe and went downstairs for coffee, Kat was already awake and dressed in a business suit. She was pacing in the living room, speaking sharply to someone on her cell phone. Her laptop and an empty cup of coffee sat on the kitchen counter.

She glanced over at Cam. He held her empty cup up in question and she nodded and mouthed a thank you, then returned to her call. Something about component tolerances and manufacturing delays. Cam hadn't known Kat was so involved in the family business. His memory was that her brother-in-law, Thomas Crowell, had been named CEO after her father's death. He hadn't seen any news that said anything about a recent shake-up in the leadership of Nestech, Inc. And that would have made headlines on every news site in the world.

Maybe Kat had stepped up. She'd always been entrepreneurial, always trying to make her own name, make her own way in the world. And she had. But every time, her father had found a way to pull her back in, usually by buying out her companies. Amicably or not, he found a way to suck her back into the family business.

Like Pacino in the Godfather. Just when she thought she was out, they pulled her back in.

So maybe she'd finally made her break, started a new business. She'd been into cybersecurity when they'd been together, if Cam's memory served. Maybe she was still working in that space. He'd have to ask her about it, if he could get her to talk about something that wasn't designed to get her in Cam's bed instead of Celina.

He set her refilled coffee cup beside her laptop, then made a fresh cup for himself. When he turned and took his first sip, Kat was off the phone and striding toward him.

"Sorry about that," she said. "This trip to California isn't all about catching up with old friends, unfortunately. I've got some business to do while I'm here." She took a sip of her coffee, then sighed. "Now it looks like I'll have to go into the office for a few hours." She gave Cam a smile that was closer to a wince. "You'd think a million-dollar salary would buy you some decent talent, but these fucking executives are all idiots. They're just rich idiots."

"I'm sorry," said Cam, and he meant it. He didn't want to sleep with Kat, but he didn't want to see her suffer, either, murderer or not. "Are you still working for Nestech or did you start another company?"

"Senior Vice President of Research and Development," said Kat. "Dad's gone, and Thomas is a hundred times worse than Dad ever was." She looked miserable. "He thinks he's smart, and there's no one with enough power to keep him in check."

"That doesn't sound like the Kat I knew."

"The Kat you knew for three days?" She snorted. "That Kat was a fabrication."

She tossed back the rest of her coffee and slammed the glass cup onto the counter, then looked sheepishly at Cam.

"I'm sorry," she said. "I'm just frustrated and fed up. I don't mean to unload on you."

"Not a problem," said Cam.

"And... I'm sorry about yesterday," she said. "Last night. Throwing myself at you like that. It was disrespectful. And demeaning." She pushed one hand through her long hair, swept it over one shoulder. "It's just, seeing you again... surprised me, I guess. Wasn't expecting it." She bit her bottom lip and dropped her eyes. "I've thought about you a lot, since those three days." She looked at him again, her eyes wide. Those deep, dark eyes that he'd fallen in love with years ago, for a time. "I wish things had turned out differently."

Cam had a thousand questions. Did she mean she wished Cam hadn't left? Did she wish she hadn't killed her father? Did she wish he hadn't died at all? But none of the questions seemed appropriate, and none of them seemed like they would be helpful to ask. Instead, Cam just looked down at his coffee and nodded.

"Apology accepted," he said, looking up and smiling at Kat.

She smiled back. She had a grateful look on her face, and it seemed to Cam like it might actually be sincere.

"You always were a good guy, Cam," she said. "I could see that much from the start, even on the train." Her eyes unfocused for a moment. She smiled. "Remember that old lady? The one we were inventing backstories for? Grand-mother visiting her family, owner of famous cookie shop."

"Russian spy," said Cam.

"Israeli assassin," said Kat.

"All of the above," they both said at the same time, then laughed.

Cam remembered. That lady had been cool as hell. Cam and Kat had been whispering their stories to each other, but the lady must have heard them. When she got off the train, she stopped and winked at them and said maybe all the stories were true.

It felt good to laugh with Kat instead of feeling so defensive toward her.

Kat's smile faded, and she sighed again. "I do wish things had turned out differently," she said quietly, then folded her laptop shut and tucked it under her arm. "But, hey," she said, stepping toward Cam and resting her hand on one cheek, "at least we had a couple good days, right?"

Cam paused for a moment, wary, then nodded.

Kat kissed him softly on the cheek, then walked past him.

"Tell Celina I'm sorry to have to leave," she called over her shoulder, "and that I'll be back this afternoon, as soon as I can."

Cam stood in the kitchen, listening to the sound of Kat's shoes fading down the hallway. He waited a beat, took another sip of his coffee, then said, "Did you get all that?"

Celina came down the stairs. Cam had known she was there. He still got a jolt of electricity whenever she was near.

"Most of it," she said. "I didn't want to interrupt. I've never heard Kat apologize for anything before."

Cam turned to make Celina some coffee. He shrugged. "Maybe she's maturing."

"Maybe," mused Celina, "but if you'd asked me before today, I wouldn't have bet on it."

Neither would Cam. He still wouldn't. The apology felt sincere enough, but Kat just didn't seem like the humble type.

He didn't know Kat well, but something told him she was up to something.

He really hoped he was wrong.

7

KAT SAT in the back of the blacked-out Mercedes Maybach sedan that Nestech had sent to pick her up. The company had them custom-built to drive Kat and her family around when they were in town, an extravagance that the company's protestors tended to overlook. It made better headlines to bitch about the environmental impact of a fleet of Gulf-streams than to complain about a fancy Mercedes.

But the Maybach was Kat's favorite. Even a fancy jet is still just a metal tube suspended thirty-five thousand feet in the air. A custom Maybach is real luxury.

They'd had Mercedes lengthen the wheelbase and install a soundproof glass partition. Kat could have a fucking rock concert in the back and her driver and body-guard, Sean, wouldn't hear a thing from the front seat.

Which was just as well, because Kat was about ready to scream into her cell phone.

She took a deep breath, though, and managed to control herself.

"I'm working on it," she said through gritted teeth.

Kat had dealt with plenty of powerful people in her life.

She was a powerful person herself. But that fact didn't blunt the egos of men with money. She could be the richest person in the world, but some man would still think he was better than her simply because she was a woman.

It was the penis. Dangling around all the time. They were always trying to stick it somewhere, and when they couldn't, it made them feel insecure. They knew a woman could close her legs and deny them, and that scared them. Fear pissed them off. Fear made them dangerous.

And male politicians were even worse. They had power without the strength that money brings, and that made their insecurity even worse. Which made them potentially even more dangerous.

Kat took a deep breath and calmed herself enough to even her voice.

"I've only been here for one day," she purred. "I will get what you need, but Celina isn't an idiot. It'll take time to figure things out."

"How much time?"

Attorney General Bill Jenkins' voice was low. Kat could hear the anger in it, which meant he wanted her to hear it. Jenkins was too skilled a politician to let his emotions come through when he didn't intend them to.

Another goddamn frightened, dangling penis.

Kat looked out the window as the car flashed down the 101 toward the Nestech office in Mountain View. When she had lived here as a little girl, before the dot-com boom, when Nestech was still a small startup, Silicon Valley had been exciting and beautiful. It still had trees and orchards and wild open spaces.

Now, everywhere she looked were buildings and bill-boards and traffic. Piddling tech company after piddling tech company with their workshopped names and logos, trying to convince the venture capitalists that they were the next unicorn company to invest in. No revenue, profits deep in the red, but massive user growth and the implicit promise that someday they'd turn on their customers and sell their data to the highest bidder for billions of dollars in profit.

That was the tech game now. The days of an honest buck were long over. It was probably good that her father was dead. He'd built Silicon Valley. He'd kill himself if he could see how low it had sunk.

No matter what justification she came up with, Kat still tasted blood on her tongue and bile in her throat.

Seeing Sam again—Cam, now—just made it worse.

"At least a week," she said into the phone.

President-to-be or not, Bill Jenkins was just another asshole. But if things went as planned, that asshole would rip her father's company out of her brother-in-law's inept hands and deliver it to Kat on a presidential silver platter.

"Give me a week," she said, "and I'll get you what you want."

She ended the call without waiting for a response.

He was an asshole, but she had to give it to Jenkins. He'd said Celina would come for the glasses, and he was right. He wasn't a total idiot.

Neither was Kat. She'd get the information Jenkins was after. She'd get her company.

And she'd get Cam, too.

And if Celina had to die in the process, so be it. It wasn't Kat's preference, but she had blood on her hands already.

A little bit more wouldn't make any difference.

8

CELINA SAT on the deck and glared at the ocean while Cam cleaned the breakfast dishes in the kitchen, her coffee cold in the cup in her hand. The waves were as angry as she was, chopping and roiling offshore and snapping at the hard-pounded sand on the beach when they broke. The sky and the sea were both iron grey, and the wind was even stronger than usual. A storm must be coming.

Celina was pissed that Kat took off, but there was nothing she could do about it. Kat warned her that she would have business to do when she got here, so Celina couldn't even complain.

But that didn't make her any less impatient. They hadn't even talked about the fucking glasses yet.

After Cam had left the night before, she and Kat had dropped the bullshit and had it out. They didn't scream or fight. Neither one of them was the Jerry Springer type. They just spoke, calmly and coldly. Celina made it clear that this wasn't like when they were younger. Cam wasn't a game for her. Kat claimed the same thing. And just like that, even though it wasn't a game, the game was on, and Cam was the prize. May the best woman win.

Celina knew that Kat would fight dirty. She always had. But she also knew that Cam was smart enough to see through Kat's bullshit. Celina just needed to keep her shit together and let Kat dig her own grave.

Easier said than done. When she was sitting on the stairs listening to Kat and Cam talk, she'd peeked through in time to see Kat kiss his cheek. Kat was changing tactics already. She'd tried the slutty frontal assault. Didn't work. She'd tried discrediting Celina. Didn't work (thank God). Now she was trying the contrite route.

Contrite was not something Kat had in her playbook five years ago, the last time Celina saw her. She had obviously changed. But was she being sincere, or was she just trying to one-up Celina one more time?

It would be interesting to see how it played out. But right now, Celina still needed to figure out what the hell Jenkins was up to with the glasses. Had he hired the Israeli assassins that had broken into Celina's mother's house? If so, were they after her mother, or after Celina and Cam? Celina's mother was the Speaker of the U.S. House of Representatives, a powerful Democrat and a powerful woman, both things that made her a target for a significant portion of the country. Celina and Cam had been there by a fluke, having broken into the house to steal a statue that had belonged to Celina's father. The assassins were not part of the plan.

But Celina needed to know if Jenkins was actively trying to kill her. She and Cam had blackmailed him with evidence of serious improprieties committed by his campaign, the kind of improprieties that would derail a career and put at least some people behind bars. Jenkins would know the evidence was still out there. Was he trying to close the loose end and make sure Celina and Cam never brought the evidence to light?

Or was it pure coincidence that the glasses made their way to Jenkins? He was powerful, soon to be even more powerful. If an ex-special forces goon had stumbled upon the glasses and recognized them as a unique high-tech item, he might try to jump a few rungs on the career ladder by bringing them straight to the boss.

But it just didn't make sense yet. Not completely. All Celina had were theories. She needed facts. Inside information. For that, she needed to get Kat to talk. She needed to know what Kat knew, if anything.

She wasn't going to get that right now. Not until Kat came back. In the meantime, she and Cam were left to their own devices once more.

Celina had closed the glass wall to the living room before bed last night. Cam came through the sliding door onto the deck and stood beside her chair. They didn't say anything, just stared at the sea in silence for a minute, each one lost in their own thoughts.

Finally shaking herself from her reverie, Celina stood up in front of Cam.

"I need to burn off some energy," she said.

Cam raised his eyebrows and smiled.

Celina put a hand against his chest. He was muscular and cut, but not in a beefy way. Lean and strong. Just the way Celina liked it. She ran her hand over his belly and around his waist to his back.

"Not that way," she said, and smacked his ass hard. "We're gonna spar."

"Spar?" said Cam.

"Yep," Celina replied, walking past him and inside. Cam followed. "I'm going to teach you how to fight."

In the two months that they'd been home, at his request, Celina had been teaching Cam how to use a handgun. The fight in the dark at Celina's mother's house had spooked him, and he wanted to be better prepared if something like that ever happened again.

Celina was all for it. You could never be too prepared to defend yourself. Even if you were against the use of violence, like Cam and his family, you might still be faced with people who were more than happy to use violence against you. Non-violent protest was all well and good, but you can't stage a sit-in against a bullet, and an assassin doesn't give a shit about your hunger strike. Knowledge is power, and Celina wanted Cam to at least know how to defend himself. After that night in Washington, Cam wanted that, too.

Celina couldn't teach him any hand-to-hand techniques while his ribs were still healing, so she'd started with handguns once his body was strong enough to absorb the force of the recoil. She'd started small, with a .22-caliber pistol, then worked up to bigger weapons as Cam healed, learned, and got more interested in the challenge of hitting a target. Even though he'd only been shooting for two months, he'd gotten pretty good. His groupings were tight and his accuracy was decent. He was a natural.

And more importantly, he'd gotten hooked. Celina sometimes found him down in the range on his own, empty brass littering the floor, working for hours on hitting smaller and smaller targets from further and further away. He was nowhere near as good a shot as Celina, but he had the work ethic. He'd get there soon.

Now that his ribs were healed, it was time for the sparring ring.

They changed into workout clothes and went downstairs. The training room was on the same floor as the gun range, but on the opposite side of the house, beside the weight room. Celina had spent a lot of time there over the years, and she still got a warm, cozy feeling when she walked in. Her father had always felt it was important that Celina be able to defend herself. Starting from when she was eight years old, she'd had many teachers across a wide variety of disciplines, from karate to Brazilian Jiu-Jitsu to Krav Maga, Muay Thai, and straight-up boxing. All in addition to her firearms training, which she'd started when she was thirteen. She'd even gotten a good dose of meditation instruction over the years. Of all the disciplines, that had always been the hardest for Celina to learn.

She was nowhere near an expert in any of the disciplines, but she knew enough and had grown strong enough that she was confident that she would be a formidable opponent to anyone who might come her way. The Israeli special-forces goon she'd taken down that night in her mother's house had found that out the hard way.

The training room was large, forty feet square, with mirrors on every wall. A door on the far side led to the weight room. The entire floor was covered in whitewashed bamboo planks, but when Celina flicked a switch on the wall, a twenty-foot-square section of the floor separated from the rest. It retracted below floor level and split in half. Each half then slid back under the floor, and a thick dark grey training mat rose up to fill the opening. It locked into place in the center of the room as if it had been there the whole time.

Cam whistled low. "Fancy," he said.

"My dad and I used this room for a lot of stuff when I was younger. Sometimes we would train or spar, hence the tatami mat. But sometimes we would do yoga or meditate or stuff like that." She shrugged. "It was my dad's design. Engineer. He liked to fuck around with stuff like this."

She felt her eye grow hot and turned away before the tears could form. She hadn't talked much about her father, and being in that room was like inviting his ghost to visit. She had so many memories of stretching with him and sparring with him, until she got too good and kept hurting him. Her dad wasn't a martial arts guy. He was more of a meditation type, so they spent a lot of time sitting and staring at the mirrored walls. He would flick her with a soft stick when she nodded off, and she would stare at him and make faces in the mirror, trying to break his meditative concentration when she was bored. They laughed a lot in that room.

Her dad was brilliant in many, many ways. Neither hand-to-hand fighting nor weapons training were one of them. But he knew how women were treated in the world, and he didn't want his daughter to be defenseless. Physically, mentally, or emotionally.

Celina looked up and saw Cam watching her in the mirror. She pulled herself together and smiled at his reflection before stepping onto the mat and waving for him to join her.

They spent a little time stretching, then stood facing each other on the mat.

"Okay," said Celina, "why don't we start with what you already know. Say I'm a big guy wearing a hoodie with the hood pulled up, looking kind of sketchy. What would you do if I were approaching you in, say, an empty subway station late at night?"

She stalked toward Cam.

"Nothing," Cam shrugged.

Celina stopped her stalking. "Nothing at all?"

"I mean, you haven't done anything, right?" he said. "You're just walking in the subway. You've got a right to exist, just like the rest of us. You can't help the fact that you look scary and it's dark outside."

Celina rolled her eyes. Just like Cam to bring a humanistic approach to a self-defense training scenario.

"Okay," she said. "Let's just say your spidey senses are tingling—"

"My spidey senses?" Cam laughed. "I don't have those."

"Everyone has those, Cam," Celina said, "and yours are tingling, telling you there's something not right about this guy."

"Why? Because he's tall and I can't see his face? That sounds more like my prejudice and my imagination than anything else."

"Instinct," said Celina. "Sometimes it makes the difference between getting away and getting yourself killed."

"We don't live in the jungle," Cam said. "Not everything is fight or flight."

Celina bristled and straightened her back. "Try being a woman," she said, her voice sharp. "Sometimes, everything is fight or flight." She forced herself to relax. "But forget about that, okay? This is a training exercise." She resumed her stalking. "Just assume that somehow, magically, you know that this guy intends to hurt you."

"Why?"

"Why does it matter why?" Celina said, stopping again, exasperated. Cam could be so naïve sometimes. Nonviolence was a good theory and a great way to plan a heist. But you can't control other people. Sometimes they bring violence to you. And you'd better be ready to respond when they do.

"It matters," Cam said, "because if he wants to steal my purse or my wallet, I might just throw it on the ground to distract him and run away. But if he wants to kill me for some reason, and he's faster or stronger or I have to get past him to get away, I'd have to take a different strategy."

That was actually really smart. Celina instantly felt bad for thinking angry thoughts about Cam.

"Good point," she said. "Let's say you don't know why he's coming after you, but it's a small subway platform and you have to get past the guy in order to get away."

She stalked toward him again.

"Okay," said Cam, thinking. "I don't carry a wallet, so I wouldn't have anything to even try to throw down except my phone. I'd probably just hold my hands up in front of me like this, so I don't seem threatening, and back away."

"Right. Say he just keeps coming at you."

"And I can't run past him?"

Cam stepped to his left to dodge past Celina.

"You try, but he blocks you each time and keeps coming."

She stepped with him to block. He dodged to the right. Celina dodged with him.

"Fuck," said Cam. "So I'm going to have to fight this guy."

"That's the idea," Celina smiled, stalking him toward the edge of the mat. It was cute watching Cam work through this scenario. She hoped he never had to face it in real life. Celina had been there more than once, and it was not fun.

"I suppose I'd get ready for him, then."

Cam shifted into the stereotypical fighting stance, with his left foot forward and his right foot back, both fists in front of his chin, ready to fight. He bounced on his toes.

And there it was. Too many movies, not enough training. That was exactly what most people would do. Or they'd do something even more stupid, like the crane pose from Karate Kid or some shit like that.

There was nothing inherently wrong with the boxing pose, but it was threatening, for one thing. And when someone is already agitated, even if you're resigned to fighting them, you don't want to antagonize them further.

Second, the boxing pose was great in a ring with rules and a referee to enforce them. But in the real world, it exposed your midsection, your crotch, your hips and knees. All targets.

And, third, the typical boxing stance put the weak foot forward. This was so the boxer could throw a punch by pivoting around the weak hip and swinging the strong arm with force. The more distance the fist traveled, the more force it would build up behind the punch.

But all that distance made the punch slower. In a boxing ring, force mattered. But in the real world, especially if your opponent was bigger than you, speed and surprise mattered more.

Celina stalked toward Cam. He bounced around like a welterweight, even threw a few shadow punches before Celina was even in range. She smiled and kept her head down, her eyes on Cam's. He'd already followed Stereotype Number One with the boxing stance. He was probably going to follow Stereotype Number Two and wait for Celina to attack, try to block, then counter-attack. That's what the karate masters always did in the movies. If you're just defending yourself, you get to be the good guy.

But in the real world, good guys die. It's better to attack first, surprise your opponent, and hopefully disable them long enough for you to get away.

As Celina expected, Cam did not do that. He just bounced on his toes, fists up, and waited, even after she was within arm's length.

With speed and precision she'd spent years developing, Celina crouched down, swung her leg in a swift arc, and swept Cam's front foot out from under him. He crashed onto his back on the mat and groaned in pain.

For a moment, Celina was afraid she'd pushed him too soon, that his ribs weren't healed enough for sparring yet. But then he looked up at her and she could see that it wasn't his ribs that were hurting him. It was his pride.

"Fuck, Celina," he said, slowly getting to his feet. "What did I ever do to you?"

He made her fall in love with him, that's what he did. But she wasn't going to say that. They hadn't said that to each other. Not yet.

She reached out a hand to help him up. He took it.

Sweeping the leg was a Karate Kid move, too, but it was a real one, at least. Still, it wasn't what Celina would have done in that scenario in the real world. The result was too unpredictable. If the guy had good balance, if he saw it coming, if he had heavy boots or thick ankles or whatever, the sweep might not work. In real life, Celina would have gone for the knee or put the heel of her palm into his nose or even put a foot in his nuts, though that had become enough of a movie cliché that a lot of guys expected it now.

But she didn't want to hurt Cam. She just wanted to teach him an object lesson. And she could see that his balance wasn't the best, so she took him down.

"You okay?" she said after pulling him to his feet.

"Yeah," he said, wincing and twisting his torso to stretch. "I guess I didn't realize that this would be that kind of training."

"What kind of training did you think it would be?"

Cam scrunched up his face, thinking, then shrugged. "The non-violent kind?"

Celina put a hand on each of Cam's cheeks and gave him a kiss. "I'll heal you later," she said. She gave him another kiss. "But, fucking hell, Cam," she said. "You need a shitload of training."

One more kiss, and then she forced herself to push him away, walked back to the other side of the mat, and turned to face him again.

"First rule of self-defense," she said, holding up one finger. "Trust your instincts."

Cam gave a heavy sigh, then his face grew serious. He nodded.

Time for the real training to begin.

9

IT WAS JUST after breakfast when they'd started sparring, maybe nine AM. By the time Celina let Cam go, sweating and sore, it was almost six in the evening. They'd skipped lunch entirely, but Cam hadn't even noticed.

He was dead set against violence in his work. His parents had taught him that, and he believed in it completely. When you plan a job, if you do it right, there was no need to bring weapons or threaten violence or put anyone's life in jeopardy. Criminals who do suffer from a lack of imagination. Period.

But that was in his work, when Cam had the luxury of time to plan and find solutions to any challenges the situation might present. When you're just going about your day and someone confronts you, it was useful to understand what was happening so you could defend yourself and your loved ones.

Cam had found that out in Washington. He'd been in the dark, helpless, while two men with guns hunted him and Celina. Celina was protecting him, but he had no idea what to do to help. He could have stolen a weapon from the men, but he didn't know how to use them. He could have disabled them hand-to-hand, like Celina did, but he didn't have the skills. He was helpless to do anything but flee, and without his glasses to help him see in the dark, he couldn't even do that.

Cam was determined never to let that situation happen again.

He'd been working in the gun range for weeks, and had been surprised to discover that he liked it. Beyond just learning how to handle a gun, he found the process interesting, even relaxing. It was the scientific method, really. Hypothesis, test, analyze. He'd sight in on a target, pull the trigger, then see how he did and adjust for the next shot. Hours passed in the range without Cam even realizing it.

Of course, it was also loud as hell, and he tried not to think about how dangerous it was, lest he slip into his usual fears about shooting off his own finger. But Celina had spent two whole days drilling gun safety into his brain before she even let him fire a shot, so his habits were good. Always keep the muzzle pointed in a safe direction. Never assume the chamber is empty or the safety is on. Be sure of the target and what's behind it. Always wear ear and eye protection, and so on.

Now she was teaching him hand-to-hand techniques, and Cam loved it. Getting into the mindset of an attacker was something he'd never even considered, but Celina forced him to think about it constantly in their training. In fact, in his first day of training, Celina spent more time talking to him about his thought processes than about his footwork or methods of blocking or striking.

Self-defense, she said, started with an awareness of your surroundings. It was easier to avoid compromising positions or locations altogether than it was to get out of them once trouble started. And if it did start, getting away should always be the first goal. Use the environment to your advantage. Dodge behind poles or parked cars, use distractions, try to understand what the attacker wants and give it to them so you can get away. That kind of thing. If it came to an actual attack, that was a failure, in Celina's telling. A failure to keep control of your situation.

Even when she did talk about the fighting, Celina drilled the conceptual principles before the techniques. Position, distance, momentum, balance, subversion. These are the keys to successful self-defense. Trust your instincts and remember that you're no longer in a social situation. You're in a fighting situation. Politeness and deference would get you killed. Strike first, strike intelligently, and strike when they're not expecting it. Then get the fuck away, if you can.

It was fascinating to learn from Celina. Her mind was quick and sharp, and she'd clearly thought so deeply about the topic that Cam felt like he was on a rocket ship, just hanging on and trying to absorb as much as he could.

Yet, at the end of the training session, drenched in sweat and breathing hard, he felt like he understood it all. Celina had poured a ton of knowledge into his mind and his body, but she'd done it in a way that it all made sense. She'd given him a framework for it, so that each piece of information had a place to sit in his mind once Cam learned it.

"You're an amazing teacher," he told her when she threw him a towel from a rack against the wall.

"I've had some amazing teachers," she said. "Whatever I do, I learned it from them."

Cam had never known Celina to be modest.

"That may be," he said, "but you've got a way of organizing all of this so that it sticks. In my brain."

She eyed him while she took a long pull from a water bottle, then capped it and tossed the bottle to Cam.

"I wasn't sure if you'd pick this stuff up or not," she said, "what with all the Gandhi shit you and Paulie talk about."

Cam unscrewed the cap of the water bottle, took a long drink, then capped it again and threw it back to Celina. He toweled off his face and his hair, then ran the towel over his chest. They'd started the session in workout gear, but quickly shed the jacket and the pants, stripping down to shorts and t-shirts. A couple hours later, Cam was bare-chested and Celina was down to her sports bra. Turned out that self-defense was sweaty work.

Cam couldn't help but notice how good Celina looked in a sports bra, her face hot, her hair wild, her body sheened in sweat. She caught the water bottle, and caught his look, too. She took another pull from the bottle and let her eye drag down and back along Cam's body.

He smiled at her. They had time for one more workout before dinner.

Kat came back around eight, well after dark. Cam and Celina had finished eating and left a plate in the oven for her.

"This is getting back as soon as you can?" said Celina as she reheated Kat's food and set it in front of her. They sat at the kitchen table while Kat ate.

"I'm sorry, darling," said Kat. "Next time I have to work late, I'll be sure to call."

Cam snorted.

Celina shot him a dark look. "Whatever," she said. "Let's cut to the chase."

Kat speared her food and chewed in silence, watching Celina while she ate.

"Those glasses you got," said Celina. "The AR glasses."

"What AR glasses?" asked Kat.

"Yeah, those ones," Celina replied. "Where did they come from?"

Celina had already told Cam the glasses had come from Jenkins. She must be checking to see how much Kat knew, and how much she would tell them.

"I don't know where they came from," Kat said. "They just showed up on my doorstep one day. Private courier."

"There was no name or address for the sender?"

"Some bullshit name. Mead Enterprises or something. Doesn't exist." She chewed another bite of food. "The address was a warehouse in Hoboken."

"Then why did you take them?"

Kat shrugged. "I don't know. I was bored, maybe? Intrigued?"

"It could have been anything," Celina frowned. "Could have been a bomb or a bio agent."

"Fucking hell, Celina," said Kat. "Who have you been pissing off these days?"

Celina ignored the question, but Cam could see the muscles flexing in the corners of her jaw.

"Okay, fine," she said. "A mysterious box showed up on your doorstep from an unknown sender, and you took it in without a second thought. What did you do then?"

"I opened it."

The muscles writhed and worked like a giant worm wriggling under Celina's skin.

"You just opened it?"

Kat sighed and pushed away her plate, half-eaten.

"Look, Celina, this wasn't some cloak-and-dagger shit, okay? I got a package, I opened it. There was tech inside, tech that looked an awful lot like Nestech technology."

She glared at Cam, who just raised his eyebrows at her

and smiled. Kat's glare softened, and a smile played at the edge of her lips before she looked back at Celina and continued.

"I took it down to the lab, took the usual precautions to isolate it from the rest of the network, and took a look."

"And disabled the GPS tracking," said Celina.

"Of course. First thing."

"And what did you find when you took a look?"

"You want me to share proprietary technical information with you?"

"You just said you got the package in the mail from an unknown sender. How could that be proprietary?"

"It's proprietary," Kat said, her voice sharpening, "because when I turned the thing on a Nestech logo appeared."

Celina glanced at Cam, then back to Kat.

Cam was positive they were his glasses. Celina had made a lot of modifications, but she'd kept the splash screen, with its glowing blue letter N and Celina's voice welcoming Cameron Hauk in one ear and Sam Davis in the other. The device used eye scanning to authenticate the user and customize the greeting, so Kat wouldn't have heard that particular welcome unless she'd dug around inside the system and found it. But she would have seen the logo.

"Then, yes," said Celina. "I want you to share proprietary information with me."

"Without our lawyers present?" said Kat. "You do still have a wild side."

"What did you find, Kat?"

Kat sighed, exasperated.

"What do you mean, what did I find? I found a ton of shit, Celina. A design more advanced than our most advanced design. An operating system more advanced than our most advanced OS. Better sensors, better processors, better everything." She glared at Celina. "I found a prototype more advanced than our most advanced prototype, and that's two years after you"—she swung her glare to Cam again—"stole it from us."

"Sounds like Nestech lost a step when your father... died." Celina smiled innocently at Kat, who glared again at Cam.

Kat had blood on her hands. That wasn't Cam's fault. He was the one who told Celina, but she was the one who murdered her own father.

And the way the tension was heating in the room, Cam wasn't at all sure she wouldn't try again.

That self-defense training could come in handy sooner than he thought.

10

CELINA FORCED HERSELF TO BREATHE, and to keep breathing. She'd learned that trick from Cam. She wanted nothing more than to slap Kat, throw her up against the wall, and make her stop being a bitch and start talking.

But she ground her teeth, forced herself to breathe, and got through it. Barely.

And then Kat did start talking.

Celina couldn't help herself with the line about Kat's father. He was kind of a dick, but who the fuck kills their own father? He wasn't beating his children or anything. Not as far as Celina knew, at least.

But what did she know, really? People did it all the time. The family that seems so perfect on the outside—fancy house, fancy cars, fancy clothes, kids getting good grades, all smiles and hugs and kisses—then ends up on the news as a triple murder-suicide, where the wife slits all their throats with a potato peeler in the middle of the night, then drinks a cold-pressed immunity juice with an arsenic booster. Christopher Nestech had always been kind to

Celina and to her father, but she'd seen him be prickly with others. Maybe he was beating his kids behind closed doors.

Or maybe his kids were just greedy fucks who killed him for his money. Who cares? She'd finally gotten Kat to stop acting like a corporate zombie and start talking like a real person. Like Kat fucking Nestrom.

"Nestrom lost a step when my brother-in-law took over," said Kat. "That's why whoever sent the glasses sent them to me instead of him."

Now Celina was getting somewhere.

"How did they know to send the package to your house?" Celina asked, adopting a musing tone. She knew Jenkins was the one who sent the glasses, which is why he sent them to Kat. Jenkins and Kat were almost as tight as Jenkins and Celina had been.

Which is why Kat's story didn't ring true. The fake sender was likely enough—Jenkins wouldn't exactly put the DOJ building as the return address—but Kat's ignorance about the true origins had to be a lie. Even if she didn't know when she got the package, it would have taken her all of fifteen minutes to trace it back using the GPS history in the glasses, or even using the tracking info from the courier.

Kat knew the glasses came from Jenkins. Celina was sure of that. But would Kat admit that to Celina, or would Kat hide that information? And if she chose to hide it, what else was she choosing to hide?

Kat glared at Celina for a long moment. Celina could see the anger in her eyes, but she could also see the calculation. Kat Nestrom was no fool.

After a moment, Kat's shoulders slumped and she let out a long sigh.

"Alright," she said. She looked at Celina, glanced at

Cam, then back to Celina. "You and I, we've known each other a long time. We go back a long way."

Celina nodded.

"Our parents were close. Our families were close."

"Are we close to your point?" asked Celina.

Kat's eyes flared for a moment, and she pressed her lips together. But she continued.

"I'm not going to bullshit you. I do know where the glasses came from."

Here it came. The big lie.

"I just don't know why," Kat said. "I came out here hoping maybe you could help me figure that part out."

"Where did they come from?" asked Celina.

Kat was taking a new tack. She'd shifted from stonewalling to asking for help, trying to get Celina on her side, playing on their friendship and trying to lull her into a position of trust. But why? What the hell did Kat want?

Kat glanced back and forth between Celina and Cam, then sighed and shook her head.

"Bill Jenkins," she said.

"Attorney General William Jenkins?" Celina adopted a dubious tone.

Kat nodded. "I know it sounds crazy." She shook her head again. "I haven't heard from him in years. Out of the blue, he calls me. Said someone brought him these glasses and they had our logo on them."

"So he was just returning them to you? Out of courtesy?" Celina let the sarcasm drip from her voice.

"He wants me to find out who had them." She looked at Cam. "Who stole them."

"But you didn't tell him that."

It wasn't a question. Celina was stating a fact.

Kat looked back at Celina and shook her head.

"Why not?"

"We're rivals, Celina," she said, "but we're still friends. At least, I like to think so."

Bullshit. Even when they were friends, Kat hadn't really cared about the friendship. To be fair, neither had Celina. They just hung out because it was fun to compete with each other. And because other people were boring. Kat Nestrom was a lot of things, most of them bad. But she had never been boring.

"Since when has friendship ever mattered to you?"

Kat sighed. "People change, Celina," she said. "I've changed."

"People only change when something makes them change."

Kat looked at Cam. "Something made me change, then."

Celina looked at Cam. He was staring into Kat's eyes. Was he actually buying this bullshit?

She changed the subject. "How did you know I was the one who had the glasses before?"

"I didn't," said Kat, swinging her gaze back to Celina. "Not really. I got into the code and found the greeting for Sam." Kat gestured toward Cam. "I realized he must have stolen a prototype we didn't know about." Cam was sitting in the chair next to Kat. She patted his knee. "Nice job, by the way."

Cam nodded thanks.

"Didn't get the significance of the Cameron Hauk thing until I came here and you introduced him," Kat continued. "Thought maybe there was more than one user."

Kat kept her hand on Cam's leg a few beats longer than necessary. A few beats longer than Celina liked. She clenched her jaw again.

"Still don't see how you traced it to me," she said, her voice strained through her clenched teeth.

"I told you. I didn't." Kat finally took her hand from Cam's knee. Her voice sharpened, but she kept it civil. "The voice in the greeting sounded familiar, but I couldn't quite place it. Then I looked at the code. You've got a distinctive style, Celina, so I suspected you might be involved, but I still couldn't prove it."

Celina unclenched her jaw. "And then I called you."

Kat nodded. "And then you called me."

That all checked out. The story made sense now. All tied up in neat little knots. Jenkins sees the logo, sends it to Kat, tells her to figure out who it came from. She figures it out and comes to California to meet with Celina in person.

But why? Why meet in person? Why meet at all? And why not just tell Jenkins what she figured out?

There were still too many unanswered questions. None of these people acted selflessly. They were all selfish assholes, including Celina. Cam was helping her become an actual person with feelings and love for fellow man and all that bullshit, but she wasn't there yet.

"Why did you come all the way out here, Kat?" Cam asked softly. "Why not just tell Celina everything on the phone when she called you?

Kat's demeanor changed when she replied to Cam's question. Where she'd been her normal bitchy self with Celina, though much more helpfully bitchy than usual, with Cam she took the tone of a secret admirer, pining for her love from afar. All soft-voiced and smiley.

Celina wanted to punch her in her perfect fucking teeth.

"I had business out here, anyway," Kat began. "And... I was afraid."

"Afraid of what?"

Cam was playing right back into Kat's act. His voice was soft, too. He even leaned forward when he asked the question, as if he was concerned for her, like he didn't want her to be frightened, like he would comfort her and protect her from the big, bad politicians. If he was doing on purpose, he was playing the role very well.

If he was actually falling for Kat's bullshit... Celina didn't want to go down that road.

"I don't know." Kat laughed nervously. A nice touch. "Afraid that Jenkins might be listening? That he might know I told Celina everything and retaliate somehow?" She shook her head and blew out a shuddering breath. She was laying it on thick. "It sounds stupid when I say it out loud."

"It is stupid," said Celina before she puked in her own mouth. "And you're smarter than that. Why did you really come out?"

Kat swung her eyes back to Celina, and the bitch came back. Kat snorted.

"You asked me to come, remember?"

"Since when does that matter?"

"Since we became friends... what... twenty years ago?"

"More like sixteen."

Kat sat back in her chair and stared at Celina.

"You never call," she said. "Or text or email or anything. I haven't heard from you in years." She shrugged. Her favorite thing to do, apparently. "You said you needed me. So I came."

Celina sat back in her own chair and nodded slowly. She didn't buy a word of it, but she didn't think she'd get anywhere by pushing. Not right then.

"That's very..." She glanced at Cam. "What's the word?"

She snapped her fingers. "Altruistic." She looked back at Kat. "That's very altruistic of you."

Kat smiled at her, a warm, broad, toothy smile that didn't reach her cold eyes.

"I'm a very altruistic person."

"Really?" Celina arched her eyebrows in surprise. "I guess you really have changed."

11

CAM KNEW ENOUGH to keep quiet while Celina was in that kind of mood. Her jaw muscles were flexing, her brows were knotted, and she stomped around the bedroom, banging her toothbrush and her water glass and her hairbrush around like a hungry bear in a pantry. He could see she was angry, but Cam wasn't entirely sure if she was angry at Kat or at him, somehow.

They got ready in silence and slid into bed. Cam rolled to his side and looked at her. She stared at the wall, chewing her cheek, stewing.

"Hey," said Cam, softly, "you okay?"

Celina didn't respond.

"What's got you so upset?"

"I'm not upset," said Celina.

"No," Cam replied with a smile, trying to lighten her mood, "you seem like you're doing great."

Celina gave him a glaring side-eye, then stared straight ahead again.

So much for lightening her mood.

"I'm not upset," she said. "I'm pissed off."

Cam didn't understand the difference between those two, but he didn't think now was a good time for a discussion of semantics.

"What are you pissed off about?"

Celina turned her head over her shoulder and gave Cam a hard stare.

His heart jumped into his throat. Celina was drop-dead gorgeous. Some of the time, his mind accepted that fact and moved on so that he could actually function during the day. But sometimes, like now, the reality of it stopped him cold.

And those stunning green eyes of hers caught him like a deer in headlights damn near every time she looked at him. This time was no different.

But right then, he had the sinking feeling that while she had him in her headlights, Celina was gunning the engine, speeding up to turn Cam into road kill.

"What did you think of that conversation?" she asked.

"With Kat?"

"Yeah," Celina said, drily. "With Kat."

The engine downshifted and revved higher in Cam's ears. He swallowed, his throat dry. He didn't know what he'd done, but it sure seemed like he'd done something.

"I thought she was hiding what she was really thinking," he said, "at first. But you got her to admit the truth."

"I got her to admit the truth?"

"Yeah," said Cam, smiling, again trying to calm Celina. "You did."

"And what was the truth?"

Her voice was quiet, but as hard as the radiator grille of a speeding truck.

"That she knew it was Jenkins who sent the glasses," he said. "That he wanted to know where they came from, and that she was afraid he might be, like, eavesdropping or tracking her somehow. She didn't want him to hear, so she came out here in person."

"To protect me."

"Yes," Cam nodded. "Out of respect. For your friendship."

"She was afraid Jenkins was monitoring her communications, so she came out here in person, to my home, with the glasses. To protect me out of respect for our friendship."

The way she kept repeating everything he said was making Cam very nervous. In his mind, the roaring engine was deafening. He could practically taste the antifreeze.

He swallowed again, his mouth now so dry it was actively pulling moisture from the air around him. If things kept going like this, he and Celina would be mummified in minutes.

Cam nodded. "Well... that's what I got out of it."

"And you buy that bullshit?" Celina said.

Cam frowned. He knew what he should say. He should say of course he didn't buy that bullshit, that it was obviously bullshit and only an idiot would believe that bullshit.

Except, he did believe it. Kat had been resistant at first. He chalked that up to habitual rivalry. But then she'd pushed past that and opened up about her reasons for coming. She'd flown all the way across the country. There had to be a reason. It made no sense for her to hide it. And she and Celina went way back. Why wouldn't Kat want to help her?

Yes, Kat was a murderer. The worst kind, the kind that would kill her own father. The only thing worse would be killing your own children.

But Cam was a killer, too. That didn't make him a bad person, right? He made a difficult choice, one he wished he could take back. He had no regret about saving Celina's life, but if he could do it again, he'd find a way to save her life without taking someone else's.

But Cam still had feelings. He loved his mother. He loved Celina. The killing didn't instantly make him an irredeemable villain.

He had to give Kat the same benefit of the doubt. She'd done a terrible thing. Maybe she regretted it. Maybe she was trying to make up for it by helping an old friend.

"Why would she come all the way out here if she wasn't trying to help?" he said.

Celina stared at him for a long moment, her green eyes searing him with their intensity.

"That's what I'm trying to figure out," she said at last.

She smacked her pillows hard, threw her head against them with her back toward Cam, and yanked the covers up over her shoulder.

Cam looked at her like that, feeling the temperature in the room slowly drop even further below freezing. He turned off the lights and lay down, but he didn't sleep.

He stared at the ceiling in the dark. He could accept that Celina was pissed off because she didn't trust Kat. Maybe Cam was being naïve. Maybe Kat didn't come all the way out here just to help an old friend. He didn't know Kat very well, and he didn't know much about the history between her and Celina.

But without evidence to prove that Kat's intentions were bad, why not assume they were good? Cam tended to think the best of people. Sure, that attitude got you into trouble once in a while, but it was right more often than not. And why would anyone want to spend their life walking around with an attitude of mistrust all the time?

But Celina was different, and that was fine. She was

pissed at Kat because she didn't trust her and she thought Kat was still hiding something.

Then why was Celina giving Cam the cold shoulder? What had he done to piss her off?

Cam lay awake in the dark for a long time, chewing on that question. He wished he could just ask her, but she hadn't exactly seemed like she was in the mood to have a frank and honest conversation about her feelings. And waking her up now would just piss her off even more.

Hours later, still unable to sleep, Cam finally gave up and got out of bed. The clock said it was almost 2am. Maybe some time in the training room working on his technique would wear him out enough to get a few hours of rest.

He stripped off his boxer briefs and pulled a pair of loose workout shorts from a drawer in the dark, not bothering with a t-shirt, and padded down two flights to what he had come to think of as The School—the floor of the house with the gun range, the training room, and the weight room.

For a moment, he considered heading to the gun range for some target practice instead, but decided that using loaded firearms while sleep-deprived in the middle of the night was probably not such a good idea. He turned the other way, down the hallway that led to the training room.

As he approached, Kat came out of the weight room at the far end of the hallway. She wore deep blue spandex workout shorts that fit low on her hips and high on her thighs. On top, she wore a matching sports bra that scooped low in the front. Her hair was pulled back in a tight ponytail, and her muscular legs and abs were bare and glistening with sweat.

The sight of Kat's body, her bare skin, immediately

brought back memories for Cam. Fond memories. Vivid ones. He felt his body reacting to the images in his mind. He swallowed hard and tried to push them away.

And then Kat looked up.

Cam was caught short again, just like he had been with Celina earlier. Kat was another one of those women with the kind of drop-dead gorgeous looks that smack you in the face and disorient you for a moment. You're not sure if you're in real life or in a movie or dreaming. And the fact that Kat could have that effect that while coming out of the gym, sweating, no makeup, was even more stunning.

She had a water bottle in one hand and was rubbing the back of her neck with a towel in the other hand when she saw Cam and startled.

"Oh," she said, then smiled with relief. "You scared me."

"Sorry," said Cam.

Cam was suddenly aware that he was wearing nothing but an old pair of workout shorts, with worn elastic in the waistband that hung low and loose.

Kat seemed to notice, too. She scanned him slowly.

"I think your shorts," she nodded toward him, "might be on backwards."

Cam glanced down at himself. She was right. His shorts were on backwards. His cheeks instantly burned.

"That's what I get for dressing in the dark, I guess," he said with a laugh.

"Well, don't worry," said Kat. She gave him her high-wattage smile as she approached. Cam remembered that smile well. It still stopped his heart every time he saw it. "I won't tell anyone."

She put one hand on his shoulder as she passed him. It stayed there, soft and lingering, before she stepped past and pulled it away. The air felt cold against Cam's skin where her hand had been.

"Kat," he called.

She stopped in the hallway and turned back to him.

"It was good of you to come all the way out here," he said, "to help Celina."

She smiled faintly.

"Celina would never say that to me."

Cam nodded. "I don't know why that is. But I'll say it. Thank you for coming."

Kat came back toward him and leaned against the wall. "Celina and I have known each other a long time," she said. "Our friendship has been..."

She bit her lip and waggled her head back and forth, thinking. Her ponytail brushed the back of her neck as it swung.

"It's been complicated," she said, and smiled wryly. "But I think Celina may understand me better than anyone in the world. Better than my own family." She laughed. "Definitely better than my family."

Her dark eyes were wide, unguarded.

"Because of that, I still think of her as my closest friend," she said. "Even if we don't talk much."

"Sometimes, Celina can be hard to talk to."

Kat gave a quick laugh and nodded. "You found that out, did you?"

This time it was Cam who laughed. "Oh, yeah. That lesson came early."

"Well, I'm here to help," she said. "And I shouldn't have to go into the office again, not for a few days, at least. As long as nothing blows up over there," she cringed, "I'm at your disposal."

"Thank you," said Cam. "I'm sure Celina will come around."

"Maybe she will, maybe she won't." Kat shrugged. "I'm still here to help. Any way I can."

She let her eyes draw slowly down from Cam's eyes, over his bare chest, to his shorts. Cam felt her eyes on him like a feather touch, became very much aware that he was not only wearing only a loose pair of shorts, but that he wasn't wearing any underwear beneath it.

He pushed from his mind the thoughts that were creeping in and prepared himself to fend off another advance from Kat.

But she didn't advance. She let her eyes fall down to the floor, bit her lip again, shook her head slightly, to herself, and sighed.

She lifted her eyes to Cam's again. "Seeing you was a surprise," she said. "I've thought about you a lot since the last time we saw each other." She gave him a smile, tight and sad, but friendly. "I'm glad to see that you're happy."

She turned and left before Cam could think of a response.

He watched her go until she turned out of sight.

12

CELINA WOKE to the sound of the shower running. A thin line of light pierced the darkness of the bedroom from beneath the bathroom door. She checked the clock on the nightstand. It was after 3am.

Celina could think of only one reason why Cam would be up at 3am taking a shower without her.

The thoughts in Celina's mind were acid. They burned in her brain. They burned in her stomach.

She tried to dilute them, to push them away, to counteract them with logic.

This was Cam. Cam was not a cheater. Cam loved her.

But he'd never said he loved her, had he? They hadn't said that to each other yet.

And people cheat all the time. Celina sure as fuck did. She'd never had a steady boyfriend to cheat on, but that was only a technicality. The tears on the faces of her ex-lovers were evidence enough that they felt betrayed. So why should Celina expect anything different from Cam?

He'd never shown any sign of cheating before, but he'd never had a woman like Kat around. There weren't many women like Kat. And having her here in the house with him—with the history they had, however brief—might be too much temptation.

Fuck.

It was Celina's own fucking fault, then. She was the one who insisted that Kat stay with them. Kat could have gotten a fucking hotel and there would be no temptation. Cam wouldn't have cheated. He might still have thought about it, but thinking is one thing and doing is another. No opportunity, no crime. Means and motive aren't enough.

But now he'd had means, motive, and opportunity. And Celina had pushed him into it. She'd frozen him out earlier that night because she thought he'd been too sympathetic to Kat's story. He'd bought her bullshit at full-price because Kat was hot and Cam was thinking with his dick.

And now he'd acted with his dick, all because Celina froze him out.

No. Fuck that. Celina would not be one of those women who blamed herself when her boyfriend acted like an asshole. Cam was a grown fucking man. He should be able to control his own impulses. Kat was hot? So was fucking Celina. If Cam was already tired of her, then fuck him. He'd miss her when Celina dumped his ass in the gutter on the side of the road.

She ground her teeth and bit her tongue when he slid back into bed beside her, when he pressed his shower-warm body against hers and put his arm over her waist. He kissed her shoulder, bare in her tank top, and snuggled in to sleep.

Fucking hell. What was she thinking? This was Cam, for fuck's sake. The Cam who spent fifteen years trying to get his mother out of jail. The Cam who wouldn't hack into the admin systems at the university because he didn't want them to think he'd doctored his grades. The Cam who had thrown himself at an armed gunman in the dark to save Celina's life.

Cam wasn't a cheater.

Celina was just being paranoid. And jealous.

Goddamn motherfucking jealous.

She took Cam's arm and pulled it up to her shoulder, pulled it tight around her and tucked it under her own arm. Cam was hers. And she was his. He wasn't some fuckboy slut who picked up any woman who would rub her ass against his crotch on a nightclub dance floor. He could have anyone, anytime, and he'd been single when she'd met him. From talking to his classmates, Sarah and Annie, he'd been single all through college. Cam was not a womanizer.

She pulled his arm tighter against her, his hand curled against her breast, his face buried against the back of her neck.

He kissed her lightly there, then again. His fingers brushed across her nipple through the thin fabric of her shirt. Celina felt it peak under his touch. A white-hot heat flared deep within her.

He was not a womanizer. He was *her* man. Hers and only hers.

She arched her back and pressed herself against him, felt him stiffen against her.

She rolled over in his embrace and took what belonged to her.

In the morning, Celina felt better. She and Cam had talked briefly after sex. She'd asked him why he was up. He told her he couldn't sleep and had gone down for a work-out. Seemed a plausible enough story. And the sex had not been the sex of a man who'd just fucked someone else.

Cam had serious stamina, so it wasn't conclusive evidence, but it did set Celina's mind more at ease.

Until Kat came down for breakfast.

Celina and Cam were at the table, eating. Cam had made them each a bowl of oatmeal with honey and freshly sliced strawberries.

Kat touched Cam on the shoulder as she passed, and they exchanged smiles that were friendly—only friendly— but why so fucking friendly? They hadn't been that friendly when they'd all gone to bed the night before, which meant they'd somehow gotten friendly during the night.

The burning in Celina's stomach came back, stronger than ever.

"I'm all yours today, Celina," said Kat as she sat at the table with them, a cup of black coffee in hand. "What's your game plan?"

Celina had lost her appetite. She stabbed at her oatmeal, her spoon clinking against the ceramic of the bowl like the clink of a chain gang prisoner using his pick to escape. She dropped the spoon in the bowl and pushed it away. Her tongue tasted like ash and she'd lost her appetite completely.

From the side of her vision, she saw Cam frown at her. She ignored him.

"My plan is to find out what you know, Kat," she said with a saccharine smile. "Then I can let you go back home and get on with your life."

Kat looked at her strangely for a long moment. Celina returned the stare, waiting, watching. Kat glanced at Cam, then back to Celina.

Was that a conspiratorial glance?

"I'm an open book," said Kat. "I'll help you any way I can."

"Uh-huh," said Celina. She pushed back from the table, her chair screeching and nearly toppling over. "Let's start with the glasses, then, okay? Where are they?"

Kat choked a little on a sip of coffee she'd just taken. Unfortunately, she didn't choke to death.

"Right now?" Kat said.

"We can at least finish eating first, can't we?" said Cam, looking down at his own half-full bowl of oatmeal.

"Bring it with you," said Celina, turning away from the table and stalking toward her lab. "Time's wasting."

She felt a prickle of sweat on her neck and her chest as she stalked away. She was halfway down the hall to the other side of the house, where her lab was located, before she heard the others push back from the table and follow her.

She was being an idiot. She knew that. A part of her brain could see that. That part was telling her to stop acting this way. Celina Maxwell was not an idiot. Celina Maxwell made fun of the idiots in the world. She ran circles around them. She used their idiocy to get what she wanted.

And now she was acting just like all the other idiots. All because she was jealous.

Was it love that made people act this way? She could see the idiocy in her mind, could see it so clearly, but she couldn't seem to counteract it. Her brain just went down a tunnel and couldn't stop until it came out the other side. The tunnel of love was more like a tunnel of jealousy. It was total bullshit, but she felt like she had no control over her own emotions anymore.

That just made her even angrier.

The door to her lab was wide and heavy, but she pushed it open hard enough to bang it against the doorstop. She stalked inside and waited for Cam and Kat to catch up.

Cam and Kat. Even their fucking names were catchy together. Cameron and Katerina. Their ship name would be Camerina. Or Kateron.

Jesus fucking Mary and goddamn Joseph H. Christ. What the fucking fuck was wrong with her?

She spread both hands wide on one of her workbenches and hung her head, desperately trying to get control of her own mind before Camerina walked in and saw her freaking out. She remembered Cam's teaching and pulled a deep breath in through her nose and blew it out her mouth, then did it again, and a third time. The idea was to breathe long and slow, but she didn't have time for that. What she was doing was less like meditative breathing and more like hyperventilation, but it did calm her a little bit. It also made her a bit lightheaded.

She stood straight again and looked around the room, trying to reorient herself and focus her mind on something other than herself freaking out.

The lab had been her father's. It was spacious, longer than it was wide, with two long workbenches running down the middle of the room. Hanging above them were a series of bright, fully adjustable lights on heavy pivoting arms, like the kind you would find in an operating theater. Celina's father had often done fine assembly work on those benches, and he could position and focus the lights exactly where he wanted them, controlling the brightness and temperature with touch controls on stalks extending from the light housings, or with foot controls under the workbench.

A slew of manufacturing devices filled two walls, from

plasma cutters to CNC machines to 3-D printers of all sizes, and everything in between. Everything her father needed to develop, prototype, and test new hardware.

Against the third wall was a long desk with several desktop computers, laptops, and tablets of various sizes. This was where her father made the 3-D designs, tracked and analyzed his test data, and generally did whatever data work he needed to do. All the computers and tablets were synced to a central server, so he could take a tablet or computer with him wherever he went without fear of losing data or not having something he needed at the moment he needed it.

Of course, most of the time toward the end, he wore his AR glasses, his last invention, which let him wear everything on his face all the time. The other machines had been rendered almost irrelevant for all but the most meticulous, input-heavy work. He'd walk around the house wearing the glasses. The earlier prototypes looked ridiculous, like the window of a welder's mask set inside a camera rig that held sensors of all kinds, wires running between the two. Her father had looked like Medusa on a ski trip in the Alps.

But that prototype had quickly gotten smaller and sleeker until it took its final shape, indistinguishable from a normal pair of eyeglasses. As she'd gotten older, he'd brought her into the lab more and more, telling her what all the equipment was for, walking her through his thought process, his process of experimentation, failure, learning, and more experimentation. Failure was a part of the process, he told her. Maybe the most important part.

By the end, she was working at his side, bouncing ideas back and forth with him, experimenting and failing together. Neatly lined up on one workbench were a few of the last prototypes they'd been working on when he was murdered seventeen months ago. She hadn't touched them since that day, hadn't been able to bring herself to touch them.

In fact, she'd barely set foot in the lab since her father's death. Too many memories. Too much there that reminded her of him. His teaching, his admonitions, his patience with her mistakes, even when they ruined months of work. Part of the process. An opportunity to rebuild it better, he would say each time one of her ideas failed. A chance to incorporate everything they'd learned and rebuild from scratch.

Celina wished she had her father's patience and calm demeanor now.

She wished she had her father. Period.

Cam and Kat came through the door, Cam still wiping oatmeal from his lips. Thankfully, neither one of them had brought any food or drink in with them. Despite what Celina had said, the lab was no place for anything that could spill or splatter, and no place to be eating.

What calm Celina had managed to gain immediately disappeared when Kat stood shoulder-to-shoulder with Cam. The lab was big. Plenty of space for three people. Yet Kat was so close to Cam their arms were practically touching. They might as well be holding fucking hands.

Celina glared at Kat. She raised her eyebrows. And smirked.

Fucking smirked.

Celina growled softly.

"The glasses," she said, holding out her hand.

"I don't have them with me."

"Where are they?"

"They're in my room."

Celina growled again, louder. She couldn't help it.

"Then go fucking get them," she said.

Kat looked at Cam with wide, innocent eyes, shrugged her shoulders, and left to get the glasses.

Cam watched her leave, then turned back to Celina and folded his arms across his chest.

Celina knew she was acting like a dickhead. Her rational mind knew that.

But her rational mind was not in control at the moment, and she could not seem to get that control back.

She had to, though. This was getting out of hand, this fucking rage she felt. She could feel it casting around the room, looking for something, anything, to grab on to, anything to serve as the focus for her anger. The fucking workbench was too messy. The light was in the wrong position. The computer screen kept waking up and going to sleep.

Cam kept looking at her like she was acting weird. So what if she was? He didn't look at Kat that way.

"Celina," he said, quietly.

Too quietly. Pissed her off. She didn't need to be handled like a bomb that could explode. She could handle herself.

He walked around the workbench, put a gentle hand on each of her arms. "What is going on with you?"

She stared around the room, everywhere but at him. How could he fucking ask that question? How could he not see what he was doing? What he and Kat were doing?

Finally, she looked into his eyes, into his deep, clear, complex brown eyes. She saw the mysterious flecks of orange and yellow in them, those colors that were uniquely Cam.

But it was what she didn't see that was more important.

No mockery. No deception. No betrayal.

Just concern. And love.

Celina looked away and shook her head, trying to clear it.

What the fuck was going on with her?

13

CAM TRIED to catch Celina's gaze, but she looked all around the lab, everywhere but at him. Holding her arms, he was trying to soothe her, but the muscles of Celina's arm were tense.

She'd been acting weird ever since Kat had arrived. Cam didn't know what to make of it. She'd been rude and secretive and touchy as hell, flying off at Kat and even at him for no apparent reason.

Celina had never cared much what other people thought, and she was always willing to tell people exactly how she felt. It was one of the things Cam loved about her, her boldness. It sometimes bordered on recklessness, but Celina Maxwell had balls, and Cam admired that.

But lately, her behavior had gone beyond mere boldness. Something was off with Celina, and it had to have had something to do with Kat. It started when Kat arrived.

Cam and Celina had talked briefly after sex the night before. Cam had asked if she was somehow jealous of Kat. He tried to reassure her that there was absolutely no need for that, that he didn't think of Kat like that at all anymore.

He clenched his fists when he said it, trying not to think about the way he'd felt when he'd seen Kat in the hallway outside the gym. Those were just sense memories, body memories. Instinctive physical responses. They came from his unconscious mind, totally out of his control. They had nothing to do with how he really felt. And he would never act on those feelings. They came into his mind of their own bidding, and he ignored them.

Celina denied being jealous. She trusted Cam, she said, and was fine with Kat being there. She was just worried about Jenkins and the glasses, worried that he was going to try to do something more, something that would permanently remove the threat of the data that Celina and Cam had claimed to have destroyed.

She said there were too many unexplained recent events. The theft of Cam's glasses from a safe house no one was supposed to know they were using. The sudden appearance of two Israeli assassins during a job. Tracking those glasses directly back to Jenkins, then to Kat. She was just worried about it all, she said.

It wasn't like Celina to worry about things like that, in Cam's experience. But as well as he had come to know her in the last ten months, it had only been ten months. Celina was the kind of person it would take a lifetime to understand. Maybe the threat Jenkins posed was serious enough that Cam should be more worried about it. If Celina was freaking out, Cam should be, too.

But she'd been fine at breakfast this morning, light and loving and full of laughter, like usual. Cam thought maybe she'd been able to move past the worry, at least for a while.

And then Kat had come down, and Celina's mood had changed again. In an instant.

It had to have something to do with Kat.

She said she wasn't jealous, and Cam believed her. There was no reason to doubt her. Cam had told her he didn't think of Kat that way, and Celina said she trusted him.

But if Kat was triggering this Jekyll and Hyde routine in Celina, there must be some reason for it. She trusted Cam, but did she not trust Kat?

Kat had come on strong on the first night, but she'd seen that Cam wasn't interested and had backed off since then. She'd made her play and lost, and now she seemed to have accepted the fact that Cam was happy with Celina and didn't feel that way about Kat any more.

So there must be something else, some other reason why Celina didn't trust Kat. Something to do with the glasses, maybe? Or Jenkins? Cam cursed himself for not taking the time to talk to Celina more about it. They'd had all day alone yesterday while Kat was at work. They could have been discussing it while they sparred, but Cam had been so focused on what he was learning that the thought hadn't even entered his mind.

Finally, Celina's eyes stopped darting all over the place and settled on his own. He fell right into them again, like he always did. A green as clear and deep as a tropical ocean. But right then, they were storm-tossed. They widened as he looked at her. Cam tried to project as much compassion, as much concern, as much love as he could through his eyes. Sometimes words weren't enough. Celina needed to feel how much he loved her. He tried to push the force of that feeling through his eyes.

And then she looked away and shook her head. For a moment, her eyes glinted like they were wet with brimming tears, but it might have been the light. Celina stared unseeing at the wall for a long moment, opened her mouth as if to say something.

"Here they are," said Kat, striding back into the lab. She set the glasses on the workbench. "Have at them."

Celina turned and broke Cam's grip on her arms. She turned toward the wall, pausing briefly before spinning the rest of the way toward Kat and the workbench. When she did, her face was composed and serious.

She repositioned one of the lights and picked up the glasses, unfolding the earpieces and examining the entire device closely. Then she set it into a kind of holster on her workbench, one with several thin wires leading to a long, thin box.

Kat seemed to know what it was, because she turned toward the bank of computers before Celina had even stepped around the workbench. Celina sat in a chair in front of a workstation and started typing away. Kat pulled up another chair. Cam stood behind them.

Several windows flashed on the screen and a bunch of computer code came up. Celina opened a second window, then a third, each of them filled with code in a language Cam didn't recognize.

"It's proprietary," said Celina as she typed in more code and watched as data streamed across the screen. "A mix of Assembly, C++, and Go, along with plenty of home-brewed stuff my father and I developed together."

"And what about that?" Cam pointed to the code on another screen.

"That part is Nestech code," said Kat. "Also proprietary. Mostly my father's invention. He was very anal about his compilers." She looked at Celina. "You didn't seem to have much trouble figuring it out. I saw a bunch of mods you made to the base code."

"I didn't touch the base code," said Celina. "Just expanded the library a bit."

"Even the top architect at Nestech couldn't make heads or tails of it," Kat said. "She said my father intentionally wrote it so no one else could ever alter his code."

"I can't imagine why," muttered Celina. When Kat didn't respond, she glanced at her and said, "My father showed some of it to me years ago. I think he and your dad would talk about this stuff."

Kat nodded. "Still," she said, "you were able to extend it. You must have understood it pretty well."

Celina shrugged. "I don't know what's wrong with your architect. It makes perfect sense to me."

"You and my dad always did get along." Kat folded her arms across her chest. "I wish he'd liked me half as much as he liked you."

Celina looked over at her, a strange look on her face. Kat stared straight ahead at the screen.

Cam had no idea what was going on, but something had just passed between the two women, some moment he didn't understand. There are times when you realize just how little you know about some people, and just how well they know each other. This was one of those times. He felt like he stood on the edge of a deep, dark well, a well filled with the years of history that Kat and Celina shared. Cam couldn't see the bottom, had no idea how deep it was. He could only see the shifting gleam of the water on the surface.

Maybe that's why he couldn't understand why Celina had been so upset lately. He just couldn't fathom all the history.

"There," said Celina as she pressed the enter key and another window opened on her computer.

A slew of numbers scrolled across the screen, too fast for Cam to read them.

"Are those... coordinates?" he asked.

Celina nodded. "Lat-long in decimal degrees. It's the GPS history for the glasses for the last three months."

She tapped out a few more keystrokes, and a map came up on the screen, along with a solid blue line in varying widths. The line traced from Celina's house in DC to her mother's house in Alexandria, then back to the DOJ building beside the National Mall. From there, it went up the coast to Kat's house in New York before arcing across the country to California.

"The width encodes the duration of time in each location," said Celina. "The wider the line, the longer the glasses stayed there."

The line was widest at the DOJ building.

"Jenkins had them at the DOJ for a long time," Cam said. "What did he do with them?"

"Let me check the usage logs," said Celina.

The keyboard clacked and rattled as she entered a series of commands.

"Doesn't look like he did anything with them," she said. "He didn't even turn them on."

"Then how did he know they were Nestech glasses?" asked Kat. "He said he saw our logo on the splash screen."

Celina didn't say anything. She was staring at the information on the computer screen, thinking. Cam could see the muscles in her jaw clenching and releasing, clenching and releasing.

"Maybe whoever stole them tried them on," he said. "The bald guy we saw in the video."

"Bald guy?" asked Kat.

With a few keystrokes, Celina brought up the last

recording the glasses had made. A broad-faced man with a double-chin and a goatee filled the screen, frowning at the camera.

"Look familiar?" asked Celina.

Kat shook her head. "Never seen him before."

Cam paced back and forth behind Celina and Kat.

"Okay," he said, "let me make sure I've got all this straight." He folded his arms and put one thumb under his chin. "Celina and I are in Alexandria when the glasses are stolen. We don't know who stole them, just what he looks like." He gestured to the image of the man on the screen.

"Have you tried to identify him?" Kat asked Celina. "Face reco, law enforcement databases, anything?"

Celina shook her head. "No hits."

Kat raised her eyebrows and grunted in surprise.

"Not long after," Cam continued, "Celina and I get attacked by Israeli special-forces."

"What?" Kat's eyes shot wide.

"Don't worry about it," said Celina.

"It's a long story," said Cam, "and we don't even really know the ending yet."

"How did I not hear about this?"

"Why would you?" asked Celina.

"Don't you think it's relevant?" said Kat. "I mean, if the Israelis are after you, I might have reconsidered staying at your house."

Cam and Celina spoke over each other.

"You're welcome to leave," said Celina.

"The Israelis aren't after us," said Cam.

Cam looked strangely at Celina for a moment. Was she trying to get Kat to leave? If so, Kat was definitely the prob-lem. And if that was the case, why didn't Celina just kick her out? It's not like she couldn't afford to find another place to stay.

"They're ex-Israeli special forces," Cam said, focusing again on the question at hand. "No affiliation with the current government."

"Not officially, anyway," Celina added.

Kat was definitely the problem.

"Anyway," Cam said, resuming his pacing, "the guy steals the glasses, the attack happens, and then the glasses go to Jenkins, then to you." He gestured to Kat. "How much of this is related?"

"Well, I don't know anything about any Israeli special forces," said Kat. "Fucking hell. I just deal with the tech."

"You haven't *just dealt with the tech* in a long time, Kat," said Celina.

The temperature in the room dropped twenty degrees as Kat and Celina glared at each other.

"You know what I mean," Kat said.

Cam sighed. They had a long list of questions and were no further toward getting any answers. With Kat and Celina going at each other all over again, Cam was starting to wonder why the hell Celina had invited her out in the first place.

Add that to the list of unanswered questions.

14

IN HER BEDROOM, Kat sat in a wide, comfortable lounge chair, feet up on an ottoman, laptop balanced on her legs. The room was nowhere near as spacious or elegant as she was used to, but for a guest room, it was generous enough. The bed was king-sized. The closet was a wide walk-in. A separate sitting area had a couch, two lounge chairs, a desk, and a huge television on the wall. Sliding doors opened from there onto a balcony wide enough for a breakfast table and four chairs. It was pitch dark now, but in the daytime, Kat could see the beach and the crashing waves below. It was cozy in a California sort of way. Nice, but a little too homey for Kat's taste.

She'd lived in Silicon Valley for almost a decade when she was younger, and she'd never gotten used to the odd combination of the crunchy granola vibe and the sleek, tech aesthetic. The result was thousand-dollar composting machines that looked like over-engineered trash cans and sat in pride of place on the kitchen counter. Look-at-me humility. It was completely stupid. The nouveau riche tech barons thought they were saving the world, but they were just getting fatter and more arrogant like the rest of the billionaires, clinging to their humble beginnings while acting as the suzerains of new-world vassal systems in the guise of tech corporations.

Kat preferred to drop the act and just accept her wealth. She didn't need to flaunt it, but she could still enjoy it. It was hers. What else was there to do with wealth but spend it or use it to make more wealth?

She tapped away on her laptop, working through a careful series of VPNs to hack into Celina's home network. She was sure Celina would track any activity on her network, so Kat had to disguise her entry point carefully. Celina had closed all of the usual vulnerabilities. No password-less appliances or smart bulbs. No unused ports left unguarded on her computers. No unsecured routers. Celina was smart. She knew what she was doing.

Kat was smart, too. She was an expert in internet security, after all. She'd found a way in, something Celina had missed. And now she was scouring Celina's network, looking for the data Jenkins had requested.

He hadn't been very specific, which made Kat's job a lot harder and irritated the fuck out of her. She'd met Jenkins once or twice when he was a young congressman, when Celina's father had just taken Jenkins under his wing. He'd been nice enough, then. Kinda hot, for an older guy. Gave off DILF vibes back then.

Not anymore. Now, he gave off pure DICK vibes. He'd had too much power for too long, with no money to back it up. That combination made people cruel and desperate, once they realized how hollow their power was. The real power came from money, not politics. Political power could be strong, but it was always fleeting. People were loyal to the office, not the person who held it. But a solid fortune made people loyal forever. Or for as long as you could buy their loyalty, anyway.

Kat searched Celina's system, using a back door she'd built into the glasses before she'd left New York. It was small, subtle. But as long as the glasses were hooked into Celina's system, Kat had an untraceable in.

Finding what she needed was another story. And Kat didn't want to set up a daemon to run while she wasn't watching. Too risky. Celina would have routines scrubbing her system for anomalies, and a new program running in the background would be an obvious red flag. She'd just have to work manually.

She'd told Jenkins to give her a week. Now that she was into the system, it shouldn't take that long. But it would take some time. If he would have told her what he was looking for, it would be simpler.

Kat noticed that she was biting the inside of her cheek and forced herself to stop. It was an old habit, one she used to do when she was younger and still living with her father. When he'd be in one of his moods and start criticizing his sister and his children—whipping sessions, Kat and her siblings used to call them—there was no recourse but to sit there and take it.

When she was very young, eight years old, Kat would cry, but that only gave her father another thing to criticize. When she was a teenager, she'd try to fight back. Her father would smile and pick apart her arguments one by one, leaving her shamed and chastened. That was even worse.

By the time she was old enough to drive, she'd taken to biting her cheeks. The pain distracted her from his words, helped her tune him out. And she got used to the taste of her own blood, even came to like it in a weird sort of way. It was warm and soothing and gave her some comfort. It became sort of like a mother's embrace, the embrace Kat had lost when she was just a little girl. Before the whipping sessions had started.

Now that she was grown and her father was dead, she was still trying to break the habit. She occasionally caught herself biting her cheeks when she was focused on something stressful.

Though he was just a politician, Jenkins was the most dangerous kind of politician: a politician on the rise. And he was about to reach the peak of a politician's power. Once he won the presidency, Jenkins would be all-powerful, for a time. The fractious Congress and the increasingly political court system had helped diffuse the power of the presidency. That masterstroke had taken decades for the power brokers to put in place. It wasn't Kat's doing, of course. She didn't bother playing those kinds of games.

But the presidency still had teeth. Manipulating Congress and the Supreme Court took time, and the power brokers wanted to keep a quick signal in their pockets. They just didn't want it to be quite such a nuisance if their calculations were off in one cycle or another.

When Jenkins got into the White House, Kat wanted him on her side. And if finding this data got him there, then she would find his fucking data, and get her father's company back in the process. She was the only rightful heir. The rest of them couldn't code their way out of an if-else statement. And her brother-in-law, Thomas Crowell, the current CEO, was running the company into the ground.

Kat had to get it back. For the sake of her fortune. For the sake of her father's name.

She would make him proud once and for all.

She focused again on the laptop, trying another way to search for the data Jenkins wanted.

As she did, Kat bit the inside of her cheeks again.

This time, she didn't notice.

15

CELINA WAS up before the others, sitting in the kitchen with a cup of coffee and her laptop, the early sun still pale through the sliding glass doors to the deck. When she heard footsteps on the stairs, she snapped the laptop shut and moved to stand by the sliding door to the deck, looking through the glass at the empty beach in the cold morning light, one last lukewarm sip in the coffee cup in her hand.

Cam slid his arms around her from behind and she melted into his embrace, feeling his warmth infuse her from back to front. He was like a walking sun, spreading his heat wherever he went. As long as Cam was with her, Celina could never be cold.

"More coffee?" he asked, his voice low, his breath hot in her ear.

She felt the usual stirrings and smiled. They'd been together for ten months, and she still felt that way when he came near. With any other lover, she would have deleted his number from her phone after two weeks.

She hoped the feelings Cam gave her never went away.

"Mmmm," she said, handing her empty coffee cup to Cam. "Yes, please."

He'd asked again last night about her and Kat. She tried to give him more background, but she'd come to realize that it was impossible for anyone else to know what she was feeling. Kat was too mesmerizing, too perfectly camouflaged. In our society, as long as she didn't piss off any men, a beautiful woman could get away with anything.

In Kat's case, she'd literally gotten away with murder. Cam knew that, and he still gave her the benefit of the doubt. And Cam wasn't some typical dick-directed guy. He was better than that, yet he was still fooled by Kat's hot-girl schtick.

Not that Celina hadn't used that schtick to her own advantage more times than she could count. And she and Kat used to team up. Double the hot girls translated to exponentially more power, and they'd leveraged that power on many occasions when they were younger. When they were friends.

But somewhere along the way, the friendship had withered and the rivalry had grown. Maybe it was when their fathers died, and they had to step up and take control of their own fortunes. Maybe it happened when Kat decided to murder her own father. Maybe something died in her then, something good.

Maybe it happened when Celina's father was murdered. Celina knew for a fact that something good in her had died that day. It didn't come back to life until Cam had come along. Different, but the same kind of goodness. Love, she supposed.

But Kat was following the old playbook, and it was working on Cam. Celina didn't know why. A hundred times, he'd told her about his murderous ex-lovers, about how the murders pushed him away. It was the sole reason why Celina hadn't killed Vernon Stratham, the man who'd ordered her father's murder, when she'd had the chance. She didn't want to be another murderous girlfriend that Cam couldn't stand to be with. So why would he forgive Kat now?

It didn't fucking matter. Whatever lies she'd told Cam, Celina knew that Kat hadn't changed. She was still up to something, up to no good. Celina would have to figure out what it was and prove it to Cam. That was the best way to show him what Kat Nestrom was really all about.

He was standing at the coffee maker in the kitchen when Kat came downstairs, looking carefree and gorgeous in flowing loungewear that looked like cozy clothes she'd pulled from the back of a drawer, but had probably cost a thousand dollars apiece. Celina watched from the sliding door, arms hugging herself, as Kat gave Cam a side-hug and a kiss on the cheek before pulling something out of the refrigerator.

She'd gone from a hand on the shoulder to a hug and a kiss. She wasn't done with Cam. She had just changed tactics, gone to a different page in the playbook. She'd been using the frontal assault before, coming in full force with her sexuality. Blunt, but usually effective enough. Celina had seen her frustration when it didn't work.

Now she was playing the girl next door routine, building trust with Cam, slowly drawing him closer with more and more physical intimacy. It would start innocuous. A touch here and there. A kiss on the cheek. Friendly. Innocent. Then there would be looks that lingered just a moment too long, maybe a head-shake, like she was trying to shake out a thought she didn't want, one she knew was inappropriate. Playing the good girl. It would pull Cam in, make him sympathetic.

Kat would slowly try to turn him against Celina, if she could do it without seeming like a villain. She'd subtly prove to Cam that Kat was the sane one, the good one, and Celina was the crazy, evil bitch.

Then, once she'd seeded Cam's mind with enough doubt, she'd look for an opening, spread her Pilates-toned legs, and suck him into her psychotic slut-maw. Fucking bitch.

Celina intended to get her the fuck out of the house before any of that could happen. She knew Kat was snooping on her network. She hadn't caught her yet, but she'd seen the back door in the code for the glasses. It was small, but it was there. Did Kat really think Celina wouldn't notice?

Celina had always been a better hacker than Kat. Maybe that's why Kat was so pissed.

Celina had found the back door and left the glasses connected all night so that Kat could walk through it. And she had. Celina knew she had.

But she'd lost her. Somehow, Kat had disappeared in Celina's network. Seemed little Kat had learned how to hunt, learned a few tricks since the last time they'd worked together.

So now it was fucking game on, all over again. Celina not only wanted to know what Kat was after, but now she wanted to know how she'd disappeared. This was Celina's house. If someone broke in, she would find out how. And she would make them pay.

Cam made three cups of coffee. He came up to Celina, handed her one, and gave her a kiss on the cheek before sliding open the door to the deck and taking the other two cups outside. Kat came along behind Cam with a stack of three plates and a bowl of fresh fruit. She raised one eyebrow at Celina and smirked as she walked past.

At least they weren't lying to each other anymore. Not when Cam wasn't there to see.

Celina followed Kat to the table. Kat sat beside Cam, forcing Celina to take the seat opposite. Celina sipped her coffee and watched Kat playfully goad Cam into eating some fruit. She selected fruit from the bowl and set them on his plate, laughing with him. The maternal part of the schtick. Make the man feel like you would take care of them. Most men are just looking for their mommies. They want a slut in the bedroom and a mommy everywhere else. Someone to take care of every need they have.

Kat didn't know that Cam wasn't like that. She could mommy him all she wanted. It wouldn't win him over. He was better than that. Smarter than that.

But Cam had the nasty habit of only seeing the best in people. Celina had to help him break that habit, but now was not a good time. It would only play into Kat's schtick.

But she couldn't have come all the way out here to try to steal Cam back. She didn't even know he was here, didn't know he was the guy she'd known as Sam Davis. No, Cam was a bonus goal. Kat had come out here for some other reason.

Some reason to do with Jenkins. He'd sent her the glasses. Celina was sure he knew she'd come out here. He would have sent Kat to get something from Celina.

Jenkins was a politician, but he was no fool. Her father had taught him well. And Jenkins knew Celina well. He would have known that the data wasn't gone. Even if he wasn't sure, with that kind of data—the kind that would end a political career, incriminate the campaign, and possibly send people to prison, even Jenkins himself—Jenkins would not want to take any chances.

But did he send Kat to destroy the data? He would have to know that was impossible. Even if Kat hacked Celina's network and found every copy, there was no guarantee she hadn't stored copies elsewhere, on cloud servers unconnected to the others and on thumb drives and hard drives stored in secure locations and so on. All of which Celina had done.

Maybe Kat was trying to figure out Celina's true intentions. Maybe Jenkins wanted to know if Celina intended to honor their pact and keep the data secret, or if she was biding her time, waiting for the opportune moment to blackmail Jenkins again. Celina would worry about the same thing, if she were him. She had no plan to blackmail Jenkins again, but most people would. They'd milk that cow for all it was worth. The only way to end that threat was to end the threatener.

Kat may have murdered her father, but she was no assassin. Jenkins wouldn't have sent her to kill Celina. Stratham was the murder broker, and he had much better options. No, Jenkins was after information. Celina just couldn't quite see what it was he wanted.

And that failure was really starting to piss her off.

16

Cam lay on a lounge chair on the deck and closed his eyes against the bright sun, watching the orange and yellow afterglow swirl behind his eyelids. A stiff, cold breeze whipped in off the ocean, and Cam was bundled against it in pants, Ugg boots, a thick sweater, and a blanket. But the sun was warm where it touched his face. It gave him a feeling of peace and comfort. Cam focused on the warmth against his eyelids, his nose, his cheeks. He focused on that peaceful feeling.

Kat and Celina were still off getting dressed for the day. Things were finally settling down between them. Kat had stopped hitting on Cam, and her true personality was coming out. She was every bit as sweet and fun as she'd seemed to Cam when he'd first met her on the train in New York years earlier. Their relationship had eventually taken a strange and horrible turn, but not before they'd had three passionate days together. He no longer thought of her as a lover, but he could not deny her physical beauty. And she was finally letting her inner beauty come out, too. She showed interest in him and Celina, helping with meals and cleanup, and working with Celina to figure out why Jenkins had sent the glasses to her in the first place.

Cam folded his hands behind his head and sighed in the sunlight. Harmony was finally returning to the house.

"You seem happy."

Kat's voice came from in front of him. Cam squinted one eye open and looked up to see Kat's silhouette. She moved to block his sun, and she came into focus, wrapping a large, flowing, very comfortable-looking sweater around her body as she smiled down at him.

"How could anyone not be happy in a place as beautiful as this?" he said.

Kat barked a bitter laugh. "You'd be surprised," she said. "I know plenty of executives with beautiful beach homes who are miserable people. Always stressed, always pushing themselves."

"They don't know how to slow down."

"Worst thing is, they actually think they're happy."

"If they think they are, doesn't that mean that they are?"

Kat crossed her arms over her stomach to hold her sweater in place and sat on the arm of Cam's chair.

"That's an interesting question," she said with a beguiling half-smile. "Can we fake our way into happiness?" She looked down at Cam. "What do you think?"

"Happiness is a state of mind, like any other. If people want to be happy, they'll find a way."

"But do most people really want to be happy?" Kat looked out at the waves cracking and thundering against the sand. "People say they do all the time, but if they're not"—she gestured toward Cam—"finding a way, or really even trying, doesn't that mean they're lying to themselves?"

"I guess the question is whether or not we really can lie to achieve a truth. Fake it till you make it, right? Isn't that what they always say?"

"Hmm," said Kat, staring into the sun, her eyes narrowed to slits. "I've never been one to lie to myself."

She turned her head to look down at Cam. The sun backlit her, streamed through her hair and around her profile, giving her a yellow and white halo.

"What about you?" she asked. "Do you lie to yourself?"

That was one thing Cam could honestly say he didn't do. He lied to others all the time. Occupational hazard of being a professional thief. But he never lied in ways that would hurt people, not emotionally. The only damage he intentionally inflicted was financial, and then only on people who could afford the hit.

"Not me," he said. "Bad business for a thief. If you lie to yourself, you can never keep your stories straight."

"I wish I'd known that when I was younger," said Kat, looking back toward the horizon. "Would have saved me a lot of heartache." She sighed, then looked back down at Cam and gave him a tight smile. "I'm working on it."

She readjusted herself on the arm of the chair, then slipped and fell into Cam's lap. His arm came down around her, instinctively.

Kat squealed in surprise when she fell, then threw back her head and laughed, a long, infectious peal. She rolled over on Cam and buried her face against his chest in embarrassment. Cam felt her weight sprawled over him, the warmth of her body a stark contrast to the cold of the chair. The wind from the ocean washed her scent—lilacs, faint and elegant—over him.

Kat's laughter set Cam laughing. He closed his eyes,

bright sunlight swirling again behind his eyelids, and they lay there together, two friends laughing.

A shadow passed over him. Cam opened his eyes and his laughter trailed off.

"Isn't this cozy," said Celina.

She stood over them, arms folded. Cam shielded his eyes with his hand against the reflections of the backlight. Celina was smiling, but the smile did not reach her eyes. Her eyes were clear and cold and brittle.

Kat rolled on Cam, set one hand casually on his chest, and looked up at Celina. She must have noticed Celina's expression, too, because she pushed herself onto one elbow, stuttered once, and looked from Cam back to Celina. She slumped and shook her head.

"Nothing's happening, Celina," she said, and gave Cam a pleading, incredulous look. "I just fell off the arm of the chair. That's all."

Cam watched Celina, waiting. He'd thought this was all behind them, and he was still hoping it was.

In the last few nights, Celina had told him a lot about the history between Kat and Celina. Similar situations in life, similar interests, similar personalities. They had a lot in common. That had made them both friends and rivals.

Kat's family situation had pushed her further and further into anger and bitterness, and her relationship with Celina had taken on a hard edge. Their bar games had become wilder and more callous. Their rivalry became more contentious than friendly. Celina had her own issues, she admitted, so she had probably contributed to the changes as much as Kat. Eventually, the contentiousness became greater than the friendship and they'd stopped hanging out. Probably for the best for both of them.

But that was then, years ago. Both of them had changed, and the games of their youth were in the past.

Or so Cam hoped. He watched Celina, watched in her eyes the struggle to maintain her composure. He could almost see the conversation happening in her head, with her impulsive side wanting to explode and her more mature side trying to keep her together.

The mature side won. Barely.

"You need to be more careful, Kat," said Celina, her voice as light as poison gas and as smooth as a razor blade. "This place is dangerous. The next time you fall, Cam might not catch you."

Kat stared at Celina for a long beat, then looked down at Cam.

"Cam's a gentleman, Celina," she said. "He wouldn't let a lady fall and hurt herself while he was around, would you, Cam?"

Cam felt his mouth flopping open and closed, but he couldn't think of a graceful way to respond. So he decided to bail out altogether. He pushed up, forcing Kat to stand and holding her hand while she did, then stood up himself. Kat got up on the left side of the chair. Cam very deliberately got up on the right, beside Celina.

"What's the plan today, Celina?" he asked, clapping his hands together and, hopefully, changing the subject.

The look on Celina's face told him she knew exactly what he was doing, and that he wasn't doing it very well. But she let him off the hook, anyway.

"Let's go through the data," said Celina, looking at Kat. "Maybe we can find something in there that explains what Jenkins is up to."

"Sounds like a plan," said Kat.

Celina crossed in front of Cam and headed toward the

door to the house. Kat followed her inside, lifting one eyebrow at Cam as she passed.

Cam closed his eyes, turned back toward the sun, and tried to feel its warmth one more time. He had a feeling he was going to need every little bit of peace and comfort he could get.

17

CELINA and the others had been at it for hours in the lab, testing and probing and searching through code and data. It was all pointless. Jenkins didn't have the wherewithal to plant anything nefarious in her glasses, either in the software or in the hardware. Especially since the glasses had been sitting in his office the whole time.

But Celina knew enough not to underestimate the man, so she did her due diligence and combed through the code and inspected the hardware carefully. So far, she'd turned up nothing unexpected.

And that worried her. Jenkins couldn't do anything, but Kat sure as hell could. Celina figured she must have fucked with the glasses somehow, even if only to install monitoring or debugging scripts. But she couldn't find a thing. And that made her very nervous.

All three of them were working on different machines. Cam and Kat sat at the workstations, looking through code, while Celina bent over the workbench with a tablet and a magnifying headset like dentists wore, inspecting the hardware. She traced every wire, every chip, every connection for signs of tampering.

She would recheck everything Kat was doing, of course. That bitch couldn't be trusted for shit. And Celina had backups of the code so she could do a diff on any files Kat touched to see if she made any changes.

But Celina knew she wouldn't find anything. Kat had upped her game since the last time Celina had worked with her. Back then, she'd been a brilliant but spoiled rich girl with no interest in anything but fucking guys and spending daddy's money.

In the years since, she'd flipped a switch and unlocked her genius. Celina had heard about the companies Kat had started, companies that her father had quickly purchased or taken over to pull her back into Nestech's clutches. The companies had barely gotten going before her father stepped in, but Celina had heard that they showed real promise. One of them was some bullshit gaming company or something, but one had something to do with internet security and another with augmented reality.

Both skills that were very fucking applicable to the present situation.

Kat seemed to be a pro now. Maybe even as good as Celina.

Okay, probably not that good. But pretty fucking good.

Kat flopped back in her chair and sighed loudly.

"Maybe we should call in some help," she said. "A data scientist or something."

Celina grunted noncommittally. There was no fucking way she was bringing in anyone else.

"What about that one woman, with the data science startup? The one that left Nestech."

"Not possible," said Celina without looking up from what she was doing. "No one would ever leave Nestech." She glanced over her shoulder at Kat. "You would have them killed."

"Good one," Kat said drily. "I'll have to update the NDAs to add that in."

She stretched back in her chair, arching her back and pushing out her tits, making sure Cam had a good view.

"Seriously, though," she groaned through her stretch. "What was her name?"

"Lindsay Rhodes," said Celina while peering at a magnified circuit board. "She was your fucking employee. You should at least remember her name."

"I wasn't involved with the company back then," replied Kat. "I had my own companies to run."

"Whatever. Lindsay doesn't do that shit anymore. Not for hire. She fucked off to England and joined a car racing team or something."

"Oh, that's right. She bought the team, didn't she?"

"Bought. Inherited. Something like that."

"Why the hell would anyone want to own a racing team?"

"Sounds pretty cool to me," said Cam.

Celina stood up at the workbench, pushed the magnifying glasses up on her forehead, and turned to face him. She and Kat just stared at him in silence.

"What?" he said. "It does."

Kat and Celina shared a look. Celina suppressed her smile, let her glasses fall back over her eyes, and turned back to what she was doing.

"Marina del Carmen runs Lindsay's data science shop now," Celina said.

"Marina," said Kat, snapping her fingers. "Right. Is her

last name still del Carmen? Didn't she marry that Indian guy she worked with?"

"What am I, fucking Instagram? What the fuck do I care who she married?"

Kat didn't reply.

"Besides, we don't need anyone else," Celina continued. "Proprietary pre-release hardware, remember?"

"Hmm," Kat murmured. "I could update that NDA first."

Celina snorted, the closest thing to a laugh she'd given Kat since she landed in California.

They worked in silence for a while longer before Celina sighed and stood up, throwing her magnifying glasses on the workbench with a clatter of frustration.

"There's nothing here," she said. "It's all just the way I left it."

Kat pushed back from her monitor. "Same. Everything checks out."

"Same here," said Cam.

Celina folded her arms and leaned back against the bench.

"What exactly did Jenkins say to you, Kat?"

"He said he found these glasses—no, he said these glasses came into his possession—and they seemed like they belonged to Nestech."

"Why didn't he send them to your brother?" asked Cam. "He's the CEO, isn't he?"

"Brother-in-law," Kat corrected him. "Jenkins and Thomas don't get along."

"Thomas is a fucking asshole," said Celina.

"Jenkins isn't?" said Kat.

"Not as bad as Thomas."

Kat paused, then nodded. "True."

"But why send them to you?" asked Cam.

"Jenkins and I go back." She glanced at Celina. "Not like that."

Celina grinned back at Kat. She knew that Kat and Jenkins had never fucked. Jenkins hadn't fucked either of them. Hadn't even tried, out of respect for their fathers. Jenkins was already a politician when Celina's father, Perry, took him under his wing, and knew that the education Perry could provide was worth more than the quick roll in the sack he'd get from Celina or Kat, no matter how mind-blowing that roll might be. Jenkins was a pragmatist, and an ambitious one. He'd already learned how to control his momentary urges in service of a longer-term goal.

"He knew I was good with tech," Kat continued, "and he knew he could trust me." She smirked at Cam. "He forgot that I had already learned not to trust him."

Cam darted a glance at Celina. She shrugged back at him.

Kat was saying she couldn't trust Jenkins, yet Cam and Celina had put a shitload of trust in him, essentially black-mailing him with incriminating evidence about his campaign in order to secure the release of Cam's mother, Paulie, from prison. Cam was worried that they'd fucked up somehow.

Celina had known at the time that it was risky. But she'd also known how badly Jenkins wanted to be president. He wouldn't do anything to jeopardize that, not now that he was so close to his prize.

And it had paid off. Paulie was free, eating and drinking and fucking her way around the world with Lord Simon Walsh, another of Perry's old friends that Celina had called in on the job at her mother's house. Simon and Paulie had hit it off and set off around the world together once the job was done. They'd been sending postcards to Celina and

Cam from their adventures along the way. Africa, Egypt, India, Vietnam, the Philippines. The last one was a letter with a photo of the two of them at some temple in Kyoto dressed in traditional Japanese kimonos, all the way down to the white socks and fucking wood sandals.

Blackmailing Jenkins had been a calculated risk on Celina's part, but one she felt pretty sure about at the time. Jenkins had never been a lightning-fast thinker. He was smart, but slow. Calculating. A planner more than an improviser. Celina and Cam had put him on the spot, and he'd gone along with what they asked because he couldn't figure out another way. Just as Celina had intended.

But now that he'd had time to think things through and formulate a plan, it seemed that Jenkins was coming back around to clean up the job. She hadn't expected that. He'd sent Kat to get the data. If that failed, Celina wondered who he'd send next, and what he would instruct them to do.

She was starting to wonder if Vernon Stratham was really the murderer, getting the dirty business done without the candidate's knowledge, or if Jenkins had been a murderous fuck the whole time.

She didn't really want to find out. Killing the president was never a good look, even in self-defense.

"And he asked you to figure out who stole the glasses?" Cam asked.

"Don't worry, Cam." Kat leaned forward, put her hand on Cam's knee, and winked at him. "I won't rat you out."

Celina clenched her jaw as she watched Kat rub Cam's knee slowly.

"I was thinking more about Celina," Cam said.

Damn right you were. Just keep thinking about Celina.

"The one thing I can't figure out," said Kat, "is why he

would care who stole the glasses? What difference does it make to him?"

Celina knew exactly why. Because Jenkins had found them across the street from Celina's mother's house the day before Celina broke in. Celina's mother had covered the whole thing up, and done a good job of it. She'd done it out of the goodness of her heart, she said. Celina was grateful for the cover, but she didn't believe her mother's motives. Her mother was just another lying fucking politician, after all.

Jenkins would put two and two together, but he'd need real evidence to connect Celina to the glasses and to the break-in. If he could get that evidence, he would have leverage on her. Just like she had leverage on him.

Not quite the same, really. Why would Celina care if she was tied to a break in? She could buy her way out of the legal trouble. What she had on Jenkins would ruin his political career forever. Not the same at all.

Jenkins was getting desperate. He was looking for anything he could get, at this point.

Good. Let that fucker twist.

"That's enough for today," said Celina. "There's nothing here." She held her hand out to Cam. "Come on, Cam. We've got training to do."

Cam took her hand and stood.

"You want to join, Kat?" said Cam. "Celina's a great teacher."

Celina wanted to scream *fuck no*, but she kept her shit together. She would not be the jealous girlfriend. She would not push Cam away like that.

"Yeah, Kat, come on," she said, teeth gritted. "I'll only kick your ass a little. All in the name of education."

Kat gave her a withering smile. Celina didn't wither one bit.

"Thanks," said Kat, "but I've got some work of my own to do. I'll see you both later."

Celina put her arm around Cam, her hand on his ass, and led him toward the door. She gave Kat a wink and a grin as she left. Kat did not look amused.

Celina knew what kind of work Kat would be doing. And she knew her network would be watching everything. Kat was good, but Celina was the best. When Kat fucked up, Celina would find it.

It was only a matter of time.

18

Cam stood in the shower for the second time that evening and let the hot spray pound the top of his head and sluice down his fatigued body. His muscles ached, but he had the worn-out relaxation that comes from hard work and good sex.

Celina had been fierce and merciless in their sparring session, driving him from one discipline to the next without a break, pushing faster and faster, attacking with more and more ferocity. And he knew she was still holding back, still being a teacher, pressing him to his limits and just beyond, but not so far that Cam would break and become discouraged.

By the end, he'd been worn and panting, sweat soaking his hair and streaming over his bare chest and back. The mat was slick and shining with it. Celina was sweaty, too, but she looked like she could go a hundred rounds more.

She called it after four hours and they went upstairs for a shower. Under the heat of the spray, their naked bodies slippery, Cam found a reserve of energy he didn't know he had. In the shower, on the floor, on the bed.

Three hours later, Celina was dozing and Cam was back in the shower.

He was thinking about Attorney General Jenkins. When he and Celina had blackmailed Jenkins, Cam had been completely focused on securing his mother's release. She'd been in prison for fifteen years, since his father's death. And for fifteen years, Cam had been trying one scheme after another to free her. Jenkins was his best shot yet, and all he cared about was getting his mother out.

Thinking back on it now, he could see that his plan would have repercussions. It had to. Blackmail is all well and good, but for the person being blackmailed, the only way to make sure it doesn't keep happening over and over is to destroy the evidence.

Cam and Celina had made a show of destroying the evidence for Jenkins. They'd wiped and destroyed hard drives, sent a copy to Jenkins on a thumb drive for him to destroy, and so on. But it was all digital theater. These days, nothing was really gone. Not if it's digital.

And Cam and Celina absolutely had copies of that data, still. Multiple copies. Backed up on servers and laptops and physical drives and even printed copies in two different safe deposit boxes.

These days, for the person being blackmailed, the only way to make sure it doesn't keep happening is to kill the blackmailers.

The evidence they'd presented to Jenkins all pointed not to him, but to his campaign finance manager, Vernon Stratham. Stratham was the one attached to the assassinations of prominent businessmen. Stratham was the one who had ordered the hit on Celina's father. Stratham was the one who would go to prison for multiple counts of murder.

This was compelling for Jenkins, of course, because of the effect such bad press would have on his campaign for the presidency. For a trusted advisor to be a murderer without the candidate's knowledge was not a campaign-ending revelation—too many presidents and high-ranking officials had weathered similarly shocking issues—but it was certainly a stumble for a candidate that was sailing to the highest office in the land. It would give new life to his opponents, life that Jenkins was eager to smother.

But Jenkins hadn't done anything since they'd given him the evidence. Cam's mother was free; Jenkins had held up his end of the deal. But Cam had seen nothing in the news about Stratham.

He hadn't expected headlines about Stratham's arrest. Jenkins would handle things quietly. But he'd expected at least a story or two about a shake-up in the Jenkins campaign, about the ouster of Stratham for one fabricated reason or another.

But there had been nothing. Nothing at all.

Which meant that either the press wasn't doing its job, or Stratham was still in his role in the campaign.

Given the volume of stories, both positive and as nega-tive as possible, about Jenkins, the press was doing its job.

That meant Stratham was still in his role.

Cam made a mental note to hack into the campaign network again to verify that. But, assuming it was true, why would Jenkins keep Stratham when he had so much evidence of Stratham's wrongdoing? When he could so easily deflect any blame from himself? There was only one possible explanation.

When Cam and Celina had shown him the evidence, Jenkins already knew.

And if Jenkins already knew, that meant he was in on it.

Whether tacitly or overtly, Jenkins sanctioned Stratham's murders.

That meant Jenkins was a hell of a lot more dangerous than Cam had thought.

And now, Jenkins was poking around, looking for Celina. And probably looking for Cam, as well.

Cam closed his eyes and tilted his head up into the stream of shower water, let it beat against his face. The water pressure was strong, an expensive indulgence in water-conscious California. It stung his forehead and his cheeks. He pulled in a mouthful of water and spit it out again, pushing back against the stream.

Celina slid her arms around Cam's sides, pressed her body against his from behind. He felt the swell of her breasts against his back, felt the strong curve of her stomach, the hard ridges of her pelvic bone.

Their wet bodies slipped easily against each other under the hot stream from the shower head. The shower was long and wide and open on one end, with a shower head on each of the walls and large glass windows on the front. Celina reached to the sides to turn on the two others. Water needled them from three sides. From behind, Celina slid her hands up over Cam's slick chest, slid them down between his legs.

As dire as Cam's thoughts had been a moment before, his mind went blank in that moment. He could not resist Celina. He could never resist her. She was his weakness. She was his greatest strength.

He turned in her arms and lifted her into his.

Afterward, Cam sat on the bench in the changing area dressed in sweatpants and a t-shirt. He propped his chin in one hand and listened to the sound of Celina's hair dryer in the bathroom. His thoughts had spun back to Jenkins, back to the threat he posed to the people Cam loved.

The hair dryer stopped. Celina came into the changing area, wearing flowing fleece pants and one of Cam's hoodies, brushing her hair with her head tilted to one side.

"You okay?" she asked. "I didn't break you, did I? That last position was a little bendy." She grinned. "But very effective."

A part of Cam's brain wanted to reply with something witty, something playful and sexy. Instead, he frowned.

"What is it?" said Celina, sitting beside Cam on the bench, concern in her tone. "What's wrong?"

Cam sighed heavily.

"Have you seen anything in the news about Stratham?" he asked. "Anything about him leaving the campaign?"

Celina's worried expression became immediately serious.

"No," she said, "I haven't. And I think I know what you're thinking."

With all the craziness over the job at Celina's mother's house, the Israeli assassins, and Cam's recovery, then Kat's arrival, he and Celina had never really had the time to talk about Jenkins and Stratham. It was long overdue.

"I'll make sure when I get downstairs," Cam said, "but if Stratham's still on the campaign—"

"It's because Jenkins wants him there."

"And if Jenkins wants him there—"

"He's okay with Stratham being a fucking killer."

"Which means he probably already knew about it."

Celina nodded. There wasn't any surprise in her eyes or in her expression. She'd already come to the same conclusion.

"And now he's trying to get to you," said Cam, "and using Kat to do it."

Celina nodded. She'd already figured that much out, too. Of course she had. Cam was smart, but Celina was a hundred times smarter. And she knew Jenkins from way back, knew how he thought, what he would do, how he would react.

"Did you know he would come after you?"

Celina shook her head. "I knew it was a possibility," she said, "but after I surprised him at dinner that night, I thought he was innocent. He didn't show any shame or remorse. Not even a little." She pressed her lips together. "That fucker fooled me. He's leveled up, too. Fucking asshole."

She said the last part almost to herself. Cam didn't know who Celina was referring to, who else had leveled up. He was about to ask when another thought stopped him. Stopped him cold.

"Would he go after my mother?" he asked, his voice a harsh whisper.

For the first time in his life, Cam felt like he could murder someone in cold blood.

Celina's eyes went wide for a moment, then narrowed as she worked through the idea in her mind.

"He might," she said, "but not at first. He'd try the easy route first and come for us directly. He sent Kat, right? Which means he doesn't want to escalate unless he has to. If he wanted us dead, he would have sent a killer."

Cam nodded. The thought gave him little comfort, but it was better than nothing.

"Besides, Simon knows what he's doing," said Celina. "He comes off all suave and chill, but he knows how to fight. He'll keep Paulie safe."

"I'll text her to warn her."

"Hmm," Celina nodded. "Yeah, good. Do that. If Jenkins is monitoring our phones, he'll see it, but that's okay. If he knows they've been alerted, he's even less likely to go after them."

"Monitoring our phones?" Jesus. The thought made Cam sick to his stomach. "Isn't that illegal?"

Celina snorted. "Are you fucking kidding? We're talking about this guy being involved in a string of murders and you think he gives a shit about some wiretapping?"

"Fair point," said Cam.

"Besides, he's the Attorney General. I think FISA takes care of all that now."

She stood and brushed out the last of her hair before setting down her brush and combing through it with her fingers. She let it fall naturally, full and long, and stood looking down at Cam with her hands on her hips.

She looked like a superhero, like a heart-stoppingly beautiful superhero.

"I'll beef up the encryption on our phones," she said, "but we should assume Jenkins can see and hear us."

"Okay," said Cam. "Then what do we do?"

Celina smiled. "We give him a show."

Cam had no idea what that meant, but he was in it. And at this point, the only way out was through.

19

Celina was sick of sitting around. She was sick of waiting. And she was sick of worrying about what other people were going to do. That had never been her style, and it didn't sit right with her. She preferred to take the fight to people herself. And if Jenkins wanted a fight, she'd give it to him.

She sat in bed with her laptop that evening, Cam beside her. They'd spent the rest of the night pretending nothing was wrong, like it was just a normal evening. The three of them made dinner, ate it under the heaters on the deck with the waves crashing in the moonlight below them. The conversation was civil, even friendly. After they cleaned up, they went inside and watched a movie, then went their separate ways to go to bed.

All acting like good friends, acting like Kat wasn't working for a man who had betrayed and killed Celina's father, like Kat wasn't trying to steal information from her, like Jenkins wasn't actively working to potentially kill Celina and Cam.

Fuck that shit.

Celina knew Kat was sniffing around her network, though she still hadn't been able to catch her in the act. But there was more than one way to trap a rat.

Celina just had to put out some bait.

The way Celina figured it, there were two things Jenkins could be looking for. If he was an idiot, he was looking for more copies of the evidence against him. Those definitely existed, but looking for them was idiotic because there was no guarantee that more copies didn't exist somewhere else. Still, Celina would dangle that bait for him.

The more likely possibility was that Jenkins wanted dirt on Celina. Something he could use against her, to counter the threat she posed to him. It would have to be big. Fucking huge.

It was also possible that Jenkins was looking for dirt on Celina's mother, Madeline Kinkaid. There were probably a hundred people trying to dig up dirt on her. As Speaker of the House of Representatives, she was a prime target for oppo research, ambitious Republicans, and eager journalists, alike.

Did Jenkins know that Madeline was Celina's mother? Celina wasn't sure. It was no secret within Celina's family, but it wasn't something they talked about widely. But Jenkins had been a trusted friend for years before he killed Celina's father. There was a good chance he knew the truth.

But Jenkins also knew Celina well enough to know that incriminating evidence regarding her mother would not sway her actions one bit. Celina didn't give a shit about her mother. Never had. No, it was more likely that Jenkins wanted dirt on Celina herself.

But then why would Jenkins' goons have been skulking around Madeline's house on that particular night? There was no reason for them to be there. It was just a random night. And they hadn't even found Cam's glasses in Madeline's house. They'd found them across the street. On the day *before* Celina and Cam broke in to her mother's house.

Jenkins could have been tracking Celina all along, but that was unlikely. Celina would have known about it. Monitoring texts and phone calls from a cell network was one thing, but tracking device movements was another. Celina had sniffers and scramblers on all her devices, the best in the world. She would have known if someone was tracking her. Especially someone too stupid to turn off the GPS on a pair of AR glasses they'd stolen.

The second explanation was that Jenkins was already spying on Celina's mother, and Celina had stumbled into that net. That was possible, but still seemed nuts. Jenkins and Madeline were from the same party. Jenkins was the heir apparent and Madeline was a newly minted leader on the rise, with enormous power and appeal. It was more likely they would work together, not be at odds with each other. There was no reason for Jenkins to be watching her that closely.

But Washington was a fucking snake pit. Maybe that's just how it was. Keep your friends close and your enemies closer, and never forget that there's no such thing as friends.

Could it be that Kat's visit had nothing to do with Celina at all? Maybe Jenkins was using Kat to gain access to Celina's network, not to find shit about Celina, but to find shit about Madeline. Fuck, if that was the case, Jenkins could have just asked. Celina didn't have any dirt, but she would gladly have given it up if she did.

Though not to Jenkins. Not to the man who killed her father.

The safest thing was to just assume everything was true.

Jenkins wanted copies of the evidence, and he wanted dirt on both Celina and her mother.

The only dirt Celina had on her mother was the fact that she was Celina's mother. That fact alone would create a lot of uncomfortable conversations for Madeline Kinkaid, and it could ruin her career. But if Jenkins already knew it, there was no need to keep digging.

If Jenkins was looking for dirt on Celina, she could expose some files that Kat could sweep up. But what could she dangle that Jenkins would believe was incriminating enough for blackmail?

The names of old lovers? There was no way Celina could remember them all, and it would be more incriminating for them than for her. Some of them were very powerful men and women, and some of them had been married at the time. Celina had always been single. Jenkins could call her a slut, but in this day and age, that would just make him seem like an asshole. It wouldn't reflect badly on Celina, certainly not in any way Jenkins could use as leverage.

Something about her father, maybe? Or about his company? That wouldn't work, either. Celina had known her dad very well, and she was pretty sure everything he did was beyond reproach, even in the ethical sludge of Silicon Valley. And he'd sold his company years before, so there was nothing for Celina to lose, nothing to damage with a bombshell revelation.

In fact, there was nothing at all that could damage her. She already had more money than she could ever use, diversified across a dizzying array of investments. Jenkins would have to destroy the entire world economy to hurt Celina financially. She didn't give a shit about her public reputation, so no amount of gossip would touch her. She'd done plenty of shit to land her in prison, but the U.S. legal system was more about equity than equality, so Celina was pretty sure she could buy herself out of anything he'd throw at her that way. She was untouchable.

But this wasn't about what would *actually* damage Celina. It was about what Jenkins *thought* would damage Celina. Would he think smearing her father's name would sway Celina in any way? Maybe. She loved her father more than anyone in the world.

Until Cam, anyway. He was definitely giving her father a run for his money.

Cam. What about Cam?

She turned her head to look at Cam, lying beside her with his head propped against a pillow, reading a Neil Gaiman novel. He noticed her looking, but didn't turn his head, just reached out one hand to hold hers.

She smiled at the unconscious gesture. Definitely giving her father a run.

Maybe even overtaking him.

She really did love this man. The thought settled in her heart with the guileless certainty of the last piece of a puzzle. She had no doubts. So why hadn't she told him? Why had she never said those three simple words out loud?

Her thoughts drifted back to her conversation with Cam in the changing room earlier that evening. If Jenkins wanted to manipulate Celina, he couldn't do it with information, no matter how incriminating.

But he could do it with people.

Maybe that's really why he sent Kat out here. Maybe she was here to see how much Cam really meant to Celina, to gauge how effective he'd be as a bargaining chip. Celina had already stuck her neck out once, and that was to free Cam's mother from prison. How much further would she go to free Cam himself? Or to keep him from going to prison in the first place?

Celina clenched her jaw and squeezed Cam's hand tight.

Too tight. Cam frowned as he read, looked at his hand in hers, then up at her face.

"What did my hand ever do to you?" he said.

Celina wanted to say something sexy, make some obvious joke, maybe even lure Cam into more sex. On any other night, that's exactly what she would have done. Cam was like a drug to her, and sex with him was the highest of highs, more than anyone Celina had ever been with. They had so much sex, but it never seemed to slake her thirst for more.

But in that moment, sex was the last thing on her mind.

20

LATE THE NEXT MORNING, after breakfast had been eaten and cleaned up, while Celina was inside getting dressed, Cam and Kat sat on the back deck. The fog had burned off early that day. The morning sun was bright and the breeze fresh and cool.

Cam watched Kat over the top of the book he was reading. He couldn't see her eyes through the stylish dark sunglasses she wore. He wasn't sure how she could even see her laptop screen with glasses that dark, but she was typing away on her keyboard, the laptop resting on her thighs, propped up in the lounge chair.

Celina had said she suspected that Kat was fishing around her network, looking for information to send to Jenkins. She could be looking for information on Cam's mother, trying to find emails or text messages or records of phone calls. She could be sending information back to Jenkins right now, information about Celina and Cam, about their movements, their relationship, what they ate for breakfast in the morning. Anything Jenkins could use.

Cam shook his head. He was being ridiculous. Kat

hadn't called Celina. Celina had called Kat. It was Celina's idea to bring Kat all the way out to California. Jenkins was the one trying to dig up dirt, not Kat. The connection between them was just a coincidence. Celina didn't trust Kat, and that was fine. But it didn't mean she was working for Jenkins. Celina herself had admitted she'd found no evidence of Kat's snooping.

In general, it didn't pay to bet against Celina. Her instincts were correct more often than not. But maybe this situation was one of the nots.

A gust of wind came off the sea and hissed over the deck, lifting tendrils of Kat's hair to one side and blowing the pages of Cam's book, losing his place. Absent-mindedly, he flipped back to where he'd been reading, but kept his eyes on Kat. She didn't seem to notice him looking, just typed away on her laptop.

If Kat was involved, maybe Jenkins was using her. Maybe she was an unwitting mole in some grander plan of his. He was a powerful man, about to become the most powerful person in the world. He could easily find a way to ensnare Kat in his scheme.

Why was Cam making excuses for her? Why was he siding with Kat instead of Celina? He and Kat had been together, but it was years ago, and only for a few days. Under other circumstances, it would have been just a fling.

Only Cam didn't do flings. They might look that way from the outside, but he fell fast and he fell hard. For those three days with Kat, Cam had been in love, such as it was.

That love was shattered when he discovered that she'd killed her father. She and her family had killed Christopher Nestrom. And Kat had lied to Cam about it.

And that was the end of the love affair. Like driving off a cliff at a hundred miles an hour, the road abruptly ending.

So why was he so quick to find excuses for her now? She had ties to Jenkins. She'd come all the way out here. The evidence was there, no matter how circumstantial. There was as good a chance that Kat was working for Jenkins as there was a chance that she wasn't.

Cam just didn't want to believe it. She was a killer, but he wanted to believe that Kat was a good person at heart.

"You could take a picture, if you want," said Kat, without looking up from her laptop.

She smiled, closed the laptop, and set it on the deck. She took off her sunglasses, squeezed her eyes shut and arched her back, stretching her arms to the sides, her legs long down the deck chair. She settled onto her side, one arm propped against the backrest.

"Or you could sketch me again," she said. "I'd be happy to pose for you."

She was wearing a loose sweatshirt over tights, her feet bare. The sweatshirt had pushed to one side, exposing one shoulder. Cam let his eye wind along the curves of her profile, down her jawline, her neck, over that bare shoulder, traversing the hourglass of her figure.

He hadn't sketched in months. He'd been so busy recovering, training, being with Celina, he hadn't even thought of it. His fingers itched for his pencil and sketchpad now.

He'd made dozens of sketches of Kat in the three days they'd been together. He still had them in an old sketch book upstairs. She was a lovely subject. She was a beautiful woman.

Cam couldn't tell if Kat was coming on to him again, or if the comment was an innocent one. He chose to believe the latter, chose to believe that she was a good person at heart, not someone who would swoop in and try to drive a wedge between him and Celina.

He smiled faintly and said, "How long are you in town?"

Kat's smile widened for a minute, her eyes flashing, before she rolled onto her back again and looked out at the sets of waves rolling in across the ocean.

"Not much longer, probably," she said, "unless something changes to give me a reason to stay."

She arched an eyebrow and gave Cam a glance, but only a brief one.

She could have been talking about anything.

"There doesn't seem to be anything unusual about the glasses," Kat continued.

"Sorry you had to come all the way out here for nothing."

"Not nothing." Kat shook her head. "Now we know for sure that the glasses weren't tampered with. Plus, I got to see Celina again." She smiled. "And you."

This time, when she looked at Cam, her look was open and friendly and honest. Cam relaxed. He'd been reading into things earlier. Kat wasn't trying to steal Cam from Celina, wasn't trying to wedge them apart. She was being sincere.

And he was happy to see her again, too. Their love affair had been brief, but it had been intense, and it had been real. Cam didn't love her anymore, but he still had fond feelings toward Kat. Mixed feelings, complicated feelings, but fond ones, on balance.

"It was good to see you, too, Kat," Cam said, nodding. "So what happens now?"

Kat shrugged. "It's up to Celina, really," she said. "I'm here for her. But if there's nothing wrong with the glasses, I suppose I'll head back east."

She looked at Cam for a moment, then looked out at the ocean again.

"You could come with me," she said. "I know Phillip would love to see you again."

"Somehow I doubt that," Cam snorted.

Phillip was Kat's butler, not an active party to Nestrom's murder, but an accessory. He would definitely not want to see Cam again.

Kat laughed softly. "Maybe so." She looked down at her hands in her lap. Her voice grew quiet. "But I would love to have you there."

She looked so sad, in that moment, that Cam's heart broke for her.

"Kat, I—"

"I know," she said.

Once again, she glanced at Cam before returning her gaze to the sea. She laughed, a short, quick laugh. When she spoke again, her voice quavered.

"I fucked that up," she said. "I know."

Cam didn't respond.

"And you love Celina," she said. "I know that, too." She sighed. "You do love her, right?"

Cam pressed his lips together, not wanting to hurt Kat more. But the truth was the truth. He nodded.

"And she loves you back?"

"I think so," Cam replied.

Kat frowned. "You think so? She hasn't said it?"

Trying another wedge.

"Kat..."

"No," Kat held up a hand. "No, I'm sure you're right. I mean, it's a little weird, though. How long have you two been together?"

Cam sighed. "About nine months."

"Nine months?" Kat shook her head. "That's a lifetime for Celina. She must love you."

Cam nodded, glad Kat was seeing things realistically.

"And I've seen the way she looks at you," Kat said, seemingly talking more to herself than to Cam. "She *must* love you." Her voice dropped, musing. "Still, I can't believe she hasn't said it yet."

"Well, I haven't said it to her yet, either."

Kat's eyes widened in surprise. "What are you waiting for?"

Cam furrowed his brow. He opened his mouth to reply, but didn't quite know what to say.

Why *hadn't* he said it yet? He'd loved Celina from the very beginning. Cam had a tendency to fall fast and fall hard, and Celina had been no exception. At the time, he'd deliberately tried not to fall for her, to change his pattern. But with Celina, there was no stopping it. He fell all the way. So why hadn't he said anything?

"Well, it's not a race," Kat said with a smile that was more polite than sincere. "I'm sure if it's meant to be, it'll happen eventually." She laughed, again a short, quick sound. "I never thought Celina would stay with anyone. I didn't think it was in her nature." She looked at Cam. "But if she's going to be with anyone, I'm glad it's you."

Cam nodded and gave her a wan smile. Kat picked up her laptop again and returned to tapping away on the keyboard.

Cam settled back into his chair with his book, but the words swam in circles on the page. He was looking at them, but all he could think about was Kat's question. Why hadn't he and Celina said I love you to each other yet?

Cam was in love with her, absolutely. He'd felt that way before and it had never worked out, but this time felt different. This time felt real. His mother had said the same thing.

But was he just deluding himself, making himself feel

that way because he wanted it to be true? Maybe Celina didn't feel that way at all. Maybe he was just another boyfriend that she happened to keep around a lot longer than the others.

No, that couldn't be right. The way he felt when they were together, it was electric. Cam had never felt that way before. That couldn't all be one-sided.

Cam shook his head lightly, to himself, trying to clear the negative thoughts. Celina loved him. He was sure of it.

But she'd never said it.

Then again, he loved her, and he'd never said it, either.

Cam shook his head once more. He gave up on reading and closed his book, rested it on his chest and stared out at the ocean. He watched the waves, unseeing, as they rolled and crashed and tumbled over the shore.

21

THE CHILL BREEZE from off the sea teased Kat's hair. Thin strands waved like shadowy snakes in her peripheral vision. She watched Cam through those shadows as she typed on her laptop, working through an endless stack of work emails. Cam had closed the novel he'd been reading. He stared at the sea, brooding.

Good. That's exactly what Kat wanted.

Well, what Kat really wanted was to fuck Celina over and get a good fuck for herself along with it. And Cam was a good fuck. No question about that.

But Cam was stubbornly loyal. She'd switched her tactics to the girl next door routine, only dropping the occasional mild innuendo to test the waters and see if they'd warmed. They had not.

Not that the thought hadn't crossed his mind. Kat was hot as fuck, if she did say so herself, and Cam was a man, after all. She'd caught Cam in a body scan or two, and she remembered the low tent in his shorts outside the gym the other night. That image—Cam shirtless and interested—

had replayed in her mind a few times as she'd relieved some of her own sexual tension on a few nights.

Yet despite Kat's best efforts, Cam wasn't going to cheat on Celina. Good for him, and good for Celina. It only made Kat want him more, of course, but so be it.

But if she couldn't have him, she could at least sow enough doubt to make Celina's life harder. Celina had it too easy. She needed to know what pain felt like.

Okay, fine, her father died. That was painful, sure. Sounds like he'd been murdered, too. Maybe even by Jenkins, his protégé and practically an older brother to Celina. Harsh. Painful.

But not as painful as being judged and tormented by your own father every day of your fucking life.

No, Celina had it easy. She deserved a little pain.

And Kat would see that she got it.

Jenkins had told Kat to find some information he could use against Celina. Kat had already found a copy of the evidence against Jenkins and his campaign finance goon, Vernon Stratham. She'd looked up Stratham. Tall, thin, glasses. He was a nerd. A deadly nerd, though.

After scanning the evidence, Kat could see why Jenkins was worried. That kind of information was not good for a political career. She'd keep that little tidbit to herself for now, though. Wouldn't make much sense to tell Jenkins she knew his secret. That would just paint a target on Kat's back, as well as Celina's.

Kat had scooped up the decoy data Celina had exposed for her. Something about one of her father's prototypes. As if Celina would give a shit about leaked plans for a prototype. That might have fooled most people, but Kat knew Celina too well. She didn't need any more money, and she couldn't give a shit if someone stole her father's idea. Like

Kat's glasses, Celina could design her own version that would be better than any copy anyone else could make.

Including Kat and Nestech. Kat clenched her fists over her keyboard at the thought. Her own fucking father had always liked Celina better, and Kat had to admit that he was right to do so. Celina was better. She was a better coder, a better designer, a more creative thinker. She better looking, in better shape. She was better, period. She was a fucking genius, just like both of their fathers.

But she apparently wasn't smart enough to know that Kat would see through her little gambit, dangling this bait for Kat and Jenkins to bite. She would take Celina's bait, let Celina think she had the upper hand. But Kat already had the information Jenkins wanted, the information Kat needed to get her company back.

She'd originally figured it would be something about Celina's mother. That was a shock to Kat when Jenkins had told her the truth. In all the years she'd been friends with Celina—okay, more frenemies than friends—she'd never once heard a thing about Celina's mother. Kat had just assumed her mother was dead. When Jenkins told her Celina's mother was Speaker Kinkaid, Kat had thought it was total bullshit.

She still thought it was bullshit, actually. But Jenkins had been adamant. And he'd given Kat the assignment to prove it.

She hadn't. There was nothing on Celina's servers about her mother. No emails or text messages. No communication of any kind. No journal entries or official documents. Nothing, aside from some news stories and videos about the speaker in Celina's internet browsing history. Hardly incriminating. She'd find the same browsing history on the computers of millions of people around the world, anyone with even a passing interest in American politics.

Whoever had covered the speaker's tracks had done a good job of it. Probably Celina's father, if Kat had to guess. And if he wanted that information hidden, no one would ever find it.

But it didn't matter. Kat had something just as good. Not for blackmail, if that's what Jenkins really wanted to do. But if he wanted something he could use to threaten Celina, to make sure she did what he wanted, Kat had just the thing.

And his name was Cameron Hauk.

In the years since Cam left, Kat had missed him. That was a first for her. She'd picked him up on the train and brought him home as a fucktoy for Christmas. A little Christmas present to herself. She'd done it before, plenty of times. Every time, she had her fun, then put the fucktoy back on the train and never thought about him again.

Except for Cam.

He had called himself Sam Davis, but he was the same man she watched in the deck chair beside her. Beautiful, smart, brave, principled. As principled a thief as you'll ever find. More principled than most of the founders and CEOs Kat worked with.

And he'd walked away from Kat.

Another first.

She'd thrown herself at him in the end, practically begged him to stay. And he probably would have, if not for that one tiny little detail, the one about how Kat and her family had worked together to murder her father in his own home at Christmas.

Those damn principles of Cam's got in the way of a good thing.

And that was probably what made him stick in Kat's

mind. The one that got away. The one thing she couldn't have.

And now Celina had him, instead.

Good for her.

And fuck her.

Kat's loss might be Celina's gain, but it was Jenkins' gain, too. Kat had seen how much Celina loved Cam. Jenkins could use that love against her. Oldest bargaining chip in the world. You give me what I want or I'll kill the people you love.

Kat smiled at her laptop. If Kat couldn't have Cam, she'd make sure Celina couldn't have him, either.

PART II

22

Celina flopped down on the couch and let out a long sigh, releasing all the stress and anguish she'd been feeling for days. It was the morning of New Year's Eve, and she and Cam had just come back from dropping Kat off at the airport.

"Thank fucking God she's gone," she said, shouting it loud enough to echo around the room.

Cam sat beside her. Celina rolled over and buried her head face-down in his lap, letting the world go dark around her. She basked in the heat coming off Cam's body, like always. The man was a fucking furnace. She pulled in a lungful of his scent, the usual Cam smell of wood and spice and warm dirt and sunshine.

And sex. With her face in his crotch, Celina could smell the sex they'd had that morning, even through his sweat-pants. She turned her head from side to side, sniffing and smelling and stroking through the fabric with her nose along the line of his cock. She felt it stiffen and smiled.

They had so much sex, all the time, in any mood, place, or situation, but Celina still felt like she could never get enough of this man and his body. They just fit together, like a mechanical exoskeleton. Separately, they were each strong. But together, they weren't just twice as strong. They were ten times stronger. Exponentially stronger.

She turned her head and lay her cheek against his crotch, felt his hardness beneath her. He stroked her hair softly, slowly slipping his fingers through the length of her silky hair. She spun around to lie on her back, her head still in his lap, and looked up at him.

"Will you miss her?" she asked.

"Kat?" asked Cam. He seemed surprised by the question. "It was nice to see her again, but I wouldn't say I'll miss her."

Celina felt a stab of jealousy, thinking about the times she'd seen them together, when they didn't know she was watching. As she approached the deck after coming down the stairs, or in the security cameras when she passed the screens. Or—fine, she was big enough to admit it—when she'd pulled up the camera recordings to see where Cam had gone that night, had seen their interaction in the hallway outside the training room. Nothing had happened. Nothing incriminating. It was all perfectly innocent.

But Celina knew Kat. There wasn't an innocent bone in her body. And there was a familiarity between Kat and Cam that irked the shit out of Celina. Kat had fucked Celina's boyfriend. With all the people they'd both fucked over the years, that was the first time they'd fucked the same person. Seemed statistically impossible, but it was true.

And she could see it in the way they interacted. Even though they were above-board the whole time—despite Kat's early attempts to seduce Cam—there was something about the way she touched his arm or his knee, the way Cam laughed with her, even the way they walked together. It was easier than with other people, more natural.

It stuck in Celina's mind like a dry-swallowed pill stuck in her throat. No matter how much water she drank to try to flush it out, the thought stuck there, tenacious and bitter, slowly burning a hole in her brain.

She rolled to her shoulder, threw an arm around Cam's back, and pulled him close, burying her face in his stomach this time, and pulling in the heat, the scent, the whole of him.

Whatever history Cam and Kat shared, Kat was on a plane back to the East coast. Cam was on *her* couch, in *her* arms. If she wanted, Celina could roll over and suck him off right now. If Kat tried that—hell, *when* she'd tried that—Cam would turn her away.

Cam was Celina's man. He knew it, and he liked it.

So why the fuck did Celina still feel so fucking jealous?

They'd taken Kat to the airport early that morning. They could have called a private car, but Celina insisted on driving Kat there herself. It was the polite thing to do. The friendly thing to do.

And the only way Celina could make sure Kat got on the fucking plane and took off. And then Celina could track the tail number all the way across the country. She wanted Kat to be as far away as possible, that fucking bitch.

Kat had taken Celina's bait, sucked up those old proto-type designs like a snot-nosed kid at the boardwalk sucks an electric-blue Slurpee. She'd left the glasses with Celina, saying she'd placate Jenkins with some story about how they'd been stolen. But Celina knew that Jenkins wouldn't care about the glasses. The whole thing had been a ploy to get dirt on Celina, something he could use against her.

And now Kat was on her way back home to deliver the supposed prize to her master. All Celina could do now was wait and see what Jenkins chose to do with the information. Most likely, he'd threaten to sell the designs to the highest bidder—probably Nestech, ironically, though Kat would probably keep a copy for herself for free—if Celina ever leaked the information about the nefarious doings of Stratham and Jenkins.

She figured Jenkins would contact her within a week or two, but they wound up waiting a lot longer than that.

New Year's came and went. Valentine's Day came and went. Saint Patty's Day, all those other bullshit holidays, even the Fourth of July came and went. Nothing from Jenkins. Not a word.

It was the end of July. The hills along the Silicon Valley freeways were baked dry and yellow, the beaches were crowded with tourists, and the silence from Jenkins was making Celina very nervous.

The Republicans had nominated Senator Thomas Deacon at their convention in a sweltering Tampa three weeks earlier. Why they would choose to hold their convention in Florida in the middle of fucking July was beyond Celina. But politicians were not known for their intelligence, and their national committee leaders even less so.

Jenkins had sewn up the Democratic nomination months before on Super Tuesday, and the party would make it official at the end of their own convention, which was starting that day. At least they had the good sense to hold the event in Chicago. Mid-August in the Midwest was no treat, but it was a hell of a lot better than Florida.

Jenkins' nomination had been a foregone conclusion. The only drama to unfold was who Jenkins would choose as his running mate. If Jenkins had followed tradition, the announcement would have come last week, but Jenkins had chosen to wait until the convention started, probably trying to inject some benign drama into what was otherwise a pretty dull election cycle.

National polls put Jenkins at least twenty points ahead of Deacon. Congress, the governor's races, even the state races were all leaning blue, drafting off Jenkins' popularity and charisma. There was expected to be a blue tsunami this year that would give the Democrats the first supermajority either party had enjoyed in decades, and pave the way for Jenkins to write his name in history with the initiatives he planned to push through.

All the more reason for him to make sure Celina wouldn't spoil it for him.

And yet, nothing. Silence.

Her phone buzzed.

Jesus, fuck. Was Jenkins bugging her thoughts now? If that was him, out of the blue... spooky.

Celina rolled over and grabbed her phone from the coffee table.

A text, but not from Jenkins.

Celina didn't recognize the number. She sat up beside Cam and frowned at her screen.

"Who is it?" asked Cam.

"Don't know."

Celina didn't like opening texts or emails from numbers she didn't recognize. In fact, her phone usually wouldn't alert her if the number wasn't in her contact list. And this number definitely wasn't. Yet the phone had buzzed anyway.

She opened a browser window on her phone and tried a reverse phone lookup. Nothing came back. That in itself was weird. It should say something like "private cell number" or something like that and give the cell carrier name. But this search came back saying the number hadn't been found. That shouldn't be possible.

She tried three other reverse phone lookup websites and got the same result each time. Celina stood and went into her lab, Cam following behind her. She had access to more powerful lookup techniques. Celina had tapped into the NSA databases years before. She'd find what she needed there, for sure.

Except she didn't. The search came up empty. If she hadn't seen a text on her own phone, Celina would say that phone number didn't exist at all.

The smart thing to do would be to delete the text and not think twice. And Celina hovered her finger over her phone screen, ready to do just that. But something made her hesitate.

The number had a 202 area code. Washington, D.C. Celina knew a lot of people in D.C., but she didn't give her private phone number to any of them. Only one person had it: Jenkins.

But she had his number, too. Why would he bother to disguise his number, or use another phone? Maybe it was a burner, so he couldn't be traced when he blackmailed Celina. But that didn't seem like Jenkins' style, either. He wouldn't blackmail her over text. He'd do it in person, off-camera, unrecorded. Politics was all about plausible deniability, and Jenkins was a master of deny and distract. If he hadn't gone into politics, he'd have been the world's greatest magician.

202-811-0635. Something about those numbers nagged at Celina's brain.

"How could it not exist?" said Cam. "It's right there on your phone."

SMS spoofing was nothing new. Hackers had been

using it for years to send texts to targets and make it seem like they came from a phone number the target knew and trusted, someone in their contacts list. It was a clever way to make it more likely for the target to click whatever link you sent them, then steal their identity or their money or both.

But it would take a master hacker to spoof Celina's phone. She was a master hacker herself, and she'd put an array of security measures on all her devices.

And even if someone had managed to spoof her, they'd chosen a number that Celina didn't recognize, a number that didn't even exist. What was the point of that?

Celina could think of only four people in the world that had the skills to spoof her phone. One was a Russian stoner who called himself Vlad the Inhaler. He was currently vacationing in a Siberian prison. Pranav from Chennai had used his ill-begotten wealth to become a big-shot movie producer in Bollywood. Billy Lin had disappeared in China four months ago and hadn't resurfaced yet.

The fourth was in Washington. Her screen name was Pussylicker. Celina had never been able to figure out her real name. She was the best of them all. She worked for the NSA by day, herself by night.

They were all friends, more or less. And they had an unspoken rule not to hack each other, lest they spiral into an unending nuclear hack war that would bring them all down. Mutually assured destruction had worked in the Cold War. It worked here, too.

They had ways to contact each other, if needed. A random text was completely unnecessary.

And even if one of them had broken the code and hacked Celina's phone, why would they choose that particular number?

"Maybe it will just route to the hacker if you reply," said

Cam when Celina shared her thoughts with him. "They sent it to you. Maybe it will just work."

"I'm not going to reply until I know who it is," said Celina. "I'm not even going to open it."

Cam nodded. A moment later, he said, "Maybe it's a code. Maybe the numbers correspond to letters, and the sender is sending you a message that way. Maybe the contents of the text don't even mean anything."

A code. Celina thought about it for a moment. "There's a zero in there," she mused. Could be a zero-indexed alphabet code. "The numbers don't go high enough. The highest is an eight. That's only the letter I, if it starts at zero."

"CAC-IBB-AGDF." Cam frowned. "What the hell does that mean?"

"Doesn't mean anything."

"Maybe they're two-digit numbers. Twenty would be..." Cam counted on his fingers. "T. There's no twenty-eight, so maybe that's single-digits. B and H. TBH."

Celina shook her head. It wasn't a substitution cypher. That was too simple. Too easy to break.

But it still might be a code, a message. Cam might be on to something there.

The number 202, used in a phone number. That had to refer to Washington.

811? 0635?

"811, Washington," Cam mumbled. "635. Washington." He furrowed his brow. "Isn't 635 the number of your house in Washington? Your mother's house, I mean. The one we stayed at."

Her mother.

It hit Celina like a bolt of lightning. That's why the numbers seemed familiar.

202 was the area code for Washington. 635, or 0635 in four digits, was the number of the house Cam mentioned. And 811 was the number of Celina's mother's house in Old Town Alexandria.

It wasn't Jenkins texting her, or one of her hacker friends—although one of them had to have been involved, and they would get an earful from Celina when she found out which one it was.

The person texting her was her mother.

And now that she knew who the text was from, Celina wasn't at all sure that she wanted to open it.

23

CAM WATCHED Celina closely as they showered together. She had both hands against the wall, her head directly under the stream of water. With her hair hanging in dark sheets along the sides of her head, Cam couldn't see her face or her eyes. But he knew her well enough to read her body language.

Normally, when they showered together—even just after sex, like now—Celina was slinky and sexy. Something about the heat and the water and their slippery skin turned her on every time. And watching her react that way turned Cam on. It was a rare shower when they didn't end up in each other's arms.

But this would be one of those rare showers. Cam could see that much, even without seeing Celina's face.

Her shoulders were hunched, her head hung low between her outstretched arms. Steam billowed around them, fogging the glass that formed one wall of the shower. She had been silent for minutes, the only sound the hiss of the water from the three shower heads, needling a hundred tiny depressions into her skin, and the gurgle of the drain between her feet.

After they'd figured out the phone number of the text, Cam had watched the color drain from Celina's face. Until a few months ago, Cam didn't even know Celina had a mother. He thought she'd died in childbirth or something like that. Celina talked about her father all the time, but had never mentioned her mother. When Cam learned—not from Celina—that her mother was the Speaker of the U.S. House of Representatives, it had felt to him like a betrayal.

He realized now how unfair that was. Even now, he and Celina had only been together for fifteen months. Back then, it had been more like five or six. He couldn't reasonably expect her to have told him her deepest, darkest secrets already, especially one as monumental as that.

But the truth had come out in the course of robbing Celina's mother's house. And Madeline Kinkaid turned out to be a real piece of work.

Cam's mother, Paulie, was his best friend in the world, before Celina. Even while exploring the world with her boyfriend, she sent postcards and letters every week describing their travels. She and Simon had covered North Africa and Asia-Pacific, had stopped in California to visit for two weeks, then had left for a tour of South America and beyond. The latest postcard had been from a city called Ushuaia in the icy southern tip of Argentina. It showed Paulie's face ringed in a faux-fur hood standing at the top of a hill, a snow-draped city street dropping against an ice-blue sky behind her, the flat grey sea in the distance. "I never thought I'd live to see the End of the World," her postcard had begun.

Madeline Kinkaid, on the other hand, not only had

never communicated with Celina since the day she was born, she'd publicly denied having a child at all. And when she and Celina had been face-to-face, she'd defended that decision, said she'd do it all again in a heartbeat.

So Cam was not surprised to learn that Celina had issues with her mother. He wouldn't talk about her either, if he were Celina.

But it was clear that the woman had sway with her daughter, even in absentia. Even after all these years. What mother wouldn't? Celina tried to deny it, to herself and to Cam, but it was clear that she was disturbed by the text. When they'd figured out who it came from, Celina had been quiet for a long moment, then had turned to Cam and said, "Okay, that's done. How about some target practice?"

Cam opened his mouth to protest, but Celina was already out the door. They'd spent two hours and thousands of rounds of ammunition in the gun range, then had sparred in the training room for six more hours. Cam's skills had advanced quite a bit, both in shooting and in sparring, in the last six months or so, but Celina held nothing back in that session. She would kick Cam's ass from one side of the room to the other, then she'd help him up off the training mat so she could kick it all over again. Time after time, for hours.

Cam didn't mind. Celina needed the release, and it was great training for him. As much as his skills had improved, he could finally see how much further he needed to go. Celina was a master. Cam wanted to get there, too, some day.

Then, after six hours, muscles aching and chests heaving, Celina had wrestled Cam to the floor and used him for a different kind of release. He didn't mind that, either.

And now they were in the shower. The sex had been

quick, by their standards. Just thirty minutes. Under normal circumstances, they'd be at it again in the shower, then the floor, the bed, the balcony. But Cam could see that wasn't going to happen this time. Even after all that physical exertion, her mind was still in tangles about her mother and that text.

"Hey," said Cam softly, laying his hand on Celina's slick, bare back. He could feel the tension in the muscles around her shoulder blades. He slid his hand to her shoulders and felt the muscles bunch underneath.

Celina's back lifted, then fell as she released a heavy sigh. She straightened and turned, the shower water running like a shroud over her face. Cam slid his hands around her waist, held her against him, looked deep into her eyes. They were as entrancing as always, a lustrous, multi-layered emerald green. But this time, they were troubled, clouded with the tumult of Celina's churning thoughts.

"Let's just open the text," he said softly.

She avoided his gaze, but he crouched down until he found it, pulled it up with him as he straightened. He set one hand on her cheek. He wanted to take her pain away, wanted to fill the empty place her mother had left with all the love he could give.

If only it were that simple.

Cam couldn't heal Celina. He could support her, love her, talk to her, and be there for her. But the healing would have to come from her.

"Let's just open the text," he said again.

Celina shook her head, an annoyed expression on her face, then looked up at Cam and nodded.

He pulled her in and held her. Amid the heat and the

steam and the needling spray, he held her in his arms. After a moment, she pulled him tight and held him, too.

Hours later, they were dressed and dried and their bellies were full. The fog had rolled in, thick and wet, from the ocean, covering the deck with an eerie murk, so they'd eaten a mostly silent meal at the table inside, in front of the fireplace.

Now, they sat across from each other in Celina's lab, her phone on the workbench between them. Celina had connected the phone to a network she used for testing. It connected to the internet, but it was isolated from the rest of her systems, completely separate, so that there was no chance of a virus or a bug of any kind degrading her network, corrupting her servers, or compromising her data in any way.

The light from overhead was bright, focused on the phone. It was completely unnecessary—the phone screen illuminated itself—but Celina had spent a good minute and a half adjusting it just so. The rest of the room was dark.

The light cast Celina's face into half-shadow. Cam watched her stare at the phone like she was facing a gunslinger in an Old West showdown in the center of town, her face set, her eyes wary, her posture poised for action.

After a long minute, Celina unlocked the phone and pulled up her text messages. Her finger hesitated for only a moment, hovering over the text from her mother, before she tapped it and pulled her finger back as if from a flame.

Celina stared down at the message, absorbing it, then spun the phone so Cam could read it.

The message was short and to the point.

Come to DC. Important.

After months without speaking, after years with no contact, out of the blue from a hidden, unidentified number, that's what Madeline Kinkaid sent to her daughter. Four words, and an order.

Cam looked up at Celina. She stared at the workbench, the shadow casting a grey pall over her face. Cam could see the muscle in her jaw working, flexing and releasing, over and over.

She pushed back from the workbench, her stool screeching against the floor, and stalked out of the lab.

Cam went after her.

He didn't bother to bring the phone.

24

Celina was seething.

Fucking Madeline.

Madeline fucking Kinkaid, the mighty Speaker of the House.

Who the fuck did she think she was, sending Celina a text from a fake number, hacking her phone, hiding like a fucking coward, then ordering her to come all the way across the country without even telling her why?

It was fucking bullshit.

It was also the first time she'd ever contacted Celina. In Celina's entire life, twenty-nine fucking years, this was the first contact she'd ever had from her own fucking mother. What a fucking bitch.

Celina had to move. Her anger was too hot. If she didn't move, it would burn her to ash.

She stomped out of the lab, down the hall, through the kitchen, out onto the deck.

The fog obscured everything. Celina could feel it on her cheeks, on her forehead. Like flop sweat.

When it blazed into life, the automatic light on the deck

just made it worse, turned the opaque black night into an opaque grey wall of fog.

Celina paced back and forth on the deck, listening to the ocean moan and thunder.

She had to move.

Down the stairs to the beach, the loose sand squeaking beneath her feet, then firming, growing coarser as she got closer to the water. It ground against her bare feet.

The sea was blackness in the night, extending out forever. The only thing she could see was the faint grey of the breaking waves, picking up the light from the porch.

Celina wanted to walk straight into the inky sea and keep going, let the cold water rise up her body and cover her, sink down to the ocean floor and walk all the way across the Pacific until she rose up again on Japanese soil. Another land. Another world.

She turned right instead. With each step, she stomped her heels into the sand, felt it form to her sole, supporting her weight.

And then a wave would come and erode that support, twist her heel and her knee, disrupt her balance.

The lights of the Golden Gate Bridge glowed in the distance ahead. Yellow lights along the deck formed a garrote around the neck of the bay. Orange towers stabbed into the soft underside of the chin of the dark sky. Quavering reflections simpered across the dark water toward her like whispered gossip.

The glow made the darkness around her deeper.

She stomped toward it, step after step, falling into rhythm with the ebb and wash of the waves. She could walk this beach for more than a mile before she ran out of land.

And then she could decide what to do next.

The wind kicked up, blew her hair against her face. She shook her head to free it, felt the breeze dry the foggy flop sweat.

A wave rolled up and over her feet, swelling around her ankles and soaking into the cuffs of her pants. She heard splashing behind her. She didn't look around.

Cam fell into step at her side. He didn't say anything, just matched her pace and walked with her.

Just having him there, close, soothed Celina. Her fevered pace slowed, her boiling anger cooled. Her mother was a fucking bitch, but Cam knew it. Cam knew all about it. The broad strokes, at least.

And he loved her anyway.

This fucked up mother-daughter bullshit didn't scare him off, like it would any other man. Any normal man. Any sane man.

Jesus, why the fuck was Cam still with her? He should have run off with Kat when he had the chance.

Celina shook her head sharply. What the fuck was she saying? First jealousy, now... whatever the fuck this shit was. Self-hatred? Self-deprecation? That was not Celina's style. There were already enough assholes in the world who would deprecate her by default, just for being a woman. She didn't need to pile on herself. Fuck that shit.

Insecurity. That's what it was.

Celina hadn't felt insecure for years. Not since she was a kid. She worked her ass off so that she didn't have to feel insecure. She was smarter, stronger, faster. And she'd earned that shit.

But it wasn't Cam that made her feel insecure.

It was her mother. Fucking Madeline fucking Kinkaid. The most powerful woman in U.S. politics.

That fucking bitch.

And what was Celina going to do about it? Cry into her cereal? Drown herself in the sea?

Fuck that. She wouldn't give her mother the satisfaction.

Her mother wanted Celina in D.C.? She'd go.

And her mother would wish she'd never asked.

Celina's stomping slowed, then stopped. The sea foam swirled over her feet. She sank deeper into the sand with each wave, her pant cuffs getting heavier and heavier as the icy water soaked into them.

The tide was coming in.

Beside her, Cam sighed. She looked at him, followed his gaze to the bridge.

"Beautiful, isn't it?" he said.

And it was. The oranges, the yellows, the lights of Sausalito peeking beneath the roadway, shimmering pastel reflections beneath it all. An Impressionist painting in life size.

Celina found Cam's hand, entwined her fingers in his. They stood and admired the view while the sea soaked their pant legs.

"What now?" asked Cam.

Celina set her jaw, squeezed Cam's hand tight, and wriggled her heels even deeper into the sand, finding support deep down where the waves couldn't erode it.

"Now," she said, "we go to Washington."

25

THEY WERE in the air early the next morning, wheels-down in Washington by California lunchtime. Cam was following Celina's lead, once again. He'd go where she went, where she needed him to be.

Celina was unusually quiet. She tried to hide it, but her chatter was too shallow, her smiles too quick, too unnaturally smooth.

And they didn't reach her eyes. That was the true tell for Celina. Those entrancing eyes were just as the poets said: windows into Celina's soul. It had taken Cam months to be able to see it. Her eyes were sirens until he'd learned to put wax in his ears. Now, he could see what Celina was thinking and feeling just by watching them.

If she knew that, she'd probably be pissed. She would not be happy knowing she had a tell. But Cam figured she was probably safe. It had taken him a long time to figure it out, and he might be the only one who could do it.

That thought made him smile, to think that he could be the only person in the world who knew Celina well enough to read her that way.

Even then, there was so much more to learn. Fifteen months together was only scratching the surface. He had learned to read Celina well enough, but there was a whole library inside her. It would take him a lifetime to truly know her.

That thought didn't scare Cam one bit.

Why the hell hadn't he told Celina that yet?

As they descended into Reagan National airport, he watched Celina stare out the window of the plane, her hands clasped tight in her lap, her mouth pulled into a frown. A streak of shadow passed over her face as the jet banked into the approach path.

Now was not the time.

A private car met them on the tarmac and took them straight to Celina's mother's house in Alexandria, Virginia, twenty minutes from downtown Washington. They parked on the curb and waited. Celina stared out the window at her mother's front door, the same pensive look on her face as she'd had when they'd landed.

"Shouldn't you text her?" said Cam.

Celina turned from the window, her expression momentarily blank, as if she'd forgotten Cam was even there.

She turned back to the window, then said, "She'll know we're here."

An hour passed, then two, and Celina didn't move. She just stared out the window at the door, silent and stony.

Cam played on his phone, checking email, social media. Wasting time. He was just settling in to read a book when a notification popped up on the top of his screen. It was a text from his mother.

On our way to Washington. Meet you there tomorrow afternoon.

Celina glanced over and saw the text.

"Who's that from?"

"It's..." Cam puzzled over the text. "It's from Paulie."

How did his mother know he was coming to D.C.?

"Did you tell her we were coming here?" Celina asked.

"No," said Cam, "but we share our locations with each other on our phones. She probably saw where I was and it fit into her travel plans."

It was the only explanation that made sense.

"You share your location with your mother? All the time?"

Cam smiled, more of an apologetic wince than a smile. "Not all mothers are... problematic."

Celina grunted, then turned back to her vigil at the window. Cam started to reply to his mother when Celina reached over and tapped his leg.

"She's here," she said.

Cam looked past her out the car window to see a man in a black suit, white shirt, and black tie exiting the front door and approaching the car. He looked to be Cam's age, early-thirties, with his hair cut in a military high and tight with a youthful, styled wave at the front. His posture was board-straight, and his gaze swept the area all around as he approached the car. Cam didn't know if these Secret Service-types were supposed to be incognito or not, but with their muscle-stuffed suits and shifty gazes, anyone could spot them from a mile away.

Celina rolled down the window. The stifling, muggy August heat immediately pushed through the air conditioning like a smothering hand over Cam's nose and mouth. The man bent to look through the window, his eyes sweeping over Cam and the driver before settling on Celina.

"Ms. Maxwell," he said, his voice as efficient as his haircut, "the speaker will see you now."

Celina kept her eyes locked on his as she slid the tinted window back up. He did not seem amused, but he stepped back onto the curb and waited, hands clasped in front of him, eyes scanning the street.

Must be a habit for them. Always looking for threats, no matter where they are. Cam wondered if they scanned for threats at the dinner table or in their bedrooms before turning out the light. Probably.

"The speaker will see you now," said Celina, mimicking the man in a childish mumble. She pulled on the door handle. "Fucking bitch."

They followed the man through the front door and into the speaker's home, down a narrow entryway and through a wide double door into a bright sitting room with high ceilings, two white couches separated by a low marble table with a tea set on a tray in the center, and artwork covering the walls. Large windows in one wall revealed a garden on the side of the house, with a wood bench, a brick wall covered in ivy, and pots of flowers overflowing with gorgeous reds and yellows and purples.

Two French doors were open to the garden, letting the warm afternoon breeze waft in, bringing with it the sweet scent of the flowers. Seemed odd to Cam to leave the doors open when the air conditioning was running, but he couldn't complain about the effect. The room felt light and airy and fragrant, not too cold and not too warm, like a pleasant walk on a lovely spring day.

That feeling fell away like a collapsing building when

Cam turned and saw through another doorway into the hall.

The hall where an Israeli assassin had been stalking Celina in the dark.

The hall where Cam had tackled that assassin, taken a rifle shot in his Kevlar vest, and fallen with the man against the stairwell where Celina was crouched.

The hall where Cam had killed the man when his head cracked open on the bottom stair.

Like a zombie, barely aware of his own movements, Cam stepped through the doorway into the hall.

The whole scene played out in front of him, like shadows moving through the space. The darkness, the adrenaline. The rush forward, barely thinking. The dry crack of the rifle shot, and the wet crunch of the man's skull against the wood stair.

It had barely registered for Cam at the time. He didn't remember much of what happened afterward. He woke on his back on the floor, staring up at the ceiling.

He looked at that ceiling now, recognized the star shape of the chandelier. That much was burned into his memory.

Then Celina's face coming into view above him, her cheeks streaked with tears. He remembered thinking how odd it was, those shiny lines across her skin. He'd touched her cheek and felt them wet. He'd never seen her cry before.

The warmth of her hand in his—so warm—as the medics lifted him onto the stretcher.

Unconsciously, he rubbed his ribs where the impact of the bullet through the vest had broken them.

"The memory will never leave you."

Cam turned to see Madeline Kinkaid standing behind him.

"The difficult ones never do," she said. "But it will fade, in time."

He'd seen her before, in the kitchen of the house he'd stayed in with Celina, Paulie, and Simon in downtown D.C. last year. But back then, Cam had still been reeling from the attack just a few days earlier, and pain bloomed in his ribs with every movement, every breath. He'd seen Madeline, but he hadn't taken her in.

She wore a vivid blue blouse under a gorgeous dark grey pantsuit, cut perfectly to her figure: trim enough to seem businesslike, shapely enough to seem feminine, but loose enough to be comfortable. The top of her head only came up to Cam's shoulder. Her straight dark hair framed and offset her pale skin. Like her daughter, she was a beautiful woman, but her hazel eyes were what pulled you in. Just like her daughter, Madeline's eyes were mesmerizing.

But it was Madeline's presence that struck Cam, struck him like the blaze of heat that hits when you open the door to a hot oven. She was short in stature, but Madeline's presence made her seem ten feet tall. She carried herself with the poise not just of someone in power, but of someone who had mastered her ability to wield it.

"Madam Speaker," Cam stammered. "It's an honor to see you again."

"Thank you, Cameron," she said, taking Cam's hand in both of hers and holding it in a two-handed handshake. "It's an honor to meet the man who saved my daughter's life."

Her grip was firm, but her skin was soft and smooth. Somehow, the handshake exuded command while also conveying a sense of safety. Maybe that mix of strength and softness, of masculinity and femininity, was part of what had allowed Madeline to climb the ranks of power in the

U.S. government, a place where, despite all the pronounce-ments and political slogans, the feminine was still seen as simultaneously both weak and threatening. The old boys' club was too brittle to bend its ways, but still too powerful for Madeline to shatter completely.

But that time would come. And looking into Madeline's hazel eyes as she shook his hand, Cam could see that she just might be the one to do it. She could be the one to bend the arc of history more squarely toward justice.

Madeline broke their eye contact. She turned toward the door to the sitting room, putting one hand on Cam's back and urging him forward more with her posture and her gaze than with her muscles.

And he went where she wanted him to go. Madeline was in charge. Softly, subtly, but absolutely clearly.

No wonder she and Celina butted heads.

"Something tells me," Madeline said as she steered Cam toward the doorway, "that Celina may not share your feel-ings about seeing me again."

Looking around the corner into the sitting room, Cam saw Celina standing in the far corner, inspecting a series of square-framed photographs that covered most of the wall. When she turned and saw Cam next to Madeline, her face darkened.

"I'm afraid you might be right about that," he said.

They stepped into the room, and Cam could have sworn he heard a low, feral growl come from the other side.

26

CELINA WAS ADMIRING Madeline's photos, the same ones that had caught her eye the first time she'd been in the speaker's sitting room. Everything else in the room was as you'd expect, D.C. proper, exuding wealth and taste without ruffling any feathers. Architectural Digest meets Plantation Owner's Monthly. Spotless white couches, fifteen-foot ceilings, a garden maintained by servants whose names Madeline probably didn't know.

But the photos were different. Gorgeous and artistic, all of them in black-and-white with square white frames. The casual eye would drift right over them, fitting them into the broader decor, the picture of a proper home for a wealthy white woman.

But when you got close, when you actually looked at them, they were not proper at all. They were borderline subversive. Each one depicted a woman with power. A gorgeous woman in a frilly gown holding a shotgun like she knew how to use it. A plus-sized woman flaunting her size, staring right at the camera, daring the viewer to deny her sex appeal. These images were statements. Subtle, in some cases. Less so, in others. But every one was a challenge to the patriarchal status quo.

There were hips and breasts and muted sensuality, but every photograph framed its subject not as an object of beauty, but as the owner of it. Every image conveyed the power of the woman over her own mind, her own body. The power of the woman to live her own life as she saw fit. And change the world in the process.

As she had been the first time she'd seen the pictures, Celina was impressed.

When she turned and saw Madeline walking beside Cam, that feeling immolated, the ash drifting away like smoke in the wind.

"Thank you for coming so quickly," said Madeline.

"Thanks for being so clear in your message," Celina responded. She made her voice sound light and friendly, but she didn't keep her true feelings out of her stare. "It's refreshing these days when someone identifies themselves and explains their intentions so openly." She took slow, strolling steps along the windows and the mirror, touching the sills and the frame and the fronds of the plants lightly with her fingers, as if casually inspecting them. "These days, too many cowards hide behind fake identities and even faker public statements." She glared across the room at Madeline. "Don't you think?"

Madeline smiled as if completely unperturbed by Celina's sarcasm. She gestured for Cam to sit on one of the couches and gave a quick tilt of her head to the security guard. He stepped from the room into the entryway and shut the double doors behind him.

"These are difficult times, I agree," said Madeline.

Celina fumed as she watched Madeline bend over the tea set in the center of the table. Madeline lifted the lid off the pot. Steam billowed out. She took the lid off a smaller cylinder and scooped loose-leaf tea into a basket in the top of the teapot, then replaced the lid to let the tea steep.

"That's not what I said," said Celina, clenching her jaw, all pretense of friendliness dropping from her voice. "At all."

Madeline straightened and shrugged. "Language is fraught with the potential for misinterpretation. It's a cross we all must bear."

Celina snorted. "Is that how you talk to the Southern evangelicals? They all think you're Satan's harpy, you know. You won't get their vote, no matter how much biblical language you use."

"I do enjoy our little chats," said Madeline, turning her back toward Celina as she sat on the couch opposite Cam. "Why don't you join us and make yourself comfortable?" she said over her shoulder. "The tea will be ready in a few minutes."

Celina actually snarled at her mother's back, but she stalked around the table and sat on the couch beside Cam.

"Is this the Armenian tea you found in Luxembourg?" she asked.

Madeline smiled. "You remembered."

Celina didn't reply, but the accidental intimacy made her blood boil even hotter than the tea. She grabbed Cam's hand where it lay beside hers on the couch and gripped it to keep herself from lunging across the table and strangling her mother.

"Celina is referring to a story I told her the last time we sat for tea together," said Madeline to Cam, seemingly immune to the waves of anger exuding from Celina. Her voice was a light and floral as the breeze wafting in from the garden.

Celina heard Cam groan softly beside her. She must have gripped his hand a little too tight. She released him, and he immediately started massaging his palm with his other hand.

"Sadly, though," said Madeline, "the last of that tea ran out last month, and I've so far been unable to source any more. This one is lovely, though. A jasmine green tea from southern China. Not as unique, but equally delicious."

"How about you stop bullshitting us about the tea and tell us why the fuck we're here?" said Celina.

The pleasant smile on Madeline's face dropped into a neutral expression. It was a small victory, but Celina felt a wave of exultation flash through her.

"Yes, I suppose it's unfair of me to delay any longer. You've gone to great trouble to come, after all."

She scooted forward to the edge of the couch and poured the tea into three simple cylindrical tea cups. The liquid was deep green and thick. Gouts of steam rose from each cup like the chimneys of an industrial plant in miniature on Madeline's coffee table.

Madeline set the teapot down again and held a cup out for Cam, who leaned forward and took it with a nod and a mumble of thanks. She held another cup out for Celina, but Celina did not move.

Madeline was fucking stalling again. Just like a politician. You ask them a question and they answer a different one. You tell them to do something, they agree, then they just do whatever the fuck they want.

Madeline pushed a coaster on the coffee table toward Celina and set the tea cup on it.

"Why are we here, Madeline?" said Celina.

Madeline paused with her hand on her own cup,

staring into the steaming liquid as if gathering her thoughts.

"I'm here because I have work to do."

She said it simply, plainly, as if stating the obvious. She lifted the cup, shifted the hot ceramic from one hand to the other, then blew gently across the top.

"You're here," she continued, "because you're important."

She took a small, breathy sip of the hot tea, then settled back into the couch, holding the cup in her lap.

"Important to who?" asked Celina.

"Important to that work," she said. "And important to me."

She leveled her gaze at Celina. It held more challenge than affection.

Celina scoffed.

"And important to the country," Madeline continued.

"What the fuck are you talking about?" asked Celina.

Madeline stared at Celina for a long moment, a warm, casual smile on her lips. She was reclined on the couch, looking relaxed and comfortable. Yet her posture was picture perfect. Her back was straight, her shoulders square. Her knees were crossed, but the fold of her dark grey slacks still led perfectly straight down the line of her leg to her spotless leather flats. She had mastered the impeccable appearance required of all women, more so of women in positions of power, where the tiniest flaw would lead her to be scorned and discounted.

If she weren't her mother, the woman who had abandoned her and denied her existence for her entire life, Madeline Kinkaid might have been a role model for Celina. She had strength. That much was clear. She had guts. No woman could rise to be third in line to the presidency of the United States without it. And she had smarts. Celina could tell that just from talking to her.

Was that all it took to be Speaker of the House? Or were there skeletons in Madeline Kinkaid's closet? Bloody knives or poisoned chalices waiting to be brought to light? What did Madeline Kinkaid have to hide?

"You know the truth, Celina," said Madeline. "You know that you're my daughter, that I've watched you your whole life, albeit from a distance."

Albeit from a distance? Madeline so easily hid twenty-nine years of child neglect behind four fancy words.

"You know that I made that choice deliberately, in full knowledge of the impact it might have, in partnership with your father."

"My father would not have agreed to that." Celina spat out the words. The idea was like poison on her lips.

"He did agree to that," said Madeline, her voice softer, but her stare no less firm, no less direct. "Though, in fairness, I didn't give him much choice."

"Why didn't you just get an abortion like a normal person?" Celina asked.

Madeline pulled in a sharp breath, but her expression did not lose its composure.

"Because I loved your father," she said, "and you are his child. Our child."

"What, like a souvenir of your summer fling at the beach? A little sand dollar necklace?" Celina snorted with derision. "Don't know if you noticed, but you left your souvenir at the rental house."

She glanced at Cam. He was staring at the steaming cup in his lap, looking like he'd rather be anywhere else in the world at that moment.

"I love you, Celina," said Madeline. "You may not believe it—"

"I don't."

"—but I do. In my own way."

"Your way sucks." Celina balled her hands into fists. "Your way is bullshit." She forced herself to release her fists, but they clenched themselves again. "Your way is a euphemism for fucking abandonment."

Madeline's cheeks flushed, just slightly.

"I never abandoned you," she said.

To her credit, she did not look away.

The woman had guts.

"It sure felt like it to me," said Celina.

Madeline didn't respond, but something softened in her eyes. Maybe Celina imagined it, but some wall seemed to crack, some block of ice began to melt inside Madeline Kinkaid.

And in that moment, something melted inside Celina, too. Her clenched fists fell open, and a flood welled in her, a flood of feelings she didn't understand and didn't want to process, but that was strong enough to drown her if she didn't get a handle on them fast.

She stood from the couch. "Excuse me for a moment."

She tripped over Cam's feet as she pushed past his legs, banged against the coffee table hard enough to slosh tea from her cup. Her cheeks burned as hot as the tea when she looked over her shoulder at the steaming pool on the table.

"I—I need to use the restroom," she mumbled, then fled the room.

27

AN AWKWARD TENSION hung in the room after Celina ran out. Cam had been burying his gaze in his tea while she and Madeline jousted, but he braved a glance up at the speaker now. She was looking at the doorway where Celina had just left, looking as deeply and profoundly sad as Cam had ever seen a person look.

He knew what she had done to Celina, and he knew the effect it had. Celina hid it well behind bluster and bravado and blinding intelligence. But once Cam had gotten to know her, he could see it. He could see Celina reacting to that wound in every moment of every day. And Madeline Kinkaid had held the knife that caused that wound.

But Cam hadn't realized how deeply Madeline had wounded herself, as well. He could see it now, the pain of a mother who not only lost her daughter, but who willingly gave her away. All the pain, all the regret, all the uncertainty was reflected in her eyes as she watched Celina walk out of the room.

And then it was all gone again, replaced by the veiled warmth of a practiced politician. She leaned forward, took a napkin from the tray, and soaked up the tea Celina had spilled. She slid her gaze to Cam. Her smile was wan, but it was a smile.

"How long have you and Celina known each other?" she asked as she folded the wet napkin loosely and set it on the tray.

"About a year and a half."

Madeline nestled back into the couch cushions and sipped her tea.

"Does that seem like a long time to you?" she asked.

Cam couldn't help the smile that turned the corners of his mouth.

"Not nearly long enough," he said.

Madeline used her hand in her lap as a saucer and let her tea cup rest there. She considered Cam with a thoughtful gaze that seemed to examine his very soul.

He could see where Celina got it from.

"You're different from the others," she said.

"Others?"

"The other men Celina has been with." She waved one hand vaguely in the air. "Such as it is."

"You've met the men Celina's been with? I wouldn't have thought—"

"I didn't meet them," Madeline said, shaking her head. "But when I said I've watched her from a distance," she gave a painful smile, "it wasn't just a rhetorical flourish."

She sipped her tea again and looked toward the doorway as if hoping for Celina to return.

"I have to say," she continued, "it hasn't been easy to keep up with her lovers. There've been quite a few." She glanced apologetically toward Cam. "I hope that doesn't come as a shock to you."

Cam smiled and shook his head. "We all have a past.

Celina is entitled to hers. And if that past involved a lot of lovers," Cam shrugged, "her body is hers to do with as she chooses."

Madeline gave him that searing stare once more, even more intensely this time. Cam squirmed under the heat of her gaze.

Madeline nodded slowly. "You are different from the others," she said.

"The other lovers?"

"The other men in the world."

Cam didn't know how to respond to that. He kept his mouth shut.

"I need to take Celina to Chicago with me, Cameron," Madeline said, matter-of-factly, "and I don't want you to accompany us."

Cam frowned. "Why is that?" he asked, then hastily added, "With respect, ma'am."

"Do you know why I chose to leave Celina with her father?" Madeline asked.

"Just what you said before," Cam said, "in the house in D.C. You wanted to make a difference for millions of women instead of just one little girl."

Madeline nodded soberly.

"I love our country and I love democracy," Madeline said, "but both are run by entitled white men who have lost the ability to care about anyone but themselves. If they ever had it." She said the last bit under her breath, with a bitterness that surprised Cam. "That's true now, and it was even more true when Celina was born."

"And you felt like you could change it?"

"I felt I needed to try," she said. "That I needed to put my shoulder to the wheel with the others. Hillary. Nancy. Michelle. Ruth."

She smiled, her eyes drifting into memory for a moment.

"Ruth was one of the originals," she said. "The rest of us pushed through the door, but she's one of the ones who opened it. In the modern era, of course."

She looked down at her tea.

"When I was young, before I met Celina's father, I wanted to be in politics. I wanted to shape law and help move America forward, keep it squarely in the center of global politics and influence."

She lifted her eyes to meet Cam's. Her gaze had become fierce.

"But when Celina was born, I wanted something more. I wanted to make sure she never had to endure what I had already endured, even at that young age. The harassment, the criticism, the double standards, the inequity."

Her face became hard, her eyes angry. She sat forward on the couch, perched on the edge.

"And when I got pregnant? Out of wedlock? The shame they tried to make me feel."

"Who tried to make you feel?"

"My parents. My friends. Even my doctors."

She shook her head, slowly, from side to side.

"I knew I couldn't change things overnight," she said, "but I was not going to let anyone make me feel that way again. Ever. And I was not going to let them make my daughter feel that way, or any other woman."

The presence Cam had felt in the hallway earlier was only a shadow of the force of will he felt in that sitting room now. It pressed on him, forced him to come along or go away. He could not sit still in the face of that conviction.

He could see how Madeline Kinkaid had risen in power and influence. To be honest, he couldn't see how she wasn't already running the country, how she hadn't already become president.

And he could see where Celina got her own force of personality. It came from her mother.

The force weakened, then faded. Madeline slid back on the couch again.

"That's why I made the choice I made," she said softly.

Cam pulled in a deep breath. He hadn't realized he'd stopped breathing.

A thick silence fell over them. Madeline seemed lost in her memories. Then she turned her gaze toward the doorway again.

"I was wrong before, Cameron," she said.

She looked at him again. That deep, profound sadness was back in her eyes.

"Not all memories fade."

28

Celina looked at herself in the mirror above the sink in her mother's powder room. She'd managed not to cry like a fucking child, but her eyes were shining, the tears amassed on her lower eyelid like an army on an international border, waiting for the command to invade her cheeks.

She stared up at the ceiling and opened her eyes wide, dabbing underneath them with balled-up toilet tissue to soak up the tears. When she looked in the mirror again, the army had stood down, but the rims of her eyes were still red and inflamed. She ran her fingers under cold water from the faucet, then pressed them against her eyes to cool them. Fortunately, she never wore much makeup, and what eyeliner she did wear was waterproof.

When she finished, the face in the mirror looked much more presentable. Tired, but no longer on the verge of emotional collapse.

Looks could definitely be deceiving.

Fucking Madeline. Celina had only cried once in the

last ten years, and that was when she'd found her father dead at his desk.

Okay, twice. She'd cried when she thought Cam had been shot and killed, too.

Yet her mother had nearly made her cry twice in the last few months alone, and all she'd had to do was speak. No deaths or threats of death. Just simple sentences spoken in that fucking politician's tone of hers. *I never loved you at all* or *I loved you, albeit from a distance.* Celina didn't know which was worse, believing that her mother had abandoned her completely or believing that her mother loved her in some fucked-up way, but had refused to see her for thirty years.

Either fucking explanation, Celina grew up without a mother.

She'd always wondered why her father never married, never took a lover. Hell, he barely even went on any dates. Maybe Madeline had told her the truth the last time they'd spoken. Maybe she and Celina's father really had continued to see each other over the years. Maybe they'd continued to be together even after Madeline married another man, adding adultery to her other sins.

That didn't seem like Celina's father's style, though. He wasn't a cheater.

But was it cheating if it was all arranged that way? Maybe Madeline's husband was in on it. Maybe he was gay or something and was trying to keep it hidden. Maybe he had a secret kid whose life he was destroying, too.

Celina dabbed the skin around her eyes with a hand towel—soft and soothing as silk against her stinging cheeks —and blew her nose in the toilet tissue before flushing it down. She pulled in a deep breath and let it out, squared her shoulders, then looked at herself in the mirror again.

That was the Celina Maxwell she knew. Strong. Tough. Formidable. Bad-ass.

That bad-ass feeling wavered as soon as she stepped through the doorway into the sitting area and saw her mother again. Goddamn it. When would that weakness ever stop? When would that fucking woman stop having control over her?

As soon as Celina stopped letting her.

"Sorry about that," she said smoothly, sliding past Cam without incident and sitting beside him on the couch again. She didn't offer any explanation for her sudden departure, just picked up her tea and sipped it, watching Madeline over the rim of the cup.

Madeline didn't seem the least bit bothered.

"Let me get right to the point," said Madeline. "I need you to come with me to Chicago, Celina. Tomorrow morning. I'm sorry for the short notice."

Sorry must mean something different inside the Beltway. By the normal definition of the word, Madeline didn't look the least bit sorry.

Celina kept her face composed and neutral. If Madeline could use her political poker face, so could Celina.

But inside, her mind was overclocking.

The only reason for Madeline to go to Chicago in the morning was for the Democratic convention. Tomorrow would be Wednesday, the third day of the four-day event. As the ranking Democrat in the House, it made sense for Madeline to feature prominently. She'd be expected to show her support for Jenkins.

As the ranking Democrat *and* a woman, it made sense for them to give her some time at the podium to highlight the supposed diversity and inclusion of the party. As if it wasn't filled with just as many misogynistic old white fuckers as the Republican party. But at least the Democrats tried to look like they were decent people.

So, it made sense for Madeline to go to Chicago, but Celina couldn't think of any reason why she would want Celina there with her. Was it like a bring-your-daughter-to-work kind of thing? Did Madeline think she could win Celina's favor after all this time by showing her how powerful she was? How many people would clap and cheer for her?

"I don't think so," said Celina sweetly, then sipped her tea again. It had cooled to lukewarm since she'd been away, but Celina drank it anyway.

Madeline smiled patiently.

"We have some important topics to discuss," she said. "More than we can cover over tea. I need to be in Chicago for a speech at the convention tomorrow, and I'd like you to accompany me so we can give ourselves an appropriate amount of time to talk them through."

Celina took another sip of tea, swallowed it. She leaned forward and set her cup back on its coaster. She took a napkin from the tray, dabbed at the corners of her mouth, folded the napkin into quarters and set it beside her cup, where it slowly opened back to its original shape.

Celina leaned back on the couch and got comfortable again. She folded her arms in her lap and smiled at Madeline.

"I don't think so," she said again, even more sweetly.

Madeline smiled that patient smile once more, unperturbed by Celina's stalling. But Celina could see the calculations happening behind her eyes.

In another setting, as a fly on the wall, she might have been fascinated by this process. To watch a master politician at the height of her powers working her will on a poor, recalcitrant subject. Celina might have been taking notes.

Instead, she was inside the fucking arena, circling the goddamn bull, waiting for the charge and lining up the spot where she'd shove her sword between the bull's fucking shoulder blades.

Only, a bullfight was a fucking sham. It was rigged. The bull was trapped, with no way out. It was dead, no matter what happened. If it gored the matador, the picadors and banderilleros would slaughter it. If it didn't gore the matador, he would sever the bull's spinal cord for its kindness.

And in a bullfight, the matador had swords honed to a razor's edge. Weapons that, if the bull could understand its situation, would strike fear into the bull's heart.

In this situation, Celina had no weapons. She had no idea what would persuade Madeline to do anything because she had no idea what Madeline wanted. Moreover, in order for Celina to persuade Madeline, she had to not only know what Madeline wanted, she had to be able to give it to her.

Madeline didn't need money. She might want more power—most politicians did—but Celina couldn't give that to her. What else was there?

Love?

Could Madeline want Celina's love?

Seemed unlikely. And she hadn't exactly been putting herself out there over the last thirty years. Even in the last year, since they'd made contact again, Celina hadn't heard a word from Madeline until the cryptic text yesterday. If Madeline wanted Celina's love, she was going about it in a very stupid way.

And whatever else she might be, Madeline Kinkaid was definitely not stupid.

Celina didn't have any swords to use against Madeline. No bargaining chips. Usually in politics, both sides make concessions to get what they want from the other. Celina had nothing Madeline could want, nothing to concede.

Was there anything Celina wanted from Madeline?

The flood welled in her again. She shut it down, dropped a manhole cover on that fucking sewer pipe and screwed the lid down tight.

There was one thing Madeline wanted from Celina. She wanted Celina to come to Chicago with her. She wanted to talk about some "important topics", whatever the fuck that meant. Celina had no idea why Madeline wanted that or what she wanted to talk about, but a trip to Chicago was the only bargaining chip Celina had.

Time to play politics.

Except Celina was in the bullfight arena with a master. Madeline had faced and defeated lobbyists, power brokers, caucus leaders, presidents, even foreign dignitaries and heads of state. She'd killed countless bulls in the past, and now Celina was in the ring with her.

Was Celina the *matadora*?

Or was she the bull?

29

CAM WATCHED Celina react to her mother. He recognized the stubborn defiance in her eyes, in the square set of her shoulders, in the way she held her neck long and straight.

She hid her defiance. Celina was nothing if not a masterful manipulator, and, for most people, if she didn't want you to see something, you wouldn't see it. But Cam knew Celina well enough now to see through the camouflage. The defiance hidden behind a veil of nonchalance. The tension in her body, masked by a posture of casual repose.

Celina was a soldier at war.

Only, Cam didn't think her mother was trying to fight her. He didn't think Madeline was an enemy. She just wanted to get some time alone with Celina so they could talk through their past, bring old wounds into the sunlight so they might start to heal.

He got it. No better time to talk than on a flight somewhere, when the two of them would essentially be trapped together in a cigar tube thirty-thousand feet in the air for a couple of hours. And on a private jet, they would be able to speak freely without fear of being overheard.

Celina needed it. She had carried a chip on her shoulder since the day Cam had met her, an anger that sprang from somewhere deep inside her. She focused it on various things—Attorney General Jenkins, Vernon Stratham, various dickhead tech bros in California. She'd learned how to harness that anger and use it to fuel her determination.

But that anger was hurting Celina. Her whole life, it had been gnawing at her, poisoning her. She needed to heal.

And maybe a flight to Chicago with Madeline would start that healing process. It was Madeline who had inflicted the wound, after all. Maybe she could help Celina heal it.

"What's in it for me?" Celina asked her mother.

Cam was not particularly practiced in the art of negotiation, but that seemed like progress. Celina had moved from flat refusals to entertaining the idea of going to Chicago.

"Have you ever been behind the scenes at a political convention?" Madeline asked. "It's fascinating to watch. Not at all like it seems from the other side."

"You're offering to let me observe a bunch of politicians behaving like assholes?" said Celina. "How is that different from what I'm observing right now?"

She put on her sweetest, most innocent smile to drive home the jab.

Madeline let it slide past her. The woman was a boulder in a stream. Nothing seemed to rile her.

"The president will be there," said Madeline. "Two presidents, actually. President Nelson is scheduled to speak tomorrow."

President Nelson had finished his second term eight years ago, yielding the office to his VP, now President Hill. It had taken Hill more than half of his first term to come out from under the shadow of his wildly popular predecessor. Rumor was that there had always been bad blood between the two, ever since a bruising primary season that led to Nelson's first term and Hill's vice-presidency.

Cam, for one, would find it fascinating to watch the dynamic between the two men. He'd love to see how they acted around each other when the cameras and the press were nowhere to be found.

Celina seemed to consider it, too.

"Hotel?"

"Blackstone," said Madeline with a slight smile. "Presidential suite."

"Two presidents in town and you've got the presidential suite?"

Madeline shrugged. "New power outranks old power."

Celina tilted her head, considering.

"No," she said. "I want a house. Lakeside."

"You want me to get you an entire house in Chicago on a day's notice?"

"Yep. A nice one. Lakeside."

Madeline stared at Celina for a long moment, that slight smile still on her lips. She sipped her tea slowly, her eyes never leaving Celina's.

She brought her tea back down to her lap. "I can do that," she said.

Cam's mouth nearly fell open. Who was this woman? Did every Speaker of the House have the power to commandeer a person's house for the night on a moment's notice? Or was this power somehow unique to Madeline Kinkaid?

Maybe Madeline was just bullshitting? Once Celina was on the plane, there was nothing she could do. Madeline would get her conversation and she could put Celina up at a Motel 6 or send her home on a Greyhound bus.

Somehow, though, he didn't think Madeline was lying.

Celina didn't seem to, either.

"And all you want to do is talk on the plane?"

"No," said Madeline. "I don't think that will be enough time. I want to talk on the plane, then I want you to come to the convention with me tomorrow night. I'll have a suitable dress waiting in the house for you."

"No dress," said Celina. "Pants."

Madeline's smile widened just a touch. She nodded.

"Then dinner. Private."

"And that will be enough time to talk?"

"It'll be a start," Madeline said.

"Cam," said Celina, turning toward him, "any requests?" She looked at Madeline. "He'll need an outfit, too. And not some cheap-shit political suit. No blue ties or red ties. Something nice." She leered at Cam and ran her hand down his arm. "He cleans up good."

Cam cleared his throat and glanced at Madeline.

Madeline returned his glance, then flicked her eyes back to Celina.

Celina watched them look at each other. Her eyes narrowed.

"This trip is just for the two of us, Celina," said Madeline. "Cameron won't be coming with us."

"Fuck that," said Celina immediately.

Cam knew she'd be upset when she found out Madeline wanted Cam to stay in Washington. But he also knew that Celina needed to work through this problem with her mother. And who knew how many opportunities they would have? She needed to seize this opportunity while it was in front of her.

He lay his hand on hers.

"It's okay, Celina," he said softly.

"No," she said, "it's not."

Cam's voice was firm. He found Celina's gaze and held it.

"Go with your mother," he said. "I've got Paulie coming tomorrow, anyway."

"She can wait," Celina said. "Or she can come to Chicago. We'll put her on my jet."

Cam shook his head slowly.

"You two have some things you need to work through," he said. "Important things. Best done just the two of you."

Celina opened her mouth to protest again, then closed it. Her eyes narrowed again. She looked back and forth between Cam and Madeline.

She was putting it together.

Cam braced himself.

"You schemed together to hatch this little plan, didn't you?" she said.

Her eyes blazed when Cam didn't deny it. Her look of furious betrayal stabbed him to his core.

"You two conspired on this shit behind my back."

She slid forward to the edge of the couch, every muscle in her body seeming to tense.

"Hardly a conspiracy," said Madeline calmly. "I told Cameron what I wanted while you were using the restroom."

"And I agreed that it was a good idea," said Cam.

"You agreed?" The fury overtook the betrayal in Celina's eyes. "The two of you agreed what would be best for me?"

Cam winced. "Not like that," he said.

He watched as Celina tensed even more, lifting off the couch an inch or two as if to stand, then somehow managed to rein herself in.

She settled back down on the couch, but Cam could see her jaw muscles working. Her fists clenched and unclenched by her side, pulsing like her heartbeat. Her breathing was quick, her chest moving rapidly in and out.

Cam watched as she slowed her breaths down, lengthened each inhalation, each exhalation. Her hands stopped clenching, but her jaw muscles didn't stop working.

"Fine," she said. "I'll go."

She looked at Cam accusingly.

"Alone," she said.

She looked back at her mother.

"But we leave tonight."

Cam's chest squeezed like she'd shoved a knife into his heart.

"Celina..." he began.

"No, Cam," she said. "If this is what's best for me, then why wait?"

The sweet smile she gave him, the same sweet smile she'd used on her mother, hurt almost as much as her decision to leave early.

"Very well," said Madeline, standing. "I'm sorry to appear rude, but I will have to make some arrangements. You're staying at the Capitol Hill house, I assume?"

Celina nodded without looking away from Cam.

"I'll send a car in a few hours," said Madeline. "Edward will see you out."

As if he'd been listening the entire time—and he probably had been—Madeline's security guard immediately opened the double doors that led to the entryway. He clasped his hands before him and stood by the door, waiting.

Cam and Celina stood, and Celina stalked out of the room ahead of Cam. He heard the front door open and shut before he'd even made it past the end of the couch.

It was going to be a long drive to the house.

If she even waited for him to get in the car.

A spear of anxiety stabbed Cam's chest. He hustled after Celina so he wouldn't miss his ride.

30

As Cameron scurried out the front door after Celina, Madeline texted her pilot about the change in flight plans and went upstairs to pack her bags. If Celina's face was any indication, Cameron was in for a rough couple of hours. Maybe a rough couple of days, if Celina didn't forgive him before she got on the plane with Madeline.

Such were the tempests of early love, and such were the tempests of Celina's temper. Madeline had to admit that she got it from her mother. But Madeline, over the years, had learned to control her temper much more skillfully than Celina.

The change in plans and the sudden departure were an annoyance. Convention week was usually a little quieter in Washington, with most of her caucus focused on the convention, and Madeline had been looking forward to a quiet night in front of the fire, catching up on some reading. But politics was a negotiation, and in a negotiation, both sides had to give up something they wanted in order to get something they wanted even more.

Madeline was scheduled to give the closing speech

tomorrow night. That might have sent some of her colleagues into a tizzy of overwork, but she did not operate that way. Madeline had always felt comfortable speaking in front of people. She knew she could keep any crowd entertained—in a political and intellectual sense; she was no entertainer—for hours without any preparation or notes.

And in this case, she had already prepared her speech. Now that Celina had agreed to be in attendance, she would make a few important modifications, but she'd prepared those in advance, as well.

She was looking forward to it.

Her pilot acknowledged the change in plans, and Madeline set to work securing a lakefront home for Celina to stay in. Celina had undoubtedly intended to stay there alone, but Madeline would stay with her.

She was quite sure the extravagant request had simply been Celina's attempt to think of ways to make the deal more difficult for Madeline. Good for her. She could recognize her strength in a negotiation and exploit it. She was her mother's daughter.

Now, she needed to work through her own history and focus on using that strength for the future, instead of as a petty scourge against her past. Celina could be a powerful force in the world, if she set her mind to it. Like her father, she lacked the kind of grand ambition such a goal required, but Madeline felt confident she could awaken it, if given the chance.

But she was her mother's daughter, after all.

Fortunately, Madeline had friends around the world, friends who would happily let her use their lakeside homes for a night on a moment's notice. She texted one of those friends now, the former CEO of one of the major US auto manufacturers, who owned several beautiful homes in the upper Midwest. He teased her briefly about the short notice, but didn't probe into Madeline's reasons for the sudden request. He sent an electronic key to her phone that would open the front door when she got close to it. Modern technology was truly a marvel.

That thought occurred to her at least once a week. And every time, she felt a pang of loss. Perry Maxwell, Celina's father, was a tech genius nonpareil. He may not have had grand ambition for the world's political stage, but his ambition to design and build better technology had influenced the entire world, thanks to that genius. Only those who followed the tech industry would recognize his name, but everyone in the world would recognize his work. He had literally changed the course of history.

And he'd changed the course of Madeline's life.

He'd taught her what it meant to love.

Pregnancy had been a surprise. They'd been careful, or so they thought. And Madeline had decided right away not to keep the child. She had plans for her life, and they didn't involve teen pregnancy.

But Perry had persuaded her otherwise. Somehow, in that gentle, wise way of his, he'd persuaded her to carry and birth another human being. And when she'd left the baby in Perry's arms and walked away without looking back, he'd stayed in touch. Not to pull her back, not to impose guilt on her, but just because he loved her and wanted her in his life.

He'd never once tried to convince her to be a mother to their child. He'd simply loved Madeline. From a distance, at first. Then more closely, more intensely, as Madeline moved past her fear of entrapment and opened her heart again to that wonderful man.

Her marriage to Bob Kinkaid had been one of expediency. They loved each other, too, but not the way Madeline loved Perry. She and Bob were friends, confidants, soldiers in the trenches of Washington together. Each of them with a secret they did not want to reveal to the world, Madeline with her illegitimate daughter and Bob with his sexuality.

Robert Kinkaid was a handsome, wealthy senator in the prime of his life. In the world of politics at the time, that meant he needed a wife. Times hadn't changed much since Jane Austen had written the opening line of *Pride and Prejudice*. And asexuality had not even been defined yet, let alone accepted by America's voting population. Bob tired of the questions, but he handled them well. He tired even more of the incessant propositions from women of all ages and social status. But he could handle those, too.

It was when his opponents started the whispers suggesting there might be a more scandalous explanation for his bachelorhood that Bob knew he needed to take action. Acceptance of homosexuality had come a long way in America, but it was still a political albatross at that time. If it had been true, Bob might have endured the whispers. But it wasn't true.

He and Madeline had confessed their secrets over their third bottle of pinot noir one late night in the congressional office building, while they were hammering out the differences in an appropriations bill. They'd agreed then and there to solve both their problems by marrying each other. They liked each other and could see a clear path to platonic love. They both recognized the physical attractiveness of the other, so pretending in public would not be odious. Bob was more than happy for Madeline to continue seeing Perry if they could do it discreetly, and felt no misgivings about Madeline's maternal decisions. It was a perfect match. A match made in Washington.

Madeline had been legitimately distraught when she'd learned of Bob's death just six years later. Her tears in front of the cameras were no act. A plane crash, of all things. Bob would have liked that. Like Buddy Holly, he'd have said. A cool way to die.

She'd been distraught then. When she learned of Perry's death almost two years ago, she'd been hollowed, an empty shell for months. She'd fought to hide it, to keep up appearances at work. She'd been a promising congressperson when Bob had died, but when Perry passed ten years later, she was the Speaker of the House. All eyes were on her at all times. She could show no weakness. She and Perry had kept their love affair very well-hidden. Even the most intrepid investigative reporters had no inkling. As far as the world knew, Perry Maxwell was just another tech billionaire to her. A valuable campaign donor, perhaps, but little else.

That was when her thoughts had changed toward Celina. Perry had left a hole in Madeline's life, in her heart. A vacuum. Celina was the only part of Perry that was left on the planet. And Madeline wanted her close. She wanted *him* close.

She knew it was foolish. Celina was not Perry. And Celina did not love Madeline.

But she didn't hate Madeline, either, despite what Celina might claim. Madeline could see that the moment she opened her front door and found Celina standing outside. That was Madeline's opportunity, and she had decided to seize it.

And when Madeline Kinkaid decided something, it usually came to pass.

As she texted a thank you back to her CEO friend, an incoming call interrupted her typing. When Madeline saw who it was, she clenched her jaw tightly, once, clicked send on her text, then relaxed her body and answered the phone.

"Well?" Bill Jenkins didn't bother saying hello. His voice was cold and curt.

"Well what?"

"Don't play coy with me, Madeline. Is she coming?"

Madeline paused for a beat to control her anger.

"We'll be there tonight," she said. "We leave in two hours."

"Tonight?" Madeline could hear the smile cross Jenkins' face. "My goodness. You do get things done, Madeline. Maybe your reputation isn't bullshit after all."

"You're too kind," said Madeline drily. "If you'll excuse me, I do have some final preparations to make."

"And the boyfriend?"

"What about the boyfriend?"

"He's staying behind?"

Madeline clenched her jaw once more. Bill Jenkins was a brilliant politician. Handsome, a powerful speaker, a skilled tactician. And he was months away from securing for himself the crown jewel of the political world, the presidency of the United States. And he'd decided to choose Madeline as his running mate.

Not her first choice. She had been planning to make her own run in four years, if Jenkins lost, or eight years, if he won. She'd told him as much when he'd first asked her to run with him.

But along with his other talents, Jenkins knew how to play dirty. Most politicians did, and it was a mark of character in Madeline's mind to see which politicians chose that route and which chose, in Michelle Obama's words, the high road.

Jenkins chose the low road.

He knew about Celina. Somehow, he'd learned the truth, and he claimed he had proof. He'd blackmailed her into accepting his offer and running as his vice-president.

Madeline knew it meant at least four years, probably eight, of being a political hood ornament. She would lose most of her political capital. New power outranked old power, but stale power ranked lowest of all, and the vice presidency was as stale as month-old bread.

But Jenkins had her over a barrel. She didn't want Jenkins to leak the truth about Celina to the press, so she agreed to Jenkins' terms.

That wasn't what bothered her. What bothered her was that she didn't know why he wanted Madeline as his running mate. There were other choices that were far more obvious, far more useful. Lisa Thomas from Maine would have been a perfect choice, with her youthful good looks and her progressive bona fides. The young voters would have shipped the ticket immediately. Willisa or Lilliam or something silly like that. It would have been political gold. Susan Shankowski from the Illinois fifth would have been another great choice, or even Tom Stracker from Nevada, if Jenkins chose not to put a woman on the ticket. All would have been better choices than Madeline.

And yet, as far as Madeline knew, Jenkins hadn't even considered another running mate. And Madeline had no clue why.

She also had no clue why it was so important to Jenkins that Celina be in attendance and Cameron stay behind in Washington. His mother's visit to town was a stroke of luck, but Madeline believed she'd convinced him to stay behind, regardless.

But she needed to find out why it mattered to Jenkins where Cameron went. Information is power. In politics, as in negotiating, the more you knew about your opponent and what he wanted, the more powerful your position will be.

"Yes, Bill," she said. "His mother is coming to town tomorrow, so he's staying to meet with her."

"Excellent," Jenkins said. She could hear in his voice that his smile had grown even wider. He hung up without another word.

A cold shiver ran over Madeline's spine. As kids, they used to say that meant someone had walked over your grave. Madeline didn't believe in those sorts of things, but she believed her instincts. And they were telling her that something was definitely not right with William Jenkins.

And Madeline wanted to know why.

31

Celina nearly told the driver to leave without Cam.

But she didn't.

She was hurt. It was bad enough that her mother had forced her to come all the way across the country, and now was forcing her to go to Chicago. But for Cam to be in on it, without even consulting with Celina, that hurt.

It pissed her off, too. But she could see the hurt behind the anger. Celina didn't like being told what to do, and she didn't like being treated like a child, like she didn't have a say in her own life. Cam had never done that to her before.

That just made the hurt even worse.

She stared out the window the entire ride home, not saying a word. She didn't reply to Cam's questions, didn't respond to his apologies, didn't react to his explanations.

His explanations made sense. Even through her anger, Celina could see that. She could see that Cam hadn't been scheming with Madeline all along, and that he really did have Celina's best interests at heart. It *would* be good if Celina and Madeline could talk things through. And it *would* be easier to do that if they were alone.

But Cam had still decided the course of her life, however minor, without consulting her first. That wasn't best interests. That was controlling. Celina did not need to be controlled.

She shook his hand from her shoulder when he touched her, kept her face close to the window glass, warm from the stifling evening air. She and Cam had spent a lot of time together in the last year and a half, but they didn't know everything about each other yet. Cam needed to learn that what he had done was not okay.

They were staying at a three-story brownstone owned by Celina's mother in downtown D.C., near the Capitol building. It was meant to be a bolt hole for Madeline, for those times when legislative sessions ran so long that she wouldn't want to go all the way home to Alexandria. In practice, though the brownstone was expensive and gorgeous, she rarely used it. Celina, Cam, and Paulie had used it as home base for a job they'd pulled the prior year, stealing a statue from Madeline herself. They'd thought Madeline was unaware of their intrusion, but it turned out she'd known the entire time.

Fucking bitch was just as smart as they said, and twice as sneaky. Celina had smothered the flame of admiration within her under deep sands of annoyance.

They got to the curb outside the brownstone and Celina was out of the car before the wheels had stopped turning. She stalked straight up to the third-floor bedroom, into the bathroom, and shut and locked the door behind her.

Locking herself in the bathroom. Pretty fucking juvenile. Even as a teenager, Celina had never stooped so low. But she needed a few minutes alone to collect herself.

She heard Cam calling her, his voice growing louder as he came through the house. She heard him come into the bedroom, saw his shadow beneath the bathroom door. To his credit, he didn't try to talk her into opening the door or force his way in. He didn't even knock. She watched his shadow hover for a few moments, then turn away. He was giving her space.

It was hard for Celina not to love Cam, even when she was pissed as fuck at him.

She slipped off her shoes, feeling the cool marble tile under her swollen feet, and splashed some cold water on her face. She didn't need to pack. She hadn't even unpacked yet. She'd told her driver to leave her bags by the front door.

And she didn't need to stall. She was not about to sit in the bathroom until Madeline's car arrived to take her to the airport. She was a grown-ass woman, and she could face her problems head-on.

She dried her face with a soft towel and opened the door, expecting to see Cam sitting on the bed, waiting. He wasn't there. Celina ignored the pang of disappointment in her chest, tuned out the thoughts in her head. *What if Cam left her? What if she'd pushed him away?* Fuck that. If Cam would go running because Celina was unhappy with him, he could keep running, for all she cared. She didn't need a man like that in her life.

But she knew Cam wasn't like that. Cam loved her, and, more importantly, he respected her. He wouldn't get pissed off and leave simply because Celina stood up to him. He was a better man than that.

She padded barefoot down the hall, her steps silent on the lush white carpet. Everything in the house was white. White carpet, white paint on the walls, white furniture. Even the towel that Celina had used to dry her face had been white. It was like living in a fucking asylum. Fitting, really. At the moment, Celina felt like she was going a little crazy.

She stepped quickly and quietly, listening for any sound of Cam's whereabouts. She heard nothing on the third floor, nothing on the second floor.

As she descended the steps to the first floor, the smell of garlic and cooking chicken hit her before she heard the sizzle of a fry pan. She came around the corner and saw Cam, his back to her, an apron tied around his waist with a bow at the small of his back, standing at the gas range.

He was cooking dinner.

He wasn't pouting or pleading or sulking or raging. He was cooking dinner for her.

Hard not to love.

A wide marble island stood in the center of the kitchen, behind Cam, with a sink and an overhanging bar and three stools. Celina slid onto one of the stools.

"Pan-seared chicken breast with sauteed vegetables," Cam said over his shoulder. "You'll need to eat before you leave."

Celina didn't know he'd even noticed her come into the kitchen.

"I'm sure they'll have food on the plane," said Celina. She wasn't ready to forgive him yet, but watching a man cook dinner for her was always a good start toward an apology.

Cam didn't reply to her comment, just kept working at the stove, the muscles in his back bunching and loosing in rhythm beneath his shirt. Celina watched those muscles move, feeling familiar stirrings deep in her core.

No. She wasn't going to forgive him that easily. Much as she might want to spend the remaining hours before Madeline's car arrived tumbling in bed with Cam, she wanted him to know that controlling her, making decisions for her, was a major red line for Celina. No one forced Celina Maxwell to do anything against her will, no matter how well-intentioned they may be. Even if Celina agreed with Cam, she needed to be involved in the decision-making process. She demanded it. It was her life, not his, and Celina made the decisions in her own life.

They ate and drank in silence. By the time they'd finished dinner and two glasses of wine each, Celina's anger had receded. But she still felt the need to keep Cam on the hook. She took little pleasure in watching him suffer —and he did seem to be suffering—but this was a real deal-breaker for Celina, and she wanted Cam to feel that, deep in his bones, from now on.

In a small gesture of goodwill, Celina took Cam's dishes and washed them herself. She figured Cam had suffered enough, and she wanted to clear the air before she left for Chicago. She meant to start the conversation when she started the dishwasher, explaining her position, making sure Cam understood and knew that she still loved him, but that what he'd done was not okay.

But just as the dishwasher hummed to life, just as Celina folded the wet dish towel and set it on its hangar to dry, Madeline's driver knocked on the front door. Cam let the man in and gestured to Celina's bags. The driver nodded and loaded them into the car.

At that point, it seemed awkward, even counterproductive, to try to have such a serious conversation with so little time to do it justice. She regretted now the hours she'd wasted giving Cam the silent treatment, hours when they could have been talking, understanding each other. Hours when they could have been making up.

She felt those stirrings deep in her core once more and gave a heavy sigh.

Celina stood before Cam in the open doorway, trying to figure out how to show him that they had some serious talking to do, but that she loved him, regardless. All she could think of was a kiss.

She stared up into those deep, clear brown eyes of his, at that tousled, sexy professor hair. He stared back, pain and longing in his eyes. Celina was sure the same emotions showed in her own eyes.

She lay one hand against Cam's cheek, stared into his eyes a moment longer, then stood on her tiptoes, pulled his head down to her, and gave him a long, soft kiss on the mouth. She savored the taste of his lips, their softness, the rough scrape of his stubble against her skin. She lingered long on that moment, on that kiss.

Then, without another word, she went out the door, got in Madeline's car, and left Cam standing in the doorway.

32

Cam watched the car drive away with Celina inside, watched until he could no longer distinguish it from the jumble of brake lights and traffic lights in the distance. He felt an aching emptiness in his chest, like an itch he couldn't scratch or a sore muscle he couldn't quite touch.

That kiss before she'd left. Why had it felt so final? She'd barely spoken to him, barely three words from the time they left Madeline's house to the time she'd gotten in the car to the airport.

And then that kiss. Like she was saying goodbye not for a day or two, but forever.

Had Cam messed everything up? By going along with Madeline, by imposing his opinions on Celina, by assuming he knew what was best for her, had he pushed her away forever?

The empty ache inside him expanded. He put a hand on his chest and clutched at his t-shirt, bunching the thin fabric in his fist. He wanted to reach into his rib cage and pull out his heart, hold it in his hand to stop the pain, to stop the vice tightening there, to stop the squeezing ache that kept getting worse and worse.

He staggered to the bedroom instead and lay in bed in the dark and curled into a ball and tried to crawl inside himself, to use his curled-up body to fill his emptiness.

He dreamt of Celina on the balcony at the back of a caboose on a train, pulling away as Cam stood in the center of the tracks. As she receded in the distance, Cam turned and waited as another train chugged toward him, its whistle shrieking over and over, its lights growing larger and brighter. He closed his eyes and held his arms out to the side, waiting for the train to strike, for the lights to envelop him.

He dreamt of Celina in a hot-air balloon, Cam holding to the drop line as the balloon lifted into the air, the burner sounding its throaty gag again and again. As the ground fell away beneath him, as the landscape blurred into a pastoral patchwork of fields and roads, Cam felt his grip weaken. He slid down the rope. The winds grew colder, stronger. The balloon rose higher. Celina stood in the basket, her face impassive, watching him slip, watching him cling to the end of the line, watching as his grip failed him and he fell. He savored the sight of her face, growing smaller and smaller, the last thing he would ever see.

He dreamt of himself in a mangled heap on the ground. Perhaps in a field after the fall from the balloon. Perhaps pressed onto and between the rails on the train tracks. Staring up at the sky, a desiccated pale blue. He couldn't move his head, couldn't close his eyes. The sun burned his retinas.

He heard a burring rattle. He heard a scratching.

A bird came into view. A crow, dark as death, eyes green as emeralds. It filled Cam's vision, blocked out the sun, glaring behind the crow's head like the halo of an avenging angel. It turned its head in staccato tilts, examining Cam through one emerald eye, then the other.

Then it pecked him.

First one cheek. Then the forehead, the other cheek.

Then the eyes.

Peck after peck, the eyes.

His vision blurred. The thin, rent skin around his eyes stung with hot blood. It ran down from his forehead and his eyes and his cheeks, ran over his nose and lips and into his mouth.

The sun emerged from behind the crow's head, glared into Cam's bloodied vision, baked the blood into a stiff mask over his face.

Until finally, with one last peck from the emerald-eyed crow, its black beak glistening with Cam's blood, everything went dark.

33

CAM WOKE in the earthless grey light of pre-dawn, heartbeat racing, pulsing in his neck.

He was still in his clothes from the night before. His t-shirt was stuck to his chest, soaked in sweat. The bedcovers were twisted and gnarled around him, also soaked.

He took in the room, unsure for a moment where he was or whether he was still dreaming. Slowly, painfully, the fabric of his reality stitched back together in his mind, more solid than his dreams had been, but no less painful.

Celina was gone. And Cam had no idea whether or not their relationship had gone with her.

He tapped his phone to check the time. Five AM. And no messages from Celina. He knew he wouldn't sleep again. He got up, stripped his clothes into a pile on the floor, and went into the bathroom to take a shower.

If he was still in California, he would probably have been arrested by the water police for how long he showered. No matter how hot he made the water, he couldn't seem to get it hot enough to rinse off his night sweats. The acid of his dreams burned his skin, even as the steaming water excoriated it.

He stood under the nozzle, his head against the wall. He sat on the ground, arms over his knees, let the water pelt his body, felt it rinse down his back, across the cool tile, and down the drain. Nothing could pull him out of the hollow feeling his dreams had left behind.

He finally gave up, turned off the water, and toweled himself semi-dry. He hung the towel. The cool morning air would finish drying his skin.

He went back into the bedroom to unpack and find some clothes to wear. A billow of steam chased after him as he stepped out of the bathroom, momentarily clouding his vision. When it cleared, he stopped short.

Kat Nestrom was there.

In his bedroom.

She was lying on his bed.

Completely nude.

Kat had propped the pillows against the wall and lay on her back against them. Her hips swiveled toward him, her legs draped lazily down the bed. Her hair was attractively mussed, like she'd just woken up. Her breasts lay full against her chest. The patch of hair between her legs was dark and sculpted into a tight arrow tip. In the half-light of early dawn, she looked like a painting, lying there amid the tangled sheets of Cam's bed.

"I don't know what you did last night," said Kat, turning her head to look at the swirl of bedcovers around her, "but why don't you come over here and show me?"

She smiled at him, a slow, alluring siren's smile.

Cam's heart had stopped when he saw a person in his bedroom, froze when he saw it was Kat, melted against his will when he saw she was naked. It stuttered now.

She was a gorgeous woman. There was no denying it.

And Cam became immediately, embarrassingly aware that he was completely naked.

Kat's smile widened as her gaze dropped to Cam's crotch. "Looks like you're interested."

Cam immediately turned back into the bathroom. He grabbed his towel off the rack and tied it around his waist, tight enough to prevent anything unwanted from popping up.

When he turned back toward the bedroom, Kat pouted theatrically.

"Don't you like me anymore, Cam?" She ran her hands over her body in a very distracting way, then shifted her legs in an even more distracting way. "Don't you find me beautiful?"

Cam stammered, unsure how to respond. His natural instinct was to counter her self-deprecating sentiments. Of course he liked her. Of course she was beautiful.

But that was a trap. She was trying to trap him, still trying to worm her way between him and Celina, like she had in California.

Only Cam didn't know if there was a "him and Celina" anymore.

He didn't know, but he wouldn't be the one to assume wrong and throw it away. Celina wouldn't throw their relationship away over an argument, would she? Not without talking it through first, at least.

But it hadn't been just any argument. Cam had crossed some kind of line in Celina's mind. And he wouldn't be the first man Celina had summarily dismissed.

"What are you doing here, Kat?" He gave Kat's side of the bed a wide berth and moved around to the other side, where his luggage lay on the floor. He lifted his suitcase onto the mattress and flipped it open.

Kat crawled across the bed toward him.

Cam did his best to keep his eyes focused on his suitcase, but his peripheral vision had a mind of its own.

Focus, Cam. Get dressed. Shirt. Pants. Socks.

Underwear.

He gulped, his mouth suddenly very dry.

"I heard you were in town," Kat said, her voice a low purr.

She lay on her side beside Cam's suitcase, put one long, bare leg over the lid. She slid her hand across one breast, down her side into the swale of her waist, then across her belly to the center of her hips, her fingers teasing the close-shaved strip of hair there.

Cam didn't look at her, stared intently into his suitcase, but all his focus was on her, nonetheless. He remembered well the shape of that body, remembered well the feel of that arrow of hair against his hands, against his lips, against...

His body remembered, too. It pressed insistently against his towel.

He ignored it. Meaningless animal instincts. Involuntary. An autonomic physical reaction.

"I thought I'd drop by and see if you wanted to spend some time together," Kat said.

"How did you get in?"

Cam pulled clothes out of his suitcase. He didn't even know what they were, didn't know if they matched, didn't care. He gathered them in an armful against his chest. Shirt. Pants. Socks.

"A woman has her ways."

She slid her leg across the main compartment of the suitcase, blocking Cam's access.

He still needed underwear.

He briefly considered going commando, but, with a gulp in his dry throat, decided against it.

He glanced at Kat.

She arched one eyebrow, challenging him.

He reached in, under her leg, to get a pair of his boxer briefs.

The back of his hand brushed against the underside of her bare thigh.

The underside of her warm, soft, bare thigh.

She moaned at his touch.

His body—instinctively, he told himself, subconsciously—responded to the familiar sound.

Kat slid her calf up his forearm, slid the top of her foot around his waist and hooked him, tried to pull him toward her.

He grabbed the underwear from the suitcase and spun out of her trap. He stood there, arms full of his clothes, uncertain for a moment what to do. He needed to dress, but he didn't want to dress in front of her.

She watched him, a sly smile spreading across her lips. She pushed his suitcase over the edge of the bed. It thumped down and spilled onto the floor.

She stretched cat-like, eyes never leaving his, and rolled to her back on the bed.

With a mind of their own, his eyes trailed the length of her naked body. Every curve, every shadow, every inch.

The towel wasn't tight enough.

Kat noticed. Her eyes husked. She moaned again and ran her tongue over her lips, then bit her lower lip.

The morning light had just begun to peek through the

windows. It glistened on her lips. It caressed her curves, painted them in a seductive chiaroscuro.

"Cam," she said, her voice low and raspy.

When he looked in her eyes, all the slyness, all the teasing, was gone. He saw only pure desire.

And he felt his body respond to it.

Cam's mouth opened, wordless.

Then he shook his head, ducked it down, and strode around the bottom of the bed toward the bathroom.

Kat skittered across the bed and stood in front of him, blocking his path. She snared his gaze in hers, held it.

"Why fight it?" she whispered.

With a flick of her hand, she undid the towel from his waist, let it fall to the floor at his ankles. With his arms full of his clothes, Cam couldn't stop her.

She leaned in, whispered.

"We both know you want to."

Her breath was hot against his ear as her hand slid between his legs, wrapped around his rock-hard cock, stroked it once, softly, loosely, teasingly.

Cam's natural fluids slicked her path. He heard her smile in his ear.

She stroked again, tighter, smoothing his fluids over his shaft. Then once more, faster.

Cam's head lolled back, and he moaned.

Involuntary. Meaningless.

"Cam," she said, her breath hot in his ear, sending a warm shiver down his spine, "I've missed you."

She ran her tongue along the outside of his ear, then bit hard on his lobe as she guided the tip of his cock along the line of her pussy. Cam groaned at how hot she felt against him, and how wet, slick and soft like silk.

He closed his eyes and pressed his head against hers,

took a long, shuddering breath. With his arms still laden with his clothes, he gently pushed Kat back.

His cock slid out through her fingers, throbbing and pulsing as it went.

Involuntarily. Autonomic.

He stepped back, head still pressed against hers, bundled arms against her chest, stretched as far out as they could go without dropping their load.

He thought about apologizing. He didn't want to hurt her. It wasn't that he didn't find her attractive. He obviously did. And it wasn't that he didn't think she was worthy. She was a good person, despite her past choices. He believed that. He had to believe that.

In the end, he didn't say anything. Didn't even look in her eyes.

He just stepped into the bathroom, shut the door behind him, and locked it.

When he came back out a few minutes later, fully dressed, Kat was gone.

34

KAT GUNNED the engine of the luxurious, rented Ferrari, weaving through the early morning traffic, racing red lights. She could barely hear the engine's roar inside the well-sealed cabin, but she could feel its power through her hands and her feet. The leather on the steering wheel crackled as she tightened her grip and twisted against it.

She was not used to rejection, especially when it was something she wanted.

And she wanted Cam. In the bedroom only minutes earlier, she'd really, really wanted Cam. And anyone who thought women couldn't get blue balls was a fucking idiot. She'd have to take care of herself later, one way or another.

But that would have to wait. For the time being, she was horny, frustrated, and really fucking pissed off.

"Well?"

Jenkins' voice over the car speaker was as abrupt as usual. Kat tightened her grip on the steering wheel and twisted again. If she twisted much harder, the leather would twist right off.

"I did what you wanted," she said, not bothering to hide the irritation in her voice.

He snorted. "Sounds like you didn't do what you wanted."

The asshole sounded smug, like that thought pleased him.

"Enough of this bullshit, Bill," she said, putting as much derision and sarcasm into his boring-ass name as she could. "Time for you to pay up."

Jenkins said something to someone in the room with him. Kat heard a keyboard clacking. She heard Jenkins tell the person to fast-forward, then stop and play.

The asshole had recorded it.

Jenkins had told Kat that Cam would be alone at the house in Washington. He'd given her the address and told her to be there the next afternoon. Seduce him, Jenkins had said. However you have to.

She'd made arrangements with her pilot.

Then, just a few hours later, Jenkins had called her again and told her plans had changed. Now she had to be there first thing in the morning, early.

She didn't know why Jenkins cared about Cam, but she figured he was pissed at Celina for something. Celina was always pissing people off. Jenkins was probably using Cam to get to Celina, and using Kat to get to Cam.

Kat was perfectly willing to oblige, and for more reason than just to get her company back. After seeing Cam again in California, Kat hadn't been able to get him off her mind. She was more than happy to have him all to herself for a while. She was sure she could convince him to come back to her.

She'd had to scramble to change her plans, had to fly in

the middle of the night to get there on time. The bed head hairdo was accidental, but sexy. It only helped her cause.

Jenkins gave her the address and a code to get in. She'd snuck through the dark house, listening for Cam. When she heard the shower, she went for it. She'd worn a loose, comfortable navy blue zip-up jumpsuit with nothing underneath. One quick zip and she was naked on the bed. No sense dicking around when all you wanted was to dick around.

That same jumpsuit rubbed against her skin like sandpaper now. What was loose and comfortable before felt mocking, restricting. Laughing at her failure to do something as simple as seducing one man alone in a house.

She swung into an oncoming lane to weave around a slow-moving Honda, gunned the engine more, then whipped the wheel back as the honk of traffic in the other lane dopplered past.

Dicking around. Pussy-footing. Beating around the bush. Why were all those idioms sexual?

And why the hell hadn't Cam fucked her?

He'd wanted her. That much was obvious. She'd held the proof in her hand, thick and throbbing.

And she'd wanted him. God, had she wanted him. She'd shown him that. She couldn't have thrown herself at him any harder.

But he'd walked away.

In Kat's entire life, Cam was the only man who'd ever walked away from her. And now he'd done it twice.

What fucking power did Celina have over him? She couldn't be that good in bed. She couldn't be better than Kat.

Kat didn't know why Jenkins had sent her on this

dumb-ass trip, but she'd been happy for the opportunity to get a tumble with Cam.

Only that hadn't happened. And now Kat had had enough.

Jenkins had recorded the whole thing, the fucking perv. She didn't relish the idea of that douchebag having a video of her naked that he could jerk off to. She didn't like the idea of him watching a video of her getting rejected, either.

She didn't know what Jenkins planned to do with the video, but she'd done her part. Now he needed to get her company back for her.

"Very nice, Kat," murmured Jenkins through the speaker. "I'm glad to see that you're taking care of yourself."

Kat gripped the wheel until her knuckles went white. Jenkins and his helper were watching the video. Kat could hear her own voice as Cam came out of the bathroom.

"Jenkins," Kat said, warning in her voice as she swerved through more traffic. She knew where Jenkins was in Chicago. She might just have to go there and fucking kill him.

She heard herself practically begging Cam, heard him try to ignore her. She squeezed the wheel tighter, sped up and ran a red light.

"Oh, no," Jenkins said through the speaker a moment later. "Oh, dear, dear, dear." He clucked his tongue. "Are you okay, Kat?" he said. His voice had all the sincerity of a daytime talk show host. "Rejection never feels good."

Kat sped through another red light.

"And that..." Jenkins whistled low.

Kat twisted the wheel like a wet towel, jerked the car into the right lane.

"That was a particularly nasty—"

"Pay the fuck up, asshole," Kat shouted at the console of

her car. She gunned the engine up the on-ramp to the free-way, slanted across four lanes into the leftmost lane, and gunned it even more.

Jenkins chuckled.

"You've done well, Katerina," he said. "Aside from the rejection, of course."

Katerina. No one called her that but her father.

"You'll get your company soon enough."

Soon enough? What the fuck did that mean?

She shouted at her console again. "Listen, asshole. I want my company now—"

The line was already dead.

Kat gripped the wheel in both hands, shook it and screamed in rage while she floored the gas. Eighty. Ninety. One hundred miles an hour. She came up fast on the car ahead of her. He must have been doing eighty-five, but she slammed on her brakes and hugged his bumper until he finally moved over.

She gunned it back up to a hundred, then kept going, screaming inside the soundless cabin of the luxurious Mercedes.

She missed the exit to the airport.

She didn't fucking care.

35

Celina watched through the porthole window of her mother's private jet as the lights around the monuments on the National Mall faded to pinpricks in the night. Cam was down there, alone. Probably confused as fuck.

Goddamn it. Celina had fucked up again. She'd gotten pissed off at Cam, given him the cold shoulder and the silent treatment for hours, then left town without telling him why she was mad.

One of these days, he was going to call it quits. Cam could have any woman he wanted. At some point, he'd decide he didn't want to deal with Celina's shit anymore and he'd just leave.

Celina needed to get her shit together before that point. She just wasn't used to doing the things people did to stay together. Talking and being vulnerable and all of that relationship fuckery. Celina had spent her life getting rid of men, not keeping them. She didn't know how to do it. She hoped she figured it out in time.

And she was shocked as fuck to realize how much she cared.

"Everything alright?"

Celina turned from the window. The interior of the jet was arranged with a couch, several luxurious single seats, a queen-sized bed in the back, and two sets of single chairs around a low table. Celina was sitting in one of those chairs, a wide, white leather recliner. She looked across the table at her mother.

It was nearly ten at night, but Madeline still looked as poised and perfectly put together as if she'd just stepped out of her room in the morning. Though the recliners were comfortable enough to sleep in, she sat perfectly straight, legs crossed casually at her knee. She held a saucer in one hand, a cup of tea tipped to her lips in the other. She was the picture of womanly wealth and power.

The only thing Celina hated more than her mother was how much she admired her. A woman in Washington. Was there ever a longer shot than that? Madeline had fucked over her own family, her own fucking daughter, but she'd clawed and scratched her way all the way to the top of the political pile.

Well, not quite to the top. There was one crown a woman had yet to wear. And in a few months, yet another in an almost unbroken line of white male assholes was going to wear it.

"I'm fine," Celina said.

She glanced out the window once more at the D.C. lights fading into the distance, then set her gaze on her mother again.

"Well, you wanted me here and I'm here," she said. "What do you want to talk about?"

Without hurry, Madeline finished her tea, which she'd held in her lap—without spilling a drop—since before takeoff. Now that the plane was leveling off, she set the cup and saucer on the table between them.

As if waiting for just that moment, the flight attendant approached, a trim and gorgeous man with sable skin, sharp cheekbones, kind eyes, and a sultry voice that sounded like warm massage oil on Celina's skin. If she didn't already have Cam, she'd have had the flight attendant in the bed in the back of the plane five minutes before takeoff.

He took Madeline's cup and saucer with a nod, then turned to Celina.

"May I get you anything, miss?"

The man smiled as he rubbed that warm oil all over Celina. Celina couldn't help but smile back.

"Black coffee, please," she said.

His eyebrows raised just a touch before the man nodded and backed away.

Madeline smiled mildly at Celina. "Femi is Nigerian," she said. "I met him in the first-class cabin on British Airways."

"You flew commercial?"

Madeline shrugged. "A congressional delegation."

"And you stole Femi away from BA?"

"When I spot talent, I try to put it to use."

Celina glanced down the aisle as Femi walked toward them with her coffee.

"You definitely spotted talent this time," she said.

Femi bowed slightly as he set the coffee down before Celina. Celina nodded her head in return, and very deliberately tried not to watch him from behind as he walked away. It required more effort than she expected.

Madeline smiled mildly at her again, as if she knew exactly what Celina was thinking. It seemed like Madeline always knew what Celina was thinking. Or had she just learned how to look that way, an expression that was the perfect mix of knowing weariness and amused acceptance?

The woman was a fucking mystery. No wonder she'd done so well in Washington.

Celina sipped her coffee and murmured in appreciation. Madeline nodded, as if in thanks. Celina waited for Madeline to tell her the provenance of the coffee beans, the name of the pregnant teenage migrant worker who'd picked them, someone Madeline had met while negotiating health care rights for indigenous mothers in the hills of Colombia.

But the nod was all she got this time.

Mystery and ambiguity. Let the listener fill in the blanks however they wished. Maybe that was Madeline's secret. Be an empty page and let her counterparts write what they like, then get what she really wanted once the actual pens were on the actual paper and the stakes were too high and too visible for her counterparts to back out.

"I want to talk about you," Madeline said.

"Why the sudden interest?"

Madeline narrowed her eyes slightly, but went on. Celina took note of the reaction, in case she'd found a gap in Madeline's armor.

"I want to talk about your reaction to our last conversation."

"The one where you and my boyfriend colluded to force me onto a plane to Chicago?"

Madeline smiled indulgently and swept an imaginary mote of dust from her pant leg.

"You're a brilliant woman, Celina," she said.

Immediately, a lump formed in Celina's throat. This fucking woman could manipulate her so easily. One casual compliment and Celina melted into a pile of quivering goop before her. Would that ever go away?

"You're a brilliant woman with a sharp mind," Madeline continued, "and an even sharper tongue."

She speared Celina with her hazel eyes. A shiver danced up Celina's spine.

"You get the sharp mind from Perry," Madeline said. "You get the sharp tongue from me."

"Is that right?" said Celina drily. In all the stories and interviews, and even in their handful of interactions, Celina had never heard Madeline say a single word that was anything less than stately and diplomatic.

"I used it more when I was younger." Madeline smiled to herself. "Too much. I've learned to control it."

"And I need to learn to control mine, too? Is that what you want to talk about? You're giving me motherly advice now?"

Madeline's smile dropped. She fixed Celina with a hard stare.

"What do you have on Bill Jenkins?" she said.

It was one of the very few times in her life that Celina was rendered speechless. The sudden change in topic. The bluntness of the question. The fact that it pointed at one of Celina's most closely guarded secrets, one that only a handful of people in the world knew about.

She managed to keep her mouth from falling open. She managed to bring her brain back online quickly, too. Hopefully quickly enough that Madeline wouldn't notice that the question had caught Celina off-guard.

She shrugged casually. "Jenkins was Dad's pet project. He got tired of hardware and software, I guess, so he went into wetware. Political wetware."

Madeline didn't reply. Her stony expression and her

hard stare didn't shift at all. She just watched Celina in silence and waited for her to say more.

Celina knew that trick. If Madeline wanted to have a staring contest, Celina would win.

Plus, it gave her time to think about what the hell Madeline was fishing for.

Celina pushed her tailbone to the back of her chair, put her ankle on her knee, and sat up as straight as Madeline. She clasped her hands in her lap and set a mild smile on her face, waiting.

The roar of the jet engines was just a throaty hiss from inside the cabin, but it filled the silence and left Celina feeling like she and Madeline were alone in a cocoon of white noise.

They stared at each other for what seemed like minutes, until one corner of Madeline's stern lips twitched upward. Her eyes softened the slightest amount. She set her forearms along the arms of her chair, looking like Lincoln with his legs demurely crossed.

"Bill Jenkins is going to announce me as his running mate," she said mildly. "Tonight, at the convention."

Celina kept her expression neutral, but inside, she was surprised. And disappointed. For all the cache of being next in line for the highest office in the land—arguably in the world—the vice-presidency seemed more of a ceremonial office than anything. Celina figured it would be a step down for Madeline. She had more power as Speaker of the House, shaping the laws of the country. As vice-president, she'd be reduced to surrogate stump speeches and toothless crusades. A senate majority was practically a shoo-in, at this point, so she wouldn't even play a real role in her function as president of the Senate.

"Congratulations," said Celina, her voice as flat as her expression.

"Do you know why?"

"He thinks you have a nice ass?"

Madeline's mouth twitched upward again. "I do have a nice ass," she said. "It's an incontrovertible fact."

For the second time in five minutes, Celina was rendered speechless. Did she just make a joke? Did she just swear *and* make a joke? Didn't that violate some kind of politician's code, a solemn pledge to offend no one, to be as bland as Wonder bread, as boring as beige?

Somehow, Celina's mother had the ability to continually surprise her. And Celina wasn't easily surprised.

"Do you know why he's selecting me as his running mate?" Madeline repeated.

Celina considered giving another snappy one-liner, but instead she just shook her head.

Madeline stared at her for a long moment, then rubbed her fingertips together in an odd expression that read to Celina as irritation. It was the first thing Celina had seen in Madeline that could qualify as an unconscious tic. A tell.

Madeline pursed her lips together and looked out the porthole window at the night sky thirty-thousand feet above the ground.

"I don't know why he's selecting me, either," she muttered, "but I want to find out."

When she turned her gaze back to Celina, her eyes were fiery and determined.

"And I think you can help me do it."

36

CELINA STARED across the table at Madeline. The air between them seemed still, as if time were suspended, but only between Celina and her mother.

Outside of that suspension, Femi, the gorgeous flight attendant, brought them dinner on white ceramic trays. Neither of them looked at the food. Neither of them looked at Femi.

Wisely, Femi set down the trays, poured them each a glass of water and a glass of white wine, and left without a word.

"Let me rephrase my earlier question," said Madeline, restarting the time clock of the universe with her words. "What do you know about Bill Jenkins?"

Celina paused before responding.

"That's a very broad question," she said.

Madeline's stare was merciless. "Not really."

Celina knew exactly what Madeline was fishing for. She just didn't know why Madeline was fishing at all. She could understand why Madeline would be suspicious of Jenkins' motives for selecting her as a running mate, but what made her think Celina was involved? Before Celina told Madeline anything—if she ever did—she wanted to know the answer to that question.

"Did you already accept his offer to be his running mate?"

"Yes," said Madeline.

"Why?"

"Because rejecting him would make my life very difficult for the next four to eight years."

"And accepting wouldn't?"

"Difficult? No. Boring?" She wagged her head back and forth in an equivocating gesture. "Possibly. Opportunities are what you make of them."

"Do you think you could make something of the opportunity to be the vice-president?" Celina scoffed. "No one else ever has."

Madeline stared at Celina for a long moment, her face screwed tight with an intensity more raw than any emotion Celina had ever seen on Madeline's face. Madeline broke the intensity, looking down at her tray.

Celina looked down as well. Some kind of chicken, the universal meat of the skies. Ironic, given that chickens can't fly. Unlike regular airline food, though, this chicken looked delicious. A white wine preparation, from the look and the smell, with tarragon, shallots, and butter. Bright green beans and crisp brown roast potatoes were on the side. It looked fresh and smelled delicious.

The wine looked equally appetizing. Pale yellow, nearly clear in Celina's glass. Probably a Sauvignon Blanc or an Albariño. And there was no condensation where the wine met the glass, indicating that the wine was at the proper temperature. Chilled, but not too cold. Femi knew his shit. Celina was sure that Madeline expected no less.

Madeline set her linen napkin on her lap, took a sip of her wine, then cut a piece of chicken and ate it, chewing slowly while staring at Celina, her face composed again. But that fierce determination was still in her eyes.

"Jenkins chose me for a reason," Madeline said at last, "and it wasn't because I could help him get elected." She cut another piece of chicken and loaded her fork. "He doesn't need me for that." She put the chicken in her mouth and chewed.

"He should have chosen a running mate who would stay out of the way, out of the spotlight."

Madeline nodded. "Someone weak. That would have been the more conventional choice."

"Is it possible Jenkins is thinking about the future? Maybe he wants to set the country up with a strong candidate for the eight years after his second term."

Madeline's voice was deadpan. "Is that your experience with William Jenkins? That he thinks about the future of the country above his own interests?"

Celina snorted.

"Exactly," said Madeline.

She chewed another bite of food, taking her time. Celina noticed her breathing, slowing as she ate, and had a realization. Madeline was agitated, but she was using her eating to hide her calming techniques. Instead of standing there doing nothing but taking deep breaths, like Celina sometimes did—thanks to Cam's instruction—Madeline used moments like the time it took to chew a forkful of food to do the same thing without calling attention to it.

Brilliant.

Again, Celina found herself admiring this woman, begrudgingly. The woman had abandoned her nearly thirty years ago. Celina had spent most of that time fostering an all-consuming hatred of Madeline Kinkaid. Now that she sat across from her, that hatred was falling apart, smashed by the sheer impressiveness of the woman herself.

Fucking hell. Things would have been so much simpler if Madeline was just a stupid bitch. Then Celina could tell her to fuck off and get on with her life.

"There's some reason that Bill chose me," said Madeline. "Some reason that helps his political ambitions. Those ambitions are all that matter to him." She used her fork to emphasize her points as she made them. "He doesn't need me to secure vulnerable votes, he wouldn't want someone as smart as me as his VP, and there are plenty of other women he could choose to show off his progressive bona fides."

Celina nodded, tracking Madeline's logic.

"Which means he's using me as a defensive play," she said. "But defense against what?"

She sliced off another piece of chicken, ate it slowly while she watched Celina's eyes. Celina felt her stare like a hot branding iron against her eyeballs, but she kept her mouth shut. Madeline could intimidate her as much as she wanted. Celina would share what she knew if and when she wanted to, and not a moment earlier.

Madeline swallowed her bite of food and pulled a long sip from her wine glass.

"I've known Bill for a long time," she said. "Your father introduced us years ago."

"Dad loved him."

Madeline nodded. "And Bill loved Perry."

Celina's face hardened. She quickly stared down at her chicken and recomposed it, but when she looked up at

Madeline again, Madeline was watching her with calculating interest.

The woman didn't miss a fucking thing. She was like a lean, hungry lioness on the hunt, seizing on the tiniest movement, acting with pure, raw, devastating instinct. That must be what people meant when they called her the ultimate political animal.

Madeline tilted her head to one side, considering. Celina wanted to look away, to avoid that lioness' stare, but she forced herself to maintain eye contact. She sipped her wine and tried to act natural.

"Bill and I were cordial," Madeline said, "but we didn't speak much. Didn't have reason to, really. The AG's office and the Speaker's office don't really need to coordinate much, even less before I became speaker. And I'm a prominent party figure, but I'm not directly involved with the campaign, from his side or the DNC side."

Celina glanced down to cut a piece of her chicken, then back up. Madeline smiled mildly, patiently, watching her. Celina raised her eyebrows and nodded with feigned interest while she chewed her food.

"So, we didn't speak much," Madeline continued, "until last June." Her voice took on a musing tone. "When did you say you and Cameron met?"

"I didn't," Celina replied around her mouthful of food.

"No," Madeline said, "that's right. You didn't." She speared another piece of chicken with her fork. "Cameron did."

Celina swallowed hard before she'd finished chewing. The chicken caught in her throat. She gulped her water. It was ice cold against her throat.

"He said you met about a year and a half ago." Madeline

took a sip of wine. "Not long before Bill started calling me more often."

Celina switched from water to wine and swallowed a mouthful, drowning and dislodging the chicken still caught in her throat. "I doubt the two are related."

"Do you?" Madeline gave Celina that mild smile again. "Hmm. Perhaps." She cut another bite of chicken, looked demurely down at her plate while she sawed at the breast. "He talked to me about Perry."

"Jenkins did?" Celina focused on her plate, on cutting another piece of chicken, smaller this time.

Madeline nodded. "He talked about how much he loved Perry, how much Perry had meant to his career, and to him as a person."

Celina's knife slipped and clinked against the ceramic tray.

"He talked about how devastating Perry's death was for him. How odd it was that Perry should die so suddenly when he had seemed so healthy."

Celina's knife screeched against her plate. She stopped cutting and stared at her chicken, clutching her utensils in bloodless fists. The thought of that asshole talking about her father's death as if he had nothing to do with it, as if he were a stricken, grieving family member, made Celina want to jam her fork through his eye and into his lying fucking brain.

"Hmm," Madeline said.

When Celina looked up, Madeline was giving her that lioness' stare again. Her mild smile seemed a little more genuine.

They finished their meal mostly in silence. The hiss of the jet engines in the cabin matched the steaming rush of

Celina's blood in her ears as she thought about Jenkins and her father's murder.

He'd fooled Celina when she'd first seen him, in a restaurant in Washington where Jenkins was meeting with the top students in the graduating class of the criminology program that bore his name at McFadden University. That program was where Celina had met Cam. She'd doctored some transcripts and faked a transfer into the school for the last semester so she could surprise Jenkins at that dinner and watch his reaction to seeing her. His face had shown surprise, but not the least bit of guilt. Celina assumed that meant Jenkins had no knowledge of her father's murder.

But it turned out that Jenkins had become either a world-class liar or a complete political monster who felt no shame in killing to get what he wanted. Or both.

If he could fool Celina like that, she was not surprised that he had fooled Madeline, too. Jenkins had taken her father's lessons to heart, then twisted them to suit his personal ambitions. Her father had been trying to teach Jenkins how to be the kind of politician who could use his personal power to move the world in a positive direction, toward peace, cooperation, compassion for others, and away from greedy warmongering and environmental devastation for short-term profit.

Instead, Jenkins had turned to the dark side. He cared only about turning that personal power into wealth and even greater power.

Even if her father had lived, Celina didn't think it would have mattered. She didn't know Jenkins well enough to know what motivated his lust for power, but she knew enough to see that he wasn't going to stop. Someone would have to stop him.

As soon as they finished their food and set their utensils

down, Femi came to clear the table. He brought Celina an espresso and Madeline another tea. The hiss of the engines lowered in pitch, and Celina felt the plane tilt as the captain announced that they'd begun their initial descent into Chicago. She peered out the window and saw the city ahead in the distance, bright lights ending in the sharp curve of the waterfront, then the inky black nothingness of Lake Michigan.

They stayed silent, Madeline and Celina, all through the descent and final approach. It wasn't until the plane had touched down, a feather soft landing with only the softest screech of the tires on the tarmac, that Madeline spoke. She unfastened her seatbelt and stood as the plane taxied toward a private hangar.

Celina, still in her chair, looked up at her mother. Madeline's face was relaxed and composed, but her eyes were hard as steel.

"When we get to the house," she said, her voice as mild as her expression, but still somehow conveying the steel of her gaze, "you're going to tell me what Bill Jenkins had to do with Perry's death."

Celina tried her best not to react, but she felt the color drain from her face.

Madeline saw it. She smiled grimly.

"And," she added in a tone that brooked no contest, "you're going to show me how you proved it to Bill."

PART III

37

William James Jenkins stood, snifter in hand, at the large, round window of his suite atop the Blackstone Hotel in downtown Chicago. His polished dress shoes sunk inches deep into the plush carpet beneath him. His suit coat hung from the rounded back of the lavishly carved and brocaded chair behind him, sat behind an equally lavish desk. With high ceilings, fine fabrics, and gold accents everywhere—not to mention enough soundproofing to muffle even Jenkins' own thoughts—the room was nothing short of opulent. They didn't call it the Presidential Suite for nothing.

No, not the Presidential Suite. The Suite of Presidents. A pretentious name for a pretentious room, and an outrageous five-figure per-night rate. Exactly what the next President of the United States deserved, especially when that next president was William James Jenkins.

The first.

His older brother had been the third. Croft Jenson Jenkins the Third, called CJ by his family and Trey by all his friends. That had bothered Bill when he was a child.

He'd wanted to be in his family's line of succession. He'd wanted the post-nominal himself, to feel an institutional bond to his own family history, a bestowal of legitimacy.

Instead, he was just little Billy, Trey's younger brother. His family called him BJ, for Billy James, and the nickname had always felt like weak venom spit in Jenkins' face.

Looking back, he could see that no one had treated him poorly. Not as poorly as he'd felt at the time. He'd been largely ignored, but not mistreated. But children are young and foolish and self-centered, and suffering, as the famous saying goes, is like a gas. No matter how slight, it will expand to completely occupy the mind of the sufferer until he has no choice but to seek a remedy.

His remedy had been extreme, both in the act and in the impact. And—again, young and foolish—the result hadn't been what little Billy had intended. Even without his brother, he was still not a third. He would never have the post-nominal.

But those were the old times. Soon, he would be William James Jenkins the First. His would be no mere post-nominal, but a regnal number. His name would carry echoes of William the Conqueror, William the Lion, William the Good.

He chuckled to himself as brought the snifter to his nose. William the Good probably wasn't appropriate, but William the Great was. Good implied morality. Useful, in its way, but not his favorite tool. Great, however. Great implied strength and power and fear and awe and the ability to do what was necessary.

The Great William James Jenkins the First stood at the window of the Suite of Presidents, gazing upon the twinkling night lights of what would soon be his demesne. He lifted his crystal tulip snifter and pulled in the honey and cinnamon aroma of his cognac, warmed by his own palm, drawing out the flavors. Fifteen hundred dollars a bottle. Sugar and spice and everything nice.

He chuckled again. Again, not quite fitting, but being nice is the goal of the weak-minded. Greatness never came to anyone who wasn't willing to get their hands dirty, to do what needed to be done to move forward. Fate rewarded the bold and punished the weak. It was one of the basest laws of the natural world. Kill or be killed. Eat or be eaten. Humans were just animals clever enough to delude themselves into believing those laws didn't apply to them.

But the smartest humans, the strongest humans, the greatest humans could see the truth through the webs of lies society had spun through the ages.

His parents had been strong. His older brother had been strong.

But little BJ had been even stronger.

And now, as the cognac warmed his tongue and his throat and burned like a honey-gold marble in his belly, as he looked through the round window, down at the towering buildings, the strings of traffic in red and white, the yellow of the streetlamps on the roads and the bridges as they crossed the inky lines of the Chicago River far below, he could feel the final step before him. The last great bestowal of power that would truly make him William the Great Conquering Lion.

A knock on the door behind him.

"Come," he called. "Ah, Vernon," he said as he turned from the window. "What brings you here at this hour?"

Vernon Stratham was as stiff and carefully mannered on the outside as he was unctuous and morally flexible on the inside. Jenkins had never seen the man in anything less than a suit coat and tie, no matter the hour or the surprise with which he'd been awakened. It wouldn't have shocked Jenkins one bit to learn that Vernon Stratham had a suit set aside strictly to sleep in. The top of his head was bald, but the ring of hair below it was neatly trimmed and combed. Even his glasses were immaculate, sparkling in the light from an ornate chandelier that hung over a mirror-polished conference table in the center of the room.

"Sorry to bother you so late, Bill," said Stratham, striding to meet Jenkins beside the conference table, "but I knew you'd want to know that Speaker Kinkaid and Ms. Maxwell touched down at PWK three minutes ago."

"Which hotel are they in?" he asked.

"They're staying at Frank Shoreson's house in Winnetka."

"Shoreson?" Jenkins frowned. "The Chrysler CEO?"

Stratham nodded. "He's in France with his family for the summer, but he gave Speaker Kinkaid the house codes."

"And the boyfriend is still in D.C.?"

"The speaker and Ms. Maxwell were the only passengers on the manifest."

Jenkins turned back toward the window, again surveying the lights. It never ceased to amaze him that big cities never stopped. They were always moving, at any hour, night or day. Like Great White sharks, always hunting. And it wasn't just a few people here and there. The strings of traffic were long and solid, the red brake lights like beads of blood across a throat, endlessly slicing open and dripping down and slicing open again. Humanity was relentless, just like the shark, and Jenkins had to be even more so.

"Get into the Wi-Fi and block any calls or texts to him from Celina or Madeline." he said. From now on, Jenkins would control what the boyfriend knew. "And get me the entry codes for the D.C. house. I'm going to bump up Kat's schedule."

Better to act early and have time for adjustment if things went wrong. Not that he expected them to go wrong, but Jenkins didn't get to where he was by being cavalier. He worked hard, he thought of everything, he prepared for everything, and he was willing to do anything to get what he wanted. That was the real secret to success in America.

By showing him the evidence she had on his campaign, Celina had unwittingly made herself Jenkins' number one target. It was a massive miscalculation on her part, but Jenkins was used to sloppy opponents. It just made his job easier.

But the information Celina had would definitely not make his job easier. She and her boyfriend had made a good show of destroying the data, but Jenkins was no fool. You couldn't destroy anything these days.

Except people. With all the wonder of modern technology, you could still destroy a person, just like they did five thousand years ago.

He could have just killed Celina and the boy toy, but Jenkins was no monster. He didn't enjoy killing people. He preferred to use them. It was more interesting, anyway. If he could worm his way into their heads, into their hearts, find the levers that would control them—their hidden desires, their deepest fears—he could turn them into tools that were far more useful than simply taking them out of the equation altogether. He could wrap them up tight in their own failings and use them as he saw fit. Some called it blackmail. Jenkins called it business.

Once Kat fucked Celina's boyfriend and Jenkins got the video, he'd have the boyfriend wrapped up. As soon as he'd learned that Celina was Kinkaid's daughter, he knew he had the speaker wrapped up. That was why he offered to bring her onto the ticket. Keep your enemies closer, especially if you can blackmail the hell out of them. That Kinkaid had kept a secret that huge for that long, even from Jenkins himself, was impressive. But Jenkins knew the truth now. And now, he had the speaker in his toolbox.

Kat herself was already wrapped up. Greed and pride were the ropes that formed the noose for her. She wanted control of her father's company, and Jenkins would give it to her. She hadn't been a perfect tool for him, but she'd been useful enough. She was a loose end, though, one that Jenkins might yet have to cut.

The only person left to wrap up was Celina herself. She already knew the truth about her mother, so he couldn't use that. In all the time she'd spent digging in Celina's home network, Kat had found nothing useful. Some prototype designs, but money wouldn't motivate Celina. He'd hoped to find proof that Kinkaid was Celina's mother, but nothing had turned up. It didn't matter. Public opinion presided over a kangaroo court these days, and mere innuendo was more than enough for a conviction. Where there's smoke, there's fire, and in the hype cycle of the entertainment news networks, smoke always meant an inferno, never a cigarette butt. But Jenkins wasn't at all sure that Celina even cared about her mother, so that conflagration wouldn't motivate her, either.

She cared about her boyfriend. Kat learned that much, and that had been a surprise to Jenkins. Celina had never been stupid enough to open herself to something as easy to manipulate as love. She knew what Jenkins was willing to do, and threatening the life of someone she claimed to love was a tactic as old as humanity itself. Jenkins would put that love to the test and see how much Celina really cared.

And, if it didn't work, at least he'd tried to find a way to use her. Celina was too gifted to throw away without a sincere effort.

But sometimes, no matter how hard you try, murder really is the only solution.

38

Celina had demanded a nice lakeside house in Chicago instead of a hotel room, and somehow, even with only a few hours to work it out, Madeline had delivered.

Over-delivered. It was almost midnight when they arrived, but the exterior lights of the home blazed, welcoming them with a wash of warm, yellow light as Madeline's driver curled them around a small circular drive to the front door of a navy-blue cedar shake Nantucket with crisp white trim. Inside the house, panoramic windows showed views of a well-lit, well-manicured bright green lawn that led to a rocky outcropping and a small beach of white sand that glowed in the light, the darkness of Lake Michigan sprawling beyond.

"I suppose this will meet your needs?" asked Madeline drily as she came up behind Celina.

"Bit cramped, but I'll make do," Celina replied without turning around. She lived in a gorgeous California beach home that overlooked the Pacific Ocean, with views of the Golden Gate Bridge, and still this house took her breath away. Beauty was beauty, whether in a painting or in a waterfront home, and this home was absolutely gorgeous.

Madeline instructed the driver where to bring their few bags. She and Celina took ten minutes to get settled, then met at the dining room table.

The table was crafted to look like uneven planks taken from a shipwreck, but the surface was smooth enough for a formal dinner setting, and the table itself was large enough to seat fourteen without bumping elbows. The casual, beachy air was all for show. The table, the high-backed leather chairs around it, the fifteen-foot ceilings, and the elegant light fixtures exuded pure elegance.

Celina opened her laptop and showed Madeline the information she had on Jenkins. Proof that his campaign was responsible for several politically motivated assassinations. Proof that Stratham had ordered the hits. Proof that her father had been murdered, and that Stratham was behind it.

Madeline said nothing when Celina showed her the last bit, but the skin on her face tightened and her eyes glinted like the edge of a razor-sharp knife.

Celina told Madeline about the dinner, about Celina's initial sense that Jenkins was unaware of the killings, that Stratham was the true mastermind. She told Madeline when and why those feelings had changed.

"But you have no concrete evidence of his direct involvement?" asked Madeline.

Celina sighed. "No," she said, "but what I have here is enough to kill his campaign."

Madeline paged back and forth through the data in silence for several minutes. Celina waited, letting her take the time she needed to soak it all in.

"Who else knows about all this?" Madeline asked.

"Me and Cam," said Celina. "And Jenkins and Stratham both know we have it. Now, you." She thought for a moment. "And probably Kat Nestrom."

Madeline frowned. "Why would Kat know?"

"She stayed my house over the holidays. I've got good network security, but she's a pro. We have to assume she saw something."

"I didn't realize you two were still close."

Celina frowned. Madeline talked like she and Celina had been in touch for years, like a real mother and daughter. But until last year, Celina hadn't spoken to the woman in her entire life. And yet Madeline seemed to know everything about her.

It pissed Celina off. But, deeper down, it felt good, too. It felt good to know that her mother had cared all along, even if it was in her own super fucked up way.

"We're not close," Celina said. "Not anymore."

Madeline turned her head and looked at Celina for a long moment, her face blank, her gaze assessing. It unnerved Celina, the way her mother had of seeming to examine the depths of her soul with a simple look.

Madeline turned back to the screen. "You two were never going to be close. Not really."

"Is that so?" The woman had some fucking audacity, making proclamations like that when she barely even knew the people she was talking about. Celina made no effort to keep her opinion out of her tone.

"You're too similar," said Madeline, unperturbed. "Two alphas in one pack. You were always going to rip each other's throats out, one way or another."

Fucking bitch. She had no right to say shit like that.

But she was always fucking right.

Madeline closed the laptop and turned toward Celina.

"What you have here isn't enough to convict Bill," she said, "but it is enough to make you a target."

"It's enough to kill his campaign."

"And once he's elected? What then?"

"It'll cause a scandal."

"And then what? Impeachment? Removal from office?"

"Why not?"

Madeline shook her head. "Impeachment is meaningless these days. People get impeached for doing their jobs, if it scores political points for the House members." She pressed her lips into a line. "Trust me, I run the House. I know."

Celina rolled her eyes.

"And the Senate would never remove him from office without absolutely unassailable proof, proof that their voters—the ones who love Jenkins as much as they hate Republicans—couldn't contest." Madeline's voice took on an edge of frustration, more emotion than Celina had ever heard in it before. "And these days, when every proven fact is fiction? That's a very high bar."

"Jenkins killed people to advance his political career," said Celina. "You're telling me that's not enough to throw him out of office?"

"One of his predecessors in that same office incited an armed insurrection to prevent a peaceful transfer of power," Madeline replied. "And you know what they did to him? They nominated him for another term."

Madeline pushed back from the table, her chair gliding soundlessly across the smooth wood floor. She pushed the chair back in and paced, pulling one hand through her hair. With a shock, Celina recognized that it was the same thing she did when she was agitated. The same pacing, the same hand through the hair. Even the length of the stride and the cadence of the pacing were the same.

She was her mother's fucking daughter.

"He'll know this, of course," Madeline mused while she paced. "He'll still want to avoid the headache, but he'll know he only needs to get into office—not just elected, but inaugurated—and this becomes a manageable issue."

"He'll try to control us until then," said Celina.

"Control us"—Madeline glanced at Celina—"or eliminate us."

Celina shrugged. "Let him come. I know how to handle myself."

Madeline stopped pacing and looked at Celina like she was a foolish child. Celina instantly felt a flush of shame, and she didn't even know why. A hot flood of anger quickly washed the shame away, but before she could snap at her mother, Madeline spoke.

"What about the people you love?" she said. "Cameron. Can he handle himself?"

Celina flushed again, thinking about the way she'd left things with Cam. Her anger fell away in an instant, replaced by a cold, brittle fear. She immediately grabbed her phone and dialed Cam's number. It rang over and over and over.

"Jenkins is a master manipulator," Madeline said while Celina waited, phone pressed to her ear, knee bouncing. "He'll find your weakness, whatever it might be, and use it to his advantage. He'll twist the truth. He'll invent lies. He'll cheat, steal. Apparently, he'll even kill." She smiled grimly. "And he might even play fair, if he knows he'll win."

Celina's call went to Cam's voicemail. She called again. And again. And again. Same result.

She pushed up and out of her chair and paced like her mother on the other side of the table. She wrote a text to Cam, then hesitated before sending it. What if Jenkins was monitoring their communications? What if he was intercepting them? Celina had installed security software on all of Cam's devices, but she hadn't secured the network at the house. Was it secure? Was it secure enough to stop Jenkins?

Her father had installed the security at her mother's house in Alexandria, and Madeline said he'd done the same in Washington. But Madeline rarely used the D.C. house. How well had they maintained the system? How well was it monitored?

And how good was Jenkins security team? He had resources. Hell, he even had Kat working for him. Maybe he'd strong-armed her into hacking the network at the D.C. house. Her father had been the best, but he'd been gone for almost two years now. Network security evolved quickly. If the system wasn't being actively maintained, it was vulnerable.

"I have to go back to Washington," said Celina.

Her mother looked at her, but said nothing.

"I have to warn Cam, and Jenkins may be blocking calls and texts. Or manipulating them." She gestured toward Madeline. "You said yourself he's a master manipulator."

"He is," Madeline nodded, "which is exactly why you shouldn't go back to Washington."

Celina practically growled with frustration. "What the fuck are you talking about?"

When Madeline spoke, her cadence was slower, her voice lower in pitch and softer in volume. She spoke so softly, Celina almost had to strain to hear her from across the table.

"He's building a web," Madeline said. "A web of interconnecting motivations that he's hoping will keep us all in line until he's done using us."

"A web." Celina dug her fingernails into her palms, staring at her mother across the table.

"He knows you have this information, so he wants to control you."

Her voice, the slowness, the softness. Celina could feel her pounding pulse slacken, could feel the tension in her muscles easing, as if that deep, slow, soft voice were lulling her to sleep.

"And Cam."

"If he controls you, he controls Cameron."

"Cam is his own person."

Madeline raised her eyebrows.

"Cameron is besotted," she said.

Again, Celina felt herself flush, though not with anger or fear this time.

Madeline tilted her head and smiled at Celina. "And so, I dare say, are you," she said.

Celina flushed even more, and looked away, down at the ground.

"That's wonderful, Celina. Truly."

Celina looked back up, and her mother's smile widened. It was a genuine smile that loosened a tightness in Celina's chest. She unballed her fists.

"But it means Bill has leverage," Madeline continued. "He will use your affection to control you both. Just as he's using his leverage against me, and probably against Kat, too."

Celina sighed, an angry snort.

"What can we do, then?" she asked.

Madeline smiled again, but this time, it was the lioness'

smile. Predatory. Calculating. Eager for the fight. Her voice had the same deep, slow, lulling calm, but the knife-edge glint was back in her eye.

"We take away his leverage," she said.

39

CAM MOVED SLOWLY, deliberately, through his morning, trying his best to shake off the encounter with Kat. Between the fight with Celina, her wordless departure the night before, the crazy nightmares he'd had, and then his traitorous body's response to finding Kat in his bed, he felt weird inside, like his skin didn't fit him anymore. He was uncomfortable in his own body.

So he did his best to focus on what was in front of him, not on what was going on inside. He made a small but elaborate breakfast of Eggs Benedict, moving slowly and taking his time. He found ham on the bone in the fridge and cut careful, thin slices. He melted the butter for the Hollandaise sauce over very low heat, beat the eggs thoroughly and tempered them far more slowly than he needed to. He watched the water come to a simmer, watched the eggs poach, trying to focus on what he was doing and seeing, trying to push out the unsettled feelings that kept intruding on his mind.

When the dish was finally done, it looked and smelled wonderful, and he didn't feel like eating a single bite. He forced the food into his mouth, anyway. He was aware that it tasted good, but he couldn't enjoy it.

He texted his mother, arranged to meet her at a small park on the corner of Pennsylvania and Ninth. It was a weird spot, but his mother said she had some things to pick up in the shopping center across the street. Also weird. His mother had never been one for shopping, and fifteen years in prison tends to cut down on your material needs even more. But the park was a short walk from where he was, and Cam had enough other stuff to worry about that he didn't question it. With everything going on, he could really use a long talk with his mom. He didn't care where it took place.

They arranged to meet later that evening, which meant that Cam had a whole day to kill. He decided it would do him no good to sit in the house and stew, so he grabbed his phone and his sunglasses and headed out the front door, joining the stream of people crowding the sidewalk.

If there was ever a place to have time to kill, Washington was the best. There was so much to see and do, and it was all within walking distance of Madeline's D.C. house. Cam figured he'd wander around the Mall, check out the National Gallery of Art, the Smithsonian museums, maybe sit in the shade at Lincoln's feet and stare at the Reflecting Pool for a while. He hadn't brought his sketchbook from California, but he figured he could pick up a cheap pad and some pencils in the museum gift shop and make some art for a few hours.

That plan changed before he made it to the corner. Halfway down the sidewalk, his phone started to buzz in his hand. Cam checked the notifications and found a dozen missed calls, all from Celina, all from late the night before.

Cam stopped short in the middle of the sidewalk, a

flush of panic sweeping through him. He hadn't heard the phone ring the night before. He must have been out cold. And why hadn't he noticed the missed calls when he woke up and looked at his phone?

A pedestrian bumped into him from behind and mumbled an apology. Cam started walking again, stopped with the crowd at the light at the corner.

Celina must be furious. Cam checked the time. It was ten AM in Washington, nine AM in Chicago. He called her number.

She picked up on the first ring.

"Are you okay?" she asked, without even saying hello. Her voice was breathless and thick, like those were the first words she'd spoken that day.

Cam hesitated, unsure how to answer the question at first. He was definitely not okay, but hearing Celina's voice, hearing the concern in it, loosened a lot of tied-up feelings in him.

Then he remembered what had happened with Kat that morning, and those feelings wound into a knot all over again.

"I'm okay," he said.

He heard a heavy sigh of relief on the other end of the line.

The light changed and the throng of pedestrians moved across the street. Cam moved with them, glancing around at them for the first time. Mostly tourists there to visit the monuments and museums or government employees trying to get to work.

As he walked, his mouth went dry and his tongue felt like it had swollen to fill his entire mouth, but he screwed up his courage and asked the question he needed answered, the question that had been darkening his thoughts since the door had clicked shut behind Celina the night before.

"Are you okay? I mean, are we—"

"Has Jenkins contacted you?" Celina interrupted. "Or Stratham?"

Cam frowned. Why would either of them contact him? "I thought Jenkins was in Chicago."

"Have either of them contacted you at all?"

"No."

"Okay," she said. "Good." Cam could hear her moving around, could hear her bare feet padding across the floor wherever she was. "It's Cam," she said to someone on the other end of the line. Madeline, presumably. "He's okay."

Most of the crowd, the tourists in shorts and t-shirts, veered to the left toward the Capitol Visitor Center. Cam stayed on the path to the right, along the street. A smaller crowd of harried-looking government workers in suits and pencil skirts followed Cam's path, picking up their pace, seeming grateful to be away from the tourists.

On the phone, Cam heard Madeline say, "He needs to get somewhere safe."

"Has anything unusual happened?" Celina asked. Cam could tell from the shift in the sound of her voice that Celina had put him on speaker. "Anything that seemed weird or off somehow?"

The knot of feelings inside Cam reached Gordian proportions. He took a deep breath, then blew it out. Alexander the Great was right. Only way to untangle it was to cut right through.

He stepped off the sidewalk, over the low stone wall that formed the border with the Capitol grounds, and stood in the shade of a tree, his back to the pedestrians. It wasn't what he would call private, but at least he wasn't walking in a crowd on a busy sidewalk.

"Kat was here this morning," Cam said.

"Kat?"

Celina's voice was instantly defensive. Cam's chest felt hollow at the sound, but he pressed on anyway.

"Can you take me off speaker?"

"It's okay," Celina said. "She knows everything."

"That's... Can you just take me off speaker for a minute?"

"What did Kat want?"

Cam sighed. He didn't want this to be a group conversation, but it seemed he had no choice.

"I got up early to take a shower," he said. "When I came back out, she was in the bed."

"Kat Nestrom was in your bed," said Celina.

"Yes," said Cam. He steeled himself for what was coming next. "And she was naked."

He heard Celina sweep the phone off the counter and take it off speaker.

"Kat fucking Nestrom was naked in your fucking bed." Her voice was close and sharp. "This morning."

Cam swallowed hard. It felt like pushing a wrecking ball through a paper straw. "Yes," he said, but his voice came out as a hoarse whisper. He cleared his throat. "Yes," he said again, "she was."

Silence.

Silence on the other end of the line.

"Hello?" said Cam. "Celina?"

He checked his phone to be sure the call hadn't dropped. It hadn't.

"Cameron."

The empty ache inside Cam's chest yawned open again.

"Hello, Madeline."

"Where are you right now?"

"I'm... I'm on the Capitol grounds," he said, confused by the question, "standing under a tree."

"Good," said Madeline. "Where are you headed? What's your plan for the day?"

"I'm meeting my mother at seven." His confusion grew. "I was just going to hang around the Mall until then. Why does it matter? What's going on?"

"We will check in with you regularly," Madeline said. "Stay in public places. The Mall, the Capitol, the museums are all perfect. Don't be alone."

"Madeline, what's going on?"

"Politics," she said with a sigh. "That's what's going on."

Cam had no idea what that meant, but he didn't get a chance to ask. To his great relief, Celina came back on the line.

"Jenkins is fucking with us," she said. "All of us. He's trying to get shit on us so he can manipulate us into doing what he wants. He's probably the one who sent Kat. He probably knew we would be there and sent Kat to fuck us." She hesitated. "To screw us, I mean." Another pause. "I mean, screw with us... fuck's sake." Her voice trailed off into an angry mutter.

"Nothing happened, Celina," said Cam, quietly.

Celina said nothing.

"Nothing. Happened."

When she spoke, Celina's voice was hard and bitter. "Yeah, well, shit's going to happen tonight." Her voice softened. "Watch your back, Cam."

The line went dead.

Stay in public places. Watch your back.

Cam still had no idea what any of that meant. But the empty ache in his chest wasn't getting any smaller.

40

THERE IS a difference between the reality of the world inside our minds and the reality of the world outside them. Most people would agree that when we use the word *reality,* we're talking about the shared reality outside our minds, the world we all inhabit and move through every day. But that doesn't make the reality inside our minds any less real.

And for some of us, like Celina, the world inside our minds can get a little fucked up.

In Celina's mind, she knew Cam had done nothing with Kat. He'd said as much, and she trusted him. She knew men lied, but Cam was not one of them. In fact, no man had ever lied to Celina. She was usually the one doing the lying, if she even bothered. Most of the time, she'd just dump the guy she cheated on rather than go to the trouble of lying to him. Lying was a pain in the ass, and she'd never cared enough to waste time and the energy on it.

Logically, she knew all of this. But the reality inside her mind wasn't all that logical at the moment.

At the moment, all Celina could see inside her mind was Kat's rocking-hot naked body on Cam's bed, no doubt willing and ready to fuck. Kat had been hitting on Cam like crazy in California, and that was with Celina standing right there. With her out of town, Kat would be all over him.

What would Cam do? In California, he'd put Kat off. But that was with Celina watching. What would he do when he knew she wouldn't find out? What would he do when she wasn't there to keep him in line, to let him know what he'd be giving up?

Because he would be giving up Celina if he fucked Kat. In a heartbeat. No one cheated on Celina. His ass would be on the curb before he could get his dick back in his pants.

But even as she thought it, Celina doubted it. The image of Cam and Kat fucking—of his back arched over her, his ass muscles clenching and loosing as his hips thrust in and pulled out, over and over, faster and faster, as Kat's claws dug red lines across Cam's back—made Celina shudder, and gave her a pain in the center of her chest that she'd never felt before.

Not true. She'd felt it once before.

When she found her father dead in his office.

Was that love? If she got that feeling at the thought of Cam cheating on her, did that mean she loved him?

Fucking hell. If that's what love was, why the fuck would she want to put herself through it? She was glad she'd never said those three words to Cam. It meant she wouldn't have to take them back, to admit she'd been wrong to say them in the first place.

"You need to stay focused."

Madeline's voice ripped Celina out of the head spin she'd been in. Like being pulled from the middle of a tornado, sucked down through the spout and back into the real world, the external reality, Celina found herself in the kitchen of the lake house again, cell phone in her hand, standing at the counter. She was barefoot, wearing panties and one of Cam's t-shirts, the clothes she'd slept in. Through the wide picture windows, the sun was already hard and bright, reflecting sharp white lines off the glittering lake. The water was greener than Celina expected, almost a Cancun green. She wanted to bust through the glass, run across the thick lawn and dive off the rocks into the water, feel the cold water numb her skin as she dove down, down, until she the water and the world blacked out around her.

"Celina."

Madeline's voice brought her back again.

Celina set her phone on the counter.

"Do you trust him?"

"What? Who?"

Madeline moved to stand in front of Celina, grabbed her by both shoulders, and pulled Celina's gaze into hers.

It was the same thing Cam did when Celina got lost in her thoughts.

"Do you trust Cameron?"

Like she did with Cam, Celine focused on Madeline's eyes. Hazel grey, flecked with yellow and orange. A lot like Cam's eyes, though not as brown.

Madeline shook Celina once, gentle, but firm. Celina shook her head, looked down, and closed her eyes. She pulled in a deep breath, then blew it out.

When she met Madeline's eyes again, Madeline stared hard at her, then nodded and released her shoulders.

"That's my girl," she said.

More thoughts poured into Celina's mind when she

heard those words, both negative, snarky thoughts and positive, tear-inducing thoughts. She pushed them all away, just like she had pushed away the thoughts about Cam and Kat.

Madeline checked her watch. "My speech is in twelve hours," she said. "Get dressed. We have work to do."

Madeline spent the next few hours on the phone with a variety of colleagues and press people while Celina worked through scenarios, writing everything on a whiteboard they'd found in a large office in the house. Madeline wanted to see Celina think through every possible outcome of what they were planning. Celina protested, saying she wouldn't usually write those kinds of things down. Madeline said she wouldn't, either, but since this was the first time they were working together and the stakes were high, they needed to be sure they were both on the same page. Celina couldn't argue with that logic. Plus, she welcomed the distraction.

Celina called Cam at noon, briefly, just to hear his voice and make sure he was safe. The call was over in ten seconds, but it took Celina another few minutes to get her mind refocused.

At one PM, Celina's outfit for the convention arrived, a white lapel wrap blouse with wide sleeves and a tapered waist worn over a waist-high taffeta skirt in midnight black with an A-line silhouette that fell all the way to the floor. The shoes were black ankle-strap Jimmy Choo sandals.

"A local designer. Talented," said Madeline, "and discreet." She spread out the skirt on the hanger with both hands and nodded. "There's a platinum snake necklace coming from Tiffany this afternoon. It'll be perfect. Elegant, but not showy."

Celina gave Cam another ten-second call at three, then

called once more at five-thirty when the car arrived to take them to the convention center.

"I won't be able to call again until late," she told him as she checked her hair one last time in the mirror in the foyer and picked up the Chanel clutch that had arrived shortly after the Tiffany necklace. She didn't know if Madeline had bought all of this stuff for Celina or if it was all on loan from one of her many connections, but she had to admit the woman had exquisite taste.

"I'm meeting my mom in half an hour," said Cam, "and then I'll go straight back to the house. I promise."

That didn't do much to settle Celina's concern, but she'd logged into the network at the house, changed all the passwords, updated the protocols, and cleared out all of the intrusive programs. And there had been several.

She watched her reflection press its lips together in the mirror, then pulled in a long, slow breath and consciously relaxed her body. Her lips went back to their natural shape. She couldn't guarantee that Jenkins wouldn't hack in again, but she felt a lot better than she had that morning.

"I'll call you later," she said. She hung up the phone, put it in her bag, and snapped the magnetic clasp shut.

"Ready?" said Madeline, stepping into the foyer beside Celina.

She wore a gathered silk draped midi dress from Giorgio Armani in a lovely soft peach with matching pumps and a suede Yves Saint Laurent clutch in light tan. With Madeline's long legs and torso and perfect posture, the dress somehow managed to simultaneously look soft and feminine, bad-ass don't-fuck-with-me boss bitch, and sexy as all fucking hell.

"Jesus fucking Christ," said Celina with a low whistle,

scanning Madeline from head to toe and back again. "With you in that dress, I'm ready for fucking anything."

Her mother arched one eyebrow.

"Let's hope so," was all she said as she led Celina to the car.

Audacious.

That was the word Vernon Stratham had been searching for.

For weeks, he'd been trying to find a single word to characterize Cameron Hauk, who he had first come to know as Paul Baker, then as Sam Davis. The man had many names, it seemed, and as many lives as a litter of mewling kittens.

He'd considered doughty and mettlesome, but they didn't encompass Mr. Hauk's irritating qualities. Plucky came closer, but the true feeling required the addition of an adjective: annoyingly plucky.

But Vernon prided himself on his ability to use language like a surgeon used a scalpel. Words had power. Like a hammer with its head covered in cotton balls, that power was diffused when too many words were used. Vernon sought economy to maximize impact.

Audacious was the word here, capturing Mr. Hauk's boldness, his unpredictability, and his impudence all in one lovely, perfect word.

The audacious Mr. Cameron Hauk.

Vernon smiled to himself as the jet tilted downward and the flight attendant came over the speaker to announce their initial descent into Washington Dulles Airport. Flying commercial was one of the many minor indignities he endured for his job. As a campaign employee—and the campaign finance chairperson, no less—it would be unseemly for Vernon to expend extraneous funds on chartered jets or even first-class seating when traveling without the candidate.

So he endured the fetid reek of the bulbous man spilling over the armrest into his window seat, like stacked plastic sacks filled with rising bread dough, pressing Vernon against the inside of the fuselage for refuge. His usual associates, potential campaign donors, were often no less obese, but the bouquet of wealth made their obesity tolerable. The man seated beside Vernon wore a polyester shirt stained with some kind of food grease, pants with an elastic waistband straining the limits of its ductility, and sandals over white socks with red and blue stripes on the cuff. The man's chortling affability only cemented his detestable character in Vernon's mind.

Mercifully, the flight from Chicago had been short, and Vernon had done what he always did: persevered in stoic silence. He would receive his due, one day.

And that day would come soon. He just had a few niggling details to sort out first.

Including the audacious Mr. Hauk.

As the plane touched down and taxied to the gate, Vernon's cell phone buzzed in the inner pocket of his suit jacket.

We still on for 7?

Speak of the devil. Vernon smiled to himself. Technology really was a marvel.

He checked his watch. Even though the time was there on his phone, long-standing habit still sent Vernon's eyes to his wrist.

4:37PM. The plane had landed twenty-two minutes late, but even with traffic, Vernon had plenty of time to get downtown.

I'll be there, he texted in reply. *Can't wait to see you.*

Love you, Mom. See you soon.

Love you, too.

Would one of those loathsome yellow faces with the kissing lips be appropriate here? Vernon decided to err on the side of restraint. When the fish is on the hook, as the man beside him might say in one of those aw-shucksy Midwest colloquialisms, there's no need to add bait.

And the audacious Mr. Cameron Hauk was most certainly on Vernon's hook.

42

CAM WALKED around the corner toward the park thirty minutes early. The air was as warm and humid as it had been all day, but the sun was nearing the horizon, two hours from sunset, and the breeze was picking up, bringing with it the hope of slightly cooler temperatures.

Nestled in the northwest corner of the grounds of the National Archives, the park contained a modest monument to Franklin Delano Roosevelt. It consisted of a block of marble about three feet by seven feet, quarried from the same location as his gravestone, with the inscription "In Memory of Franklin Delano Roosevelt" carved on one side. This was the original FDR memorial, the location and design specified by FDR himself before his death. The sprawling, mawkish exhibition in the tidal basin was built decades after the original, and likely would not have pleased the former president much at all.

Cam felt the same way. He appreciated the simplicity of the little park. Tucked unassumingly in a tiny corner away from the crowds on the Mall, it had green grass, mature shade trees, several double-sided benches, and the majestic and symbolic beauty of the National Archives Building beside it.

It was also the park he sat in the night he broke into the Department of Justice building next door for the second time, the night he had intended to attack Vernon Stratham and steal a thumb drive that contained evidence Cam could use to blackmail Attorney General Jenkins into setting his mother free from prison.

The same night Celina—who Cam knew then as the woman in black—saved him from what probably would have been a suicidal mistake. Stratham had been walking with Jenkins, who was very well-guarded. Cam had some solid self-defense skills now, thanks to Celina's training, but back then, he didn't know a karate chop from a chopped salad. Instead of watching Cam get himself killed, Celina had drugged him and dragged him out of the building.

It turned out she had different evidence, better evidence, that she was willing to use to set Cam's mother free. There had been a few bumps along the way between them, but that was the end result, and along with all his other feelings for her, Cam was still eternally grateful for Celina's generosity in that moment. She'd had her own plans for that evidence, but she scrapped them to free Cam's mother. She didn't have to do it, but she did it anyway.

Out of... love?

The warm, cozy feelings the park gave Cam melted away. He still wasn't sure where he and Celina stood. After she'd left so quickly for Chicago, he'd felt awful. The concern in her voice on the phone had buoyed his spirits, only for them to fall again when he told her about Kat. His phone had practically frosted over with Celina's icy response. Since then, their talks had been short, her voice clipped and flat.

But at least she was still calling. She cared enough about his safety to check in with him. That was something.

He had no idea what Celina and Madeline were planning, but he assumed it had something to do with the Democratic convention. They had left for the convention hall already. Madeline was the closing speaker that night. Cam figured he'd catch the speech on YouTube later, if he didn't have a chance to stream it live. He hadn't seen his mother in over a year. A convention speech could wait.

When Cam arrived, the only other visitor in the park was a tall, thin man in a dark suit sitting on a bench on the east side, by the entrance to the Archives. He was looking down at his phone, his back toward Cam. Giving the man his privacy, Cam chose a bench on the north side of the park and sat on the side facing the street. He would normally face the park and avoid having to watch the traffic, but the Market Square shopping center was across the street, and that's where he figured his mother would be coming from. He wanted to catch sight of her as soon as he could.

He was still shocked that Paulie was in Washington at all. From her most recent postcard a week ago, she and Simon were still in China after spending several months in Japan and Korea, enjoying the food and the culture there. He'd thought their plan was to head to Australia and New Zealand next, then hop to South America before swinging north back to America.

Not that he was complaining. His mother was his best friend in the world, rivaled now only by Celina. He'd visited her nearly every weekend for fifteen years while she was in prison. He'd had a few months with her after she got out, and then she'd left with Simon for a trip around the world that had lasted more than a year so far, and still going. Or so Cam had thought.

It briefly occurred to him that something bad might have happened to cut their trip short, but he banished the notion almost as soon as it came up. If something really bad had happened, his mother wouldn't text to meet him in a park after a shopping trip. She would call him directly and come home. And even if something bad had happened, there was no point in worrying over it. Cam could wait for the bad news and deal with it, if and when it came.

He crossed his arms, leaned back on the bench, and stretched his legs out straight. They were sore and stiff from walking around the Mall all day. But, despite all the emotional turmoil and the cloak-and-dagger talk from Celina, it had actually been a pretty good day for Cam. He loved museums, and the museums in Washington were world-class. And as a bonus, he'd filled half of a sketchbook with drawings of tourists and buildings and some of the exhibits. And a few drawings of Celina, of course, from memory. He drew what was on his mind, and Celina rarely left it anymore.

Pedestrian traffic when he sat down consisted mostly of weary workers heading home. As he waited on the bench, the crowd morphed into a dinner crowd. The sagging faces and downcast eyes became smiles and laughter. The rumpled suits and pencil skirts became shorts, collared shirts, summer dresses, and sandals, all streaming toward the restaurants at the shopping center across the street. His mother should be coming along any minute now.

He felt someone sit behind him on the bench.

"Be careful extending your legs so far," said the person, a

man's voice. "You wouldn't want to trip someone accidentally. Not in this town. With all the lawyers, you'd be sued before you could help the person up."

Cam didn't know how to respond at first. Seemed weird enough that a random stranger would sit down directly behind him in a park with several empty benches, even weirder for the stranger to make conversation, and weirder yet to make a comment like that. But he'd said it with well-meaning humor in his voice. Probably a tourist from somewhere a lot friendlier than Washington. Some kind of Mayberry in the south or the Midwest, where striking up a casual conversation with a complete stranger was a matter of course. Cam would not be the rude East-coaster who left the man with a sour taste in his mouth from his trip to the big city.

"Thanks for the warning," he said. "On the bright side, I'd have as many lawyers offering to defend me as there would be looking to prosecute."

He tried to turn his head to see the speaker, but the man had sat directly behind him, and Cam didn't feel like shifting his comfortable position to look all the way around. Over his shoulder from the corner of his eye, he could see that the man was wearing a dark suit.

As he looked, he noticed idly that the man across the park was no longer there. Just a coincidence, though. Men in dark suits were not exactly rare in D.C., and there was no reason for the man to have changed seats just to exchange pleasantries with Cam.

"Are you visiting Washington?" Cam asked.

"Here on business," replied the man. "You?"

"Meeting my mother."

"A loving son. Rare, these days, it seems."

"What line of work are you in?"

The man hesitated, but only for a moment. "Insurance."

Insurance. The world's most boring line of work. Cam had always wondered if there was anyone, anyone at all, who went into the insurance business because they actually loved it, or if everyone in that industry was either a greedy executive or a mindless corporate zombie.

"What got you into the insurance business?"

The man chuckled softly, probably guessing what Cam had been thinking. He probably heard it from people a lot.

"Practicality, at first," he said. "But now I love it for the thrills."

Cam laughed, then realized the man wasn't laughing with him.

"Sorry," he said. "I didn't realize insurance could be thrilling."

The man chuckled again.

"Well, it depends what kind of insurance we're talking about."

Cam couldn't imagine any kind of insurance that might be even remotely thrilling, but to each their own.

He felt a cold circle of metal press against the nape of his neck. The cold ran down his spine.

"I work in the killing kind of insurance," said the man, amiably.

This time, Cam turned his head enough to see over his shoulder. The man tilted his head so Cam could clearly see his face.

Vernon Stratham.

"It's nice to see you again, Mr..." He frowned thoughtfully. "What shall we call you today? Mr. Davis? Mr. Baker? Mr. Hauk? Or do you have a new pseudonym to add to the collection?"

Cam turned his head back toward the shopping mall

across the street. It seemed far away now, the throngs of smiling, laughing people completely oblivious to the man threatening Cam with a gun in the park across the street.

"Why don't I just call you my latest insurance policy," Stratham said. He pressed the gun harder into Cam's neck. "Get up, Mr. Hauk. We're going to my office."

Cam could hear Stratham smile behind him.

"I'm sure you remember the way," Stratham said.

43

Stratham led Cam through a side door into the Department of Justice building, bypassing the metal detectors and security guards. He steered Cam up the stairs to his office on the third floor and pushed him roughly through the door.

Stratham's office was a far cry from the Attorney General's office two floors above. Jenkins had a massive, elegant space with high ceilings and windows covering two walls. Stratham's office, by contrast, was a dark hole crowded with filing cabinets, barely wide enough for the cheap particle-board desk and faux-leather swivel chair. If it weren't for the security camera in one corner of the ceiling, Cam would have said the office hadn't changed since the Fifties.

The air in the office carried the same stink of drudgery that permeated the maze of cubicles outside. At least to Cam's nose, it did, but probably not for the workers themselves. The people who actually worked for the Department of Justice tended to be high-minded idealists. Their idealism had usually been worn down to a sharp-edged pragmatism, but it still drove them out of bed and into their cubicle every morning to work a job where they were paid half of what most of them could command in the private sector. These people weren't the talentless hacks most outside of government assumed. They just tended to value their idealism above their paycheck.

"Have a seat, Mr. Hauk," said Stratham. He closed the door, set his gun on his desk, and settled primly into the chair behind it, the sterile fluorescent light glinting off his wire-rimmed glasses.

Cam sat in an armless plastic chair in front of Stratham's desk. Stratham didn't bother to restrain his hands or feet, probably assuming the gun would be enough deterrent against escape. Cam glanced at the weapon, a compact Ruger revolver. Looked to be small-caliber, no more than a .22, but Stratham probably used LR Punch ammo. A normal .22 round didn't have much stopping force, but the LR ammo packed enough power to make Cam's life miserable. Or end it altogether at close range.

All of that came to Cam in a moment, with just a glance, followed by the realization of how much Celina had taught him about guns and self-defense in the last year alone. A little over a year ago, when he'd sat in this same office, in this same plastic chair, he'd had no clue how to defend himself. And if he'd seen a gun then, his only feeling would have been fear. Now, he knew he could take down Stratham, knew how to disarm him in hand-to-hand close-quarters combat, knew how to operate the Ruger once he got hold of it. This time, as he sat in front of Stratham, his concern wasn't how to protect himself, but when and whether it would be to his advantage.

What the hell was Stratham up to? Why did he care about Cam? And why was he in Washington at all?

"Shouldn't you be in Chicago, working your donors?"

Stratham smiled faintly. "Major donors don't attend political conferences, as a rule. Too plebeian for their tastes."

Cam nodded slowly.

"Should I let my mother know I'll be late for our meeting?"

Stratham sighed. "Technology is a double-edged sword, isn't it? It can do so much good—"

"So it was you the whole time. She was never coming."

Stratham pressed his lips in irritation at Cam's interruption, then relaxed into that faint smile once more.

"Did you enjoy seeing your old friend this morning, Mr. Hauk?"

Cam felt the color drain from his face. He didn't respond.

Stratham raised his eyebrows. "Don't you remember?" He chuckled and shifted in his chair to pull his cell phone from his pocket. "You always did have an odd effect on women," he said as he tapped on the screen. "Melantha was a beauty, was she not?"

Cam reddened at the memory of the woman he'd met two years earlier, on the same Russian billionaire's yacht where he'd met Stratham. She'd been Stratham's girlfriend once, a notion Cam still could not believe. She and Cam had had... a moment, until he found out she was the one who'd killed the Russian billionaire.

"Never saw the appeal, myself, but then can any man truly understand the mysteries of the unfairer sex?" His expression soured for a moment, then relaxed into a faint smile again. "But we're talking about today, not ancient history." He turned the phone toward Cam. "This might jog your memory."

On the screen, a video began to play. Cam saw the

bedroom of Celina's D.C. house, in high definition and full color. The bed was empty, sheets rumpled where Cam had tossed and turned all night. He could hear the faint hiss of the shower in the background.

As he watched, Kat entered the room, slowly at first, looking around. When she saw the room was empty, she pressed her ear to the bathroom door, thought for a moment, then stripped naked and slid into bed, arranging the sheets around her and auditioning several poses before settling in to wait.

"I'll skip to the good part," said Stratham, tapping the screen.

The video skipped ahead. Cam saw himself emerge from the bathroom in a cloud of steam, saw himself turn back for a towel, saw that the towel was not enough to conceal his body's interest in the gorgeous naked woman in his bed.

He looked away from the screen. "What do you want, Stratham?"

"A moment, if you please," said Stratham, holding up one finger and watching intently, a lurid smile on his face. "The good part is coming up."

"What do you want?" Cam repeated.

Through the small speakers of the phone, he could hear Kat seducing him, could hear his own feeble attempts to resist. He should have stayed in the bathroom. He should have pushed Kat out of the bedroom and locked the door. He should have just walked out himself.

He thought of Celina, the coldness in her voice after he told her about the incident, and felt a flush of shame.

Stratham cackled with delight as Kat flicked the towel from Cam's waist, then shook his head as Cam rebuffed her. "Maybe I can see the appeal," Stratham said. "You do have enviable self-control, Mr. Hauk."

Cam wanted to smash Stratham's phone. Sure, Kat had baited him, and, sure, he hadn't gone through with it. But he'd obviously wanted to. Now, all he wanted was to shatter the phone into a thousand pieces, erase all evidence of that embarrassing episode.

But he knew better. He knew there were other copies of the video, for starters. Just like Jenkins must know there were other copies of the evidence against him.

And he knew that smashing the phone or reacting in any way would play right into Stratham's hands. He was trying to intimidate Cam, to get under his skin. If Cam showed that it was working, Stratham would have the upper hand.

Cam settled back in his chair, crossed his legs and folded his arms, and breathed, in and out, waiting for the video to end.

He watched himself push away from Kat, walk into the bathroom, and close the door. He watched Kat stand there in disbelief for a moment. Cam almost felt bad for her. She dressed in a rush and hurried from the room.

Stratham sighed contentedly, stopped the video, and set his phone face-down on the desk.

"I never tire of watching that," he said. "So satisfying, for so many reasons. Don't you agree?"

Cam said nothing, just gave Stratham a polite, patient smile. He knew Stratham would get to the point, eventually.

"How do you think Ms. Maxwell would feel about this video, Mr. Hauk?"

There it was. Emotional blackmail. Of course.

"Do you think she would find it as amusing as I do,"

Stratham continued, "or do you think she would react... differently?"

Cam kept the polite smile on his face. It was becoming more difficult to do so.

Stratham frowned theatrically. "Now that I think of it, she might not see the humor in this video." He frowned further. "She might not find it amusing at all, would she? Oh, dear." He clucked his tongue. "No, now that I think of it, she might find this video quite... what would be the word?" He leaned forward, resting his elbows on the desk and clasping his hands together. "Shocking, perhaps? Infuriating?" He furrowed his brow. "Devastating?" His frown became a broad smile. "What word would you choose?"

Cam kept silent, but the smile was gone from his face, as was all pretense of maintaining it. Stratham had laid out the punishment. Now he needed to explain the stipulations.

"Boring, probably." Cam did his best to sell the bluff. "Celina already knows about Kat."

"Yes, you are irritatingly honest with her. An odd quality for a professional thief." Stratham chuckled. "But hearing is one thing. Seeing is quite another. I hardly think Ms. Maxwell will be bored when she sees this video."

"*When* she sees it?"

"I couldn't in good conscience keep such important information from her, could I? She deserves to know what type of man she's dating."

"What do you want, Stratham?"

Stratham put an expression of mock shock on his face. "Are you suggesting I withhold this information in exchange for some kind of favor or payment? That would be immoral."

Cam went back to waiting in silence. No polite, patient smile this time.

"Still, I can see how this kind of visual evidence would absolutely destroy what is otherwise a lovely relationship, I'm sure." Stratham dropped the shocked act, his face in an instant turning hard and cruel. "I will agree not to deliver this video to your lover"—his mouth released the word with evident distaste—"if you agree never to reveal the evidence you have against the Attorney General."

"Don't you mean the evidence against you *and* the Attorney General?"

Stratham didn't respond, but the cruelty in his eyes glittered behind the silver wire rims of his glasses. He leaned back, his cheap office chair screeching, and folded his arms across his chest.

Cam stared back, musing. He knew agreement meant nothing. The video would still be there and Stratham could deliver it at any time. The only way to defeat blackmail in the digital age was to confess, to take the teeth out of the threat by facing it head-on. Stratham got the video from the security system at Celina's house. Cam would get a copy, too, and show it to Celina himself.

He could play along with Stratham for now. But how far would Stratham take this? And how long would he keep it up?

"What if I refuse?" Cam asked.

Stratham paused for a moment. A slow smile crept over his face, matched by a slow creep along Cam's spine.

Stratham leaned forward. The chair screeched again.

"Refuse?" he said. "Oh, please do, Mr. Hauk." He picked up the revolver and pointed it at Cam. His smile widened. "Please do."

44

OF ALL THE images Celina had in her mind, she never would have expected a political convention to be like this.

Her mother had called it a convention hall, but it wasn't. It was an arena, the same place where the Bulls and the Blackhawks played, where Aerosmith and Justin Timberlake had recently held their concerts. It had a capacity of twenty-four thousand, and every bit of that capacity was taken up by women in sensible shoes and men with conservative haircuts. From the look of the audience, it could as easily have been a convention for drain stopper salespeople as for the nomination of the next President of the United States.

But the energy. The energy was absolutely wild. These people were political nerds, but they were hard-core political nerds, and this was their wedding, their Mardi Gras, and their Olympics, all rolled into one. It only came once every four years, and they were making the most of it. Even more so this year, when their candidate was a shoo-in for the presidency. Every seat in the arena was filled, a swath of political humanity that spread across the floor and up the walls, dotted with colorful banners and placards, looking like the milk left over after eating a bowl of sugary cereal. And the energy in the arena was the sugar high, the walls practically flexing with nerd power.

Backstage, the effect was even more palpable. The stage had been constructed at one end of the arena, allowing direct access from behind through a tunnel at floor level. The hallways in that entire end of the arena had been blocked off, and a surprisingly large group of speakers and their coteries were milling about in the makeshift green room area that resulted. The floor and the walls were bare concrete. The concession stands were filled with complimentary (watered-down) drinks and (cheap) snacks. And the people in the crowd were as happy as if they were in the Oval Office itself.

As Celina and her mother weaved through the crowd, her mother glad-handing countless minor politicians and party officials, Celina watched a group of young girls point at Madeline and squeal with the excitement normally reserved for meeting a pop star or a teen idol. She saw her mother notice them from the corner of her eye, coyly ignore them for a moment, then deftly work her way toward them for an autograph and a quick word. As they passed on through the crowd, Celina looked back to see the girls comparing their autographed programs and swooning. Apparently, political nerds were born, not made.

Madeline had the option to avoid that crowd. She could have taken the VIP elevator straight to the box seats on the higher levels, where the true power players were hanging out. But she'd deliberately steered Celina and her security detail through the throng on the lower level. She was a woman of the people. Celina didn't know if her mother actually enjoyed those people or if it was all just good politics, but, regardless, Madeline Kinkaid was good at her job. She was tireless in her ability to greet people, press their flesh and give them their moment in the spotlight, and leave them feeling like they'd touched the hand of God. Celina admired it. She wondered how she'd wound up such a people-hating grinch, if her mother was so skilled.

Then she remembered that her mother hadn't been around to teach her how to use whatever innate abilities she might have. Celina clenched her teeth and focused on what was happening around her.

Eventually, they did take the elevator to the higher levels, and there Celina found a much different scene. Gone was the giddy excitement from the floor below, but the energy here was no less electric. In fact, it was even stronger. But it had a different quality. Instead of the bubbly party energy, this was the energy of intense power, and an intense pleasure derived from that power. These were people who craved the ability to control others, people who had worked hard to earn the opportunity. In some cases—maybe in many cases—they'd seized that opportunity by standing on a pile of corpses, figuratively or literally.

These were the real power brokers. Most of them didn't have money—a fact that left them constantly scrabbling and insecure—but they held the reins of government, and so they danced in a tense pas de deux with the wealthy, each of them smiling and collaborating with the other while looking for the moment when they could rob their partner blind.

But this night was not for the wealthy. The wealthy were watching from home, by and large. This night was purely for the politicians and their sycophants.

The upper hallway was wide, long, and curved around the short end of the arena. As below, a concession stand had been transformed into a bar, this one serving slightly higher-end beverages. The space was filled with women in more expensive, but just as sensible, shoes and men with the same cheap, conservative haircuts, but a higher quality of suit worn beneath them.

As in any hierarchy, this crowd contained both the powerful and those on the periphery of that power. The King and his court. The murmur of the crowd grew louder as the elevator doors slid open. Celina and Madeline stepped into the viper pit itself.

And there Celina witnessed her mother's true power for the first time.

Power exists in many forms and is measured in many ways. It can be defined as the ability to get things, or as the ability to get things done. It can be defined as the amount of money one possesses to achieve both goals.

But in the end, power is defined as the ability to get others to bend to you and your will. As Madeline entered the wide hallway, Celina watched as one after another of the milling guests glanced their way, drink in hand, mouth open in ongoing conversation, then did a double-take, mouths now silent, but still hanging open for a moment before the guest composed themselves.

The reorientation was subtle, but absolute. Where the energy had been frenetic and scattered, a hundred different conversations all happening at once, when Madeline waded into the crowd, all of that energy shifted to focus on her. The conversations went on as before, but the focus was all on Madeline.

The effect was startling. Celina felt the weight of that focus like an anvil, and she wasn't even the focal point. Yet Madeline took it in stride, her easy smile never wavering, her light banter no less light, no less energetic.

She was used to this. Celina realized for the first time how powerful her mother really was. She wasn't the president or even the VP, but she handled the mantle of power with the ease that can only come from experience and natural ability. Madeline Kinkaid was born to be powerful.

She made her way through the crowd slowly, offering the same quick handshakes and greetings she had on the floor below, only occasionally stopping for a leaned-in whisper or a short, quiet exchange mid-handshake. Celina watched as people in the crowd jockeyed to situate themselves in Madeline's path. One woman, young and round-faced, dressed in a dazzling powder white pantsuit with a seersucker-like texture, her shining hair pressed into plastic-perfect straightness, stepped into Madeline's path, holding her hand out, elbow at her hip, practically bouncing in her flats. Her smile split her face like a cut cantaloupe. Celina could not help but be astounded by the woman's unabashed enthusiasm.

"Speaker Kinkaid," the woman said, breathless. "It's an honor to meet you, Madeline Speaker." Her smile faltered, her cheeks flushed. "Madame Madeline." She frowned and shook her head, her cheeks now fire-red. The joy in her eyes turned to shame and self-recrimination. She looked down at the floor. "Madame Speaker," she said correctly, at last.

Madeline took the woman's hand in both of hers, softly. She bent her knees to catch the woman's gaze and drew it gently up again until they both stood tall and straight.

"Governor Fernley-Crenshaw," she said, her voice warm and sincere. "Is it alright if I call you Susan?"

The governor's face opened in shock, all shame washed away. She nodded, open-mouthed. "Sue," she muttered. "My friends call me Sue."

"Sue, then," said Madeline, "and I hope I can earn the right to call you that." She flashed a bright smile and leaned toward the governor, pulling her in slightly, conspiratorially. Just two ladies sticking together, taking on the world. "What you've done in Alabama with criminal justice reform is remarkable, and your work on abortion rights in your state is inspiring." She leaned in further. "Taking on the Alabama Supreme Court like you did? As a defense attorney?" Madeline clucked her tongue admiringly. "I wish I had your chutzpah."

The governor's eyes were wide as the full moon. "Thank you, Madame Speaker," she stammered. "I'm just following your example."

"I was thrilled when you won your special election, truly." Madeline patted her hand lightly. "I know it's not easy settling in to a new role, but I want you to know that we're all rooting for you, the entire caucus."

The governor's mouth opened, but no words came out.

"I'm looking forward to your speech tonight," said Madeline with a bright smile. "Knock 'em dead."

"Th-Thank you, Madame Speaker," the governor stuttered.

"Call me Madeline."

The governor's mouth flapped, too astounded to speak further. She just nodded, her cheeks now red for an entirely different reason. When Madeline finally released her hand and moved on to the next guest, Celina, trailing behind, watched the governor stare at that hand as if she would never wash it again, as if she was considering cutting it off, having it bronzed, and keeping it on the corner of her desk for the rest of time.

Celina followed Madeline through the rest of the throng in similar fashion. She'd wondered why they'd left the house at five-thirty when Madeline's speech wasn't scheduled until 9pm Central time. Now she understood. It took the woman forty-five minutes just to cross a room.

But, finally, they did cross it, arriving at a set of glass double doors, thrown wide open in a welcoming way, but guarded by two burly men in dark suits, making sure it was clear that the welcome was conditional, and anyone who did not meet the conditions would be dismissed in the manner of a nightclub bouncer.

The two men nodded respectfully toward Madeline, their eyes drifting over Celina with scant notice. They didn't recognize her, but Celina recognized them. She'd seen them in the Department of Justice building a year ago. They were both part of Attorney General Jenkins' personal security detail.

As they stepped through the doors, Madeline stopped to survey the room. The crowd here was smaller, even more exclusive, and even more powerful. This was the inner circle, and here the vipers' fangs were the sharpest.

Madeline scanned the room and spotted Jenkins himself in the far corner, speaking with a handful of men in suits. He was tall, affording him a clear view of the room above the heads of the crowd. His eye caught Madeline's, and he lifted his glass in silent greeting mid-conversation. He started toward them.

Madeline turned back and offered Celina a quiet smile.

"Okay," she said softly to Celina. "It's showtime."

45

IT HAD BEEN MORE than a year since Celina had seen Bill Jenkins in person, and it hadn't been nearly long enough.

She watched him slip through the crowd toward them from across the room. He was tall and handsome, with a wide, bright smile and a thick head of hair swept back off his forehead, a hint of grey making him look statesmanlike and distinguished. No conservative haircut here. Bill Jenkins looked like a movie star.

And he dressed the part of a successful politician. His suits were well-tailored, using fabrics that were expensive, but not ostentatious. He exuded a power that was understated, but undeniable. And while Bill Jenkins had the same ability as Madeline to dazzle people, to make them feel like they were the only people in the world, and to inspire people to follow him, Jenkins did it with a diamond-cold beauty that evoked awe, but not affection. Loyalty, but not love. He was a spectacle, a specimen of political perfection, whereas Madeline was a human being. One left you awed but cold, while the other left you inspired and aglow.

Celina watched the crowd part for Jenkins like paper

slowly ripping, making way for their leader with a bowing deference that was a stark contrast to the eager affection they'd shown to Madeline. For Madeline, they'd all wanted to touch her. With Jenkins, they waited and hoped for him to touch them.

Maybe that's why Jenkins wanted Madeline as a running mate, to harness her ability to draw people in. No, he wouldn't care about that. As long as he had their votes, Jenkins would sooner ignore them than interact with them. He was an elitist, at heart, despite the teaching Celina's father had given him. Celina's father was not a particularly social man, but he loved people all the same, and he had been trying to teach Jenkins how to love them, too. Instead, Jenkins had learned how to make people think he cared about them, while he went about his self-advancing political schemes.

What would he do once he reached the top, once he became president? With nowhere else to advance himself, what would he do then?

Celina's mouth twisted in a rueful smile. Then he would chase the one thing he still didn't have, the thing he probably resented most about Madeline and about Celina: their wealth. Jenkins was rich by most people's standards, but he still had to beg donors for the big bucks. He still had to employ Vernon Stratham to collect, still had to promise things he didn't want to give in exchange for the donations, to debase himself for money. He still relied on the largesse of the wealthy for trips on their luxury yachts or rides on their private jets or vacations in their secluded mountain villas. Celina knew Jenkins well enough to know how much that chafed him. If he could use the power of the presidency to enrich himself privately without damaging his public legacy, he would. If he couldn't, he'd be even more ruthless after the presidency than he had been before. And that was a scary thought.

"Hello, Madeline," Jenkins said with a broad smile as he approached, holding both hands out. Madeline took them graciously and leaned in as Jenkins air-kissed her on one cheek. Jenkins leaned back, still holding both of Madeline's hands, and scanned her from head to toe. "You look absolutely stunning," he said.

No one ever greets a man by scanning their full body and saying something about their appearance. No one ever says *Hey there, Tom. You're looking like a fine cut of beef tonight. Your ass looks amazing in that suit.* Why do they think it's okay to do that with women?

"Thank you, Bill," Madeline replied. Knowing her true feelings for the man, Celina marveled at the warmth in Madeline's voice. "This is quite a party you're throwing here."

"I begged them to tone it down," said Jenkins, looking sheepishly at the crowd in the room and through the glass partitions at the crazed arena beyond, where Celina could hear someone speaking from the stage, the crowd responding with cheers, "but they said they couldn't do it. 'Give the people what they want', they said." He shrugged. "Who am I to argue?" He grinned that movie star grin, then slid his eyes to Celina.

"Celina," he said. "What a surprise. It's lovely to see you here."

"Bill," said Celina flatly.

He scanned Celina, too, then raised his eyebrows theatrically. "You two will turn some heads tonight. Just gorgeous."

Jenkins turned back to Madeline.

"I read your speech," he said. "It's perfect. You're going to floor them." He grinned. "I'm glad my speech is tomorrow. No one would remember it if it were tonight."

As if anyone would remember it, anyway. If you could pick one word to describe the speeches at political conventions, *memorable* would not be the one.

Madeline bowed her head in thanks.

When Jenkins said he'd read Madeline's speech, he really meant he'd approved it. All of these conventions were carefully orchestrated to build the mythos of the candidate, to build the tension from the first night, ramping it up to a crescendo at the end of the fourth night, when the candidate took the stage. They wouldn't even let the candidate appear on stage until that moment, lest it release some of that tension. Jenkins hadn't announced his running mate—yet another tension-building technique. He would announce tonight just before Madeline's speech as her introduction to the stage, but he'd do it via video on the massive television screens that hung around the arena, giving the people in the cheap seats a better view. Even though he would be standing twenty yards above and behind the stage, Jenkins would make the announcement via pre-recorded video.

And he'd be twenty feet tall. Cheap parlor tricks, like the wizard behind the curtain. But that was modern politics.

Madeline and Celina had cooked up a few tricks of their own.

The crowd cheered again, the sound coming through the open doors of the room, which was one of the arena's executive suites. A wall of glass partitions, several of which had been slid open, led to four steep, stadium-style rows of cushy leather seats. The view was obstructed, of course, by the stage and the curtains around it. It would not do for the crowd to glimpse this year's hero too soon. The stage itself could only be seen through the countless televisions arrayed around the room and in the hallway, even erected on stands in front of the stadium seats. But the sound of the cheers and party horns reverberated around the arena, as loud as any playoff game, filtering through the open doors to provide a backdrop to the conversations in the room.

All these political fucks probably imagining—consciously or subconsciously—the cheers were for them. That's what they all really wanted, anyway. They just wanted to be loved.

That, and sex with underage girls, the sick fucks. Why were so many men with power so fucking twisted?

Celina scanned the room for the first time and saw several faces she recognized. She was no political junkie, but she recognized the two senators from California, her home state. They'd both been in office for decades. She saw several congresspeople in their second or third terms who had been stirring shit up on the House floor since they started, getting lots of press and generally making Madeline's job harder. She even saw a handful of moderate Republicans, those among the more reasonable members of their caucus. One was Senator Zachar, a stoop-backed senator from Utah who was serving his hundredth term, it seemed. His bald head was horseshoed with long, wispy white hairs, like they'd drifted off a feather boa and somehow gotten stuck on his scalp.

He was speaking to a tall, thin man with his back toward Celina, no doubt regaling him with the story of that time George Washington got wasted on the Senator's back porch and nearly blew his head off with a musket. The old man leaned in to deliver the punch line, probably something along the lines of *And I grabbed the bumper of rattle skull from his hand just as old George fell off the damn veranda!*. The two men laughed together, a bright flare in the dark sky of the murmuring crowd. The tall man clapped Senator Zachar on one shoulder and turned to escape, turning toward Celina.

Celina Maxwell didn't get star-struck often. She was usually the star doing the striking. But in that moment, she was as starry-eyed as the teen girls on the first floor had been with her mother.

The tall, thin man was former President Jalandhari, the predecessor to the current president, President Hill. Madeline had told Celina there would be several former presidents in attendance tonight, but Celina hadn't thought much about it. Now, it was all she could think about.

The president caught her eye and smiled, then smiled more broadly as his gaze slid to Madeline. He started through the crowd toward them both.

Celina's heart stuttered for a moment. President Jalandhari was the first U.S. president of non-European heritage, the first non-white president, the first president younger than forty when he took office. The man was a walking record book. He had served for eight years, and it had been eight years since he left office. That put him in his mid-fifties. The office had definitely aged him, turning his dark beard salt-and-pepper grey. But his black hair was still as thick and lustrous as it had been, his chestnut skin as smooth as ever, his body as lithe and lean as it had been nearly twenty years earlier. The man was an undeniable PILF—Politician I'd Like to Fuck—for Celina. She was creaming her panties just watching him come closer.

"Madeline," he said, his rich, low voice sending a shiver through Celina's body. "I was hoping I'd see you here."

He took one of her hands in both of his and bowed

slightly. His eyes stayed locked on Madeline's. No body scans or comments on her appearance here.

Not from him, anyway. Celina had already scanned Jalandhari several times. He was wearing his trademark three-piece suit, and it fit the man like melted fudge fit a rock-hard nipple.

"Hello, Ravi." Madeline's greeting was just as warm as it had been for Jenkins a moment earlier, but Celina could feel a difference, could feel that this one was more sincere. Or maybe she was just projecting.

"I was just complimenting Madeline on the text of her upcoming speech," said Jenkins.

His smile was just as wide as before, but it had become more brittle. He had stood just a little bit taller when President Jalandhari walked up, puffed his chest out just a bit. The man had an ego the size of Texas, but he was insecure as fuck.

"I'm sure it will be brilliant," said Jalandhari.

His eyes slid to Celina. She nearly passed out right there, her blood suddenly pulsing in her neck.

"Ravi, this is—"

"Celina Maxwell," Jalandhari said, holding out one hand toward Celina. "I've followed your career with great interest."

Celina's mouth felt as dry as the martini she desperately wanted in that moment. She took Jalandhari's hand. It was smooth and warm and somehow both soft and firm at the same time. Which was good, because she needed it to keep from falling over.

"M-My career?" said Celina, struggling to get enough moisture into her mouth for her tongue to work properly. "What career?"

Jalandhari smiled that wry smile that adorned the walls

of countless teenage girls. So weird to have a president be a sex symbol. But it had inspired an entire generation of young women to get interested in politics. Sex appeal was not such a bad thing.

"The career I'm sure you'll have one day," said Jalandhari. "A woman as powerful as you can't stay silent for long." He leaned in toward Celina. "And shouldn't," he said, his gaze pointed and earnest.

Celina didn't know what to say to that. She just nodded in response. When Jalandhari took his hand away, she immediately felt the lack.

Another cheer rose from the crowd. They were coming more frequently now, the energy in the arena growing more frenetic as the night wore on. President Jalandhari must have noticed, too. He looked at the closest television screen, then at his watch.

"The crowd is getting boisterous," he said. "When is your speech, Madeline?"

Madeline checked her own watch. "Overdue, actually," she said.

"The schedules have been running long," said Jenkins. "We should make our way down to the stage."

He turned and offered one crooked arm toward Madeline, who took it gracefully.

"Would you be so kind as to watch the speech with me?" Jalandhari asked Celina with a slight bow. "A few of us have a viewing area set aside in an adjoining room."

Celina would have liked nothing more than to watch just about anything with the man, but she had other things she had to do.

"Celina's going to accompany me, Ravi," said Madeline, smiling. "I'm sorry to deprive you."

"Celina's coming backstage?" Jenkins frowned.

"Moral support," said Madeline, her smile sparkling, her gaze steady on Jenkins' eyes.

"Another time, I hope," said Jalandhari, again with that slight bow of his. "Good luck with your speech, Madeline." He glanced back and forth between the three of them, a smile playing at the corners of his mouth. Celina had to wonder how much he knew, or how much he suspected. "I look forward to watching it."

They said their goodbyes, and Celina followed Madeline and Jenkins to a private elevator. As the doors slid shut, Celina felt a surge of adrenaline. She and Madeline were in a confined space with the man who was soon to be the most powerful person in the world.

They were already on his hit list.

And they were about to really piss him off.

She couldn't fucking wait.

46

CAM STARED at the barrel of the compact revolver on Stratham's desk. The gun was aimed toward him, but Stratham wasn't holding it. His hand rested on the desk, his finger tapping idly beside the grip.

There was a fifty-fifty chance Cam could lunge for the gun and grab it before Stratham realized what was happening.

Fifty percent chance he'd get the gun. Fifty percent chance he'd get the bullet.

Not good odds.

So Cam waited to see how the evening played out, biding his time.

And there was a lot of time to bide. He and Stratham had been sitting largely in silence for what felt like forever, Stratham patiently tapping his finger and staring at Cam.

"So..." said Cam, finally, his voice sounding out of place after so much silence, "can I go now? You made your blackmail pitch. I get it. Are we done here?"

Stratham smiled faintly at Cam and checked his watch.

"Why don't we visit a while longer?" he said. "I so rarely get to spend time with you these days."

"Lovely," said Cam.

"Let's see," said Stratham, leaning back in his chair, careful not to let his hand stray far from the grip of the revolver. "You've led a very interesting life, Mr. Hauk. A criminal childhood, the tragic death of your father, your mother incarcerated for over a decade, your sad crusade to secure her release."

"You mean my successful crusade to secure her release?"

Stratham shrugged. "Sad and, ultimately, successful. One cannot account for luck in life."

Cam snorted. "I worked a long time to earn that luck."

Stratham waved his hand—the hand that was not near the gun—dismissively. "This is just one way to justify the luck that befalls us. Hard work has no impact on luck. Luck is like sunshine. It falls equally on the deserving and the undeserving."

"That must drive you crazy."

Stratham slid his eyes to Cam and cocked an eyebrow. He wasn't going to take that bait.

"Your luck was not in freeing your mother, Mr. Hauk."

Cam waited for the explanation.

"Your luck was in meeting Ms. Maxwell."

Cam nodded slowly. "I can't argue with you there."

"A beautiful woman, to be sure," Stratham said, "but a powerful one, too. And an intelligent one."

"Don't tell me you're one of those men who thinks intelligent women are a myth? Or an inconvenience?"

Stratham chuckled. "I hope you know me better than that by now, Mr. Hauk. Intelligent women—women who actually show and use their intelligence—are a rarity, but not because of any weakness of the gender. Intelligent people are a rarity, regardless of their biological sex. And intelligent women seem rarer only because our society compels women to mute whatever natural intelligence they may have, to the point where that muting becomes so ingrained they eventually forget they possess any intelligence at all."

"I wouldn't have pegged you for a women's rights advocate, Vernon."

Stratham didn't chuckle then. He sat forward in his chair, his hands flat on the table, his face set in an intense expression.

"I believe in meritocracy." His hands formed into fists. "Those who are smartest, boldest"—he picked up the gun and pointed it at Cam—"most powerful, and most able to retain that power. Those are the ones who should have the rights. All others should be subordinate, unless and until they can demonstrate their own merit."

"Might makes right?"

Stratham dropped one fist on the desk, rattling some pens in a metal mesh cylinder in front of Cam.

"Merit earns power," he said. "It is the natural order of things."

"You're a real bleeding heart," said Cam. "You don't think the powerful have an obligation to help the weak, to help those less fortunate?"

"The powerful have an obligation to obey the laws of nature."

"And that means killing people?"

"That means using your power to achieve your ends. The lioness does not spare the feeble wildebeest. She kills it, quickly and mercifully, and in so doing makes the herd stronger."

"Selfishness for the greater good? That's a new one."

Stratham picked up the revolver, smiled, and leaned back, his chair creaking. He aimed the gun casually at Cam. "On the contrary, Mr. Hauk. It's as old as humanity. As old as life on Earth."

"So, in your philosophy, I should come over there and snap your neck."

Stratham's smile widened, and a gleam of pleasure shone in his eyes. He held the gun more upright in his lap.

"You should try," he said, "if you think you can succeed." He checked his watch again. "But let's wait another hour or so before we test nature's will."

Cam kept the scowl off of his face. Stratham was waiting for something, but what? He'd already made his play. He had the video of Cam and Kat. He'd made his blackmail pitch.

What the hell was he keeping Cam here for?

47

THE SOUND of the crowd in the arena faded in Celina's ears, then abruptly stopped, cut short as the doors slid softly shut. The elevator was luxurious, with thick carpet and padded walls. All external sound was muted as the car started down, save for the soft whine of the elevator mechanism.

Celine and Madeline stood near the back of the small space, Jenkins a step in front of them. He blew out a breath and laughed.

"Thank goodness that's all done," he said over his shoulder. "For the moment, at least. I hate parties. All that smiling and glad-handing gives me indigestion." He turned in the car to face Celina and Madeline, a smile on his face. "Now it's just the three of us," he said.

His smile dropped like a dead body from a rooftop.

"And we can drop the bullshit."

His expression was neutral, but it somehow conveyed a menace that made the small hairs on Celina's neck stand up. It was the eyes. Jenkins' eyes were as cold and hard as granite.

"What, exactly, are you doing here, Celina?" he asked, biting out his words, fixing those cold, hard eyes on her.

"You told me to bring her here, Bill," Madeline replied. Her voice retained the lilt of pleasantry, but it had lost all its warmth.

"I told you to bring her to the convention," he snapped, spearing Madeline with his gaze before pulling it back to Celina. "Not backstage with you."

"She told you before," Celina said, standing up tall and squaring her shoulders. Jenkins might be a scary fucker, but so was she. "I'm here for moral support."

A low growl came from Jenkins' throat. He turned and jabbed his thumb against the stop button on the elevator panel. The car jerked to a halt. Celina and Madeline had to put their hands on the wall to steady themselves. Celina expected a bell to ring, something to alert others, but she heard nothing. Jenkins must have had them disable the alarm.

"You were always a smug pain in the ass," said Jenkins. "Smart," he smiled, his teeth gleaming in the single over-head light, "but smug. A spoiled little rich girl." He laughed bitterly. "I thought maybe you'd grow out of it, but..." He gestured toward her with one hand. "Obviously, that hasn't happened."

"I'm sorry to disappoint you."

"You can't possibly disappoint me," said Jenkins. "My expectations are far too low for that." He looked at Madeline, spat out each word. "Why is she here?"

Madeline looked back at him, her expression completely blank.

Celina made a mental note never to play poker with her mother.

Jenkins' expression remained neutral, but Celina could see the muscles in his jaw work as he waited for a response. Madeline remained silent, maintained that same blank expression. Celina watched Jenkins' composure erode, heard his teeth grind, saw the skin of his neck redden, his hands flexing into white-knuckled fists and releasing, over and over.

And still Madeline waited in silence, her expression completely blank.

Celina amended her mental note: never play anything with her mother, unless they were on the same team.

Finally, when Jenkins seemed ready to explode, pulled in a deep breath and blew it out. In the tiny elevator, Celina could smell white wine and garlic canapes on his breath. He pulled his phone from his jacket pocket, leaned back against the elevator door, and tapped the screen. When he looked up at Celina, his face was relaxed and pleasant again.

That's when the shiver ran down her back.

The alarm bell in the elevator was turned off, but the alarm bells inside Celina's head were blaring.

Jenkins held the phone in front of him, the bluish glow giving his face a ghoulish cast.

"You ready?" said Jenkins into the phone.

He tapped the screen once more, then turned it toward Celina and Madeline.

A face filled the screen. That fucking weasel Vernon Stratham. His grin was so wide, Celina could almost see brown flecks in his teeth from the shit he'd just eaten.

"Ms. Maxwell," Stratham crooned. "How wonderful that you could join us."

Us?

Another shiver ran down Celina's back.

"And Madame Speaker," Stratham continued. "An honor, as always."

He was too happy, too smug. The alarms in Celina's head had gone from shrill bells to blaring klaxons.

Stratham clucked his tongue in mock self-derision. "I'm so sorry," he said. "Where are my manners? I have a guest with me. Rude of me not to include him."

The shiver down Celina's back, the klaxons in her head, and now the acid in her stomach burning.

"Someone I think you both already know," continued Stratham, turning the camera, "quite well."

Celina looked at the face on the screen and felt like the elevator cables had suddenly snapped loose. Her stomach felt like she was falling down the shaft, through the floor, into a dark abyss below. Her world had come untethered, shrunk to a single tiny screen and a seizing panic in her heart.

Stratham had Cam.

48

Cam sat on his armless plastic chair in front of Stratham's desk, looking at Celina's shocked face on the phone screen Stratham was holding toward him, the revolver aimed in the other hand.

It all made sense to Cam now.

Stratham had blackmailed him with the video of Kat. Now Jenkins was blackmailing Celina with the threat of violence toward Cam.

And he was probably blackmailing Madeline somehow, too. Clever.

But as Celina would say, *fuck that*. Cam hadn't spent countless hours in the gun range and the training room with Celina just to let a power-hungry egomaniac and a glorified accountant with a superiority complex use him to force the woman he loved to do anything against her will.

Before, he'd been looking for opportunities to escape from Stratham and weighing the costs against the odds. That equation had never worked in his favor. Now, he didn't care what the odds were. The cost of letting Stratham and Jenkins get away with this was too high.

He shifted his body—slowly, subtly—slipping forward toward the edge of the chair, setting his feet squarely underneath.

"Celina," he said, staring into the camera and trying to use the force of his mind to will her to believe him, "I'm okay. I'm completely fine."

"Well," chuckled Stratham, turning the camera back around toward himself and holding up his revolver, "not completely fine."

Cam might have tried something right then, while Stratham was distracted. But while Stratham may have been an arrogant ass, he was no fool. Except for an initial glance at the screen, he kept his eyes on Cam even while mugging for the camera.

Stratham turned the phone around again so Cam could see Celina's face. His chest tightened when he saw the tight line of her mouth, the pursed curves between her brows, the anxiety in her eyes.

"What do you want?" she said to someone off-camera.

"Simple." It was Jenkins. "Go back upstairs and watch your mother's speech with President Jalandhari. I'm sure he'll be delighted to regale you with stories of his own unsurpassable administration."

Jenkins' voice was low and menacing and filled with sarcasm. Cam had met the man before, even bargained with him for his mother's release from prison. And Celina had told him countless stories about Jenkins, none of them flattering. But even while Cam was showing him evidence that would severely hinder his presidential campaign, he'd never heard Jenkins be anything but politic and completely professional.

That was not what he heard now.

What he heard now was the threat of an animal cornered.

An animal going for its opponent's throat.

Cam had always heard that politics was a kill-or-be-killed kind of business. He knew that Stratham and Jenkins took that saying at face value. He had evidence to prove it.

But he would not let them get away with it this time. Not with Celina's life in jeopardy. He shifted more in his chair, readying his body, waiting for his opportunity. Stratham was too good, too sharp. Cam knew that he'd only have a moment to act, if he got an opening at all.

"That's it?" Celina replied on screen. "I go back upstairs and you let Cam go?"

"That's it," said Jenkins. "As easy as can be." His voice was smooth and pleasant now, but that menace still lurked just beneath the surface.

Cam didn't believe him. From the look in her eyes, Celina didn't, either.

"What are you so afraid of, Bill?" asked Madeline.

The smooth, pleasant veneer fell away from Jenkins' face in an instant.

"I'm not afraid of anything," he snarled.

Cam could see Celina flinch in response. And Celina Maxwell didn't flinch at anything. Ever.

He didn't know what Celina and Madeline had planned. He didn't know what was making Jenkins act out so fiercely in this moment. He'd gone for more than a year knowing that Celina and Cam had evidence against him, but doing nothing to stop them. Why was he acting out now?

Madeline's speech.

That had to be it.

He was afraid of her speech, afraid she'd do something

or say something, maybe even show the evidence at the convention, in front of the television cameras broadcasting all over the world.

He must be blackmailing her to keep her in line. That was his MO.

Or maybe not. He'd given her the VP nomination. Maybe he hoped that would earn her loyalty.

But why Celina? Why use Cam to threaten her?

He and Stratham had been waiting for hours. They must have planned this. Or were using it as a contingency, in case Celina did something out of line.

Like, apparently, going backstage at her mother's speech.

It still made no sense to Cam, but he didn't care. All he cared about was Celina, and Jenkins was trying to get Celina to do something she didn't want to do.

Cam could not allow that.

Stratham hadn't bothered to tie him up. Cam would make him regret that decision.

"Just stay on the elevator," said Jenkins to Celina, his smooth voice back again, "and go back upstairs. That's all you have to do."

"What if I don't?"

Jenkins laughed. Cam heard the elevator whir to life, saw Celina waver as the car started moving again.

"Vernon?" said Jenkins. "Would you like to field that question?"

Stratham chuckled and turned the camera back toward himself, his eyes still on Cam.

"I can see why you and your boyfriend get along so well, Ms. Maxwell. Your minds both work in similar ways." He chuckled again. "He asked me the same question a short time ago."

Cam leaned forward, ever so slowly shifting his weight over the balls of his feet.

"I'll tell you the same thing I told him," Stratham continued, leaning closer to the camera, eyes still on Cam. "Please do refuse, Ms. Maxwell." He held the camera out far enough for it to show him cocking the revolver, his eyes and his aim still squarely on Cam. "Please do."

"Cam?" said Celina.

Stratham swung the camera around so Cam could see the screen. He could see the strain on Celina's face.

"I'm okay, Celina," he said, his eyes on Stratham.

He slid his weight further forward, sliding himself off the front edge of the chair as he bunched his muscles, ready to pounce.

He shifted his gaze to look straight into the camera.

"I'm completely fine."

49

ONE SECOND, Cam was on the screen in front of Celina, saying he was completely fine.

The next second, he was gone.

"Cam!"

Her scream was involuntary, shrill and loud in the tiny elevator. The padded walls gobbled the sound greedily.

The view on the phone screen jounced wildly. Celina could see the ceiling, then a filing cabinet, then something that must have been a leg or an arm.

Jenkins turned the screen away from her and toward himself, watching with his brow furrowed. Celina wanted to rip the phone from his hands, beat him with it until he was bloody and weeping for mercy.

She heard the crack of bone on bone, then a screech and a groan, then a scream of pain.

Madeline put a hand on her shoulder. Celina shook it off, started toward Jenkins, her fist already cocking behind her again.

From the phone, she heard a gunshot.

She stopped dead. Her arm was still pulled back, but all

of her muscles were slack. Her anger was gone, replaced by emptiness.

Jenkins turned the phone so she could see.

The screen was dark. The call ended.

Cut off.

The elevator dinged softly and settled to a stop.

"Guess your boyfriend is dumber than I thought," said Jenkins. With a smirk, he slipped the phone back into his jacket pocket and stepped off the elevator.

That was enough to yank Celina back to her senses.

Her first thought was to go after Jenkins. He'd put the phone away, but she could still beat him to a pulp with her fists.

Her second thought, half an instant later, was to go after Cam.

She jabbed at the button to go back upstairs, then repeatedly stabbed the button to close the elevator doors. The doors slid quietly shut as Jenkins looked over his shoulder in surprise.

Madeline reached out and pressed the stop button.

"I'm going back to Washington," Celina said through gritted teeth. "Right now."

"Celina," her mother said softly.

"I'm going to help Cam."

She reached for the elevator panel. Her mother rested one hand on hers.

"How will you help?"

Her voice was quiet. Celina glanced at her. Madeline raised her eyebrows.

"If he's dead," Madeline said, "there's nothing you can do."

Celina's mind spun off-axis at the thought, her chest tightening.

"If he's not dead," Madeline continued, "it'll take you an hour to get to the airport, ninety minutes of flight time, another thirty minutes to get to where Cam is. It'll all be over by then."

Celina set both palms on the elevator doors, hung her head between her arms, and forced herself to focus. She used her breathing—like Cam had taught her—to calm herself, to slow her heart rate.

Her mother, wisely, stayed silent, letting Celina process her thoughts.

Madeline was right. Celina could do nothing from here. Cam was on his own with Stratham.

Celina had a quick thought, pulled her cellphone from her pocket and dialed Cam's number.

Straight to voicemail.

She sent him a text, all-caps. *YOU OK?* Stared at the screen, waiting, hoping.

No reply.

No dots indicating that he was typing a reply.

Nothing.

Cam was on his own with Stratham.

Celina could do nothing from here.

Madeline put a hand on Celina's shoulder.

"There is something we can do," she said, as if she'd been listening to Celina's mind.

Celina stood and turned toward her mother. Madeline's face was stern, stony, her jaw set. Gone was the warm, people-loving politician. In front of Celina was a woman robed in fury. It strengthened her stance. It blazed in her eyes. It lent power to her conviction.

"We can finish our plan," she said, "and give Jenkins exactly what he deserves."

With those words, Celina's mind cleared. Madeline's

fury had purified the tumult of feeling within Celina, focused it enough to burn away all other thoughts, all other emotions. It left nothing behind but that same fury, that same strength, that same power, and that same conviction that she saw in Madeline.

That she saw in her mother.

Celina straightened her body, standing tall. She looked down at her clothes and straightened her outfit. For a woman, appearance was a constant ball and chain. But, used correctly, a ball and chain made an effective weapon.

Madeline stared hard into Celina's eyes.

Celina stared back, calm, collected, focused.

And furious.

Madeline nodded, then pushed the button to open the elevator door.

50

MADELINE STEPPED off the elevator first. Celina stayed behind in the elevator, holding the door open.

Jenkins smiled smugly. "I'm glad you came to your senses," he said.

"Me, too," said Celina, delighting in watching Jenkins' smug smile melt into an angry sneer as she stepped off the elevator and followed her mother.

The door slid quietly shut behind her. They were standing at the intersection of two concrete hallways. To Celina's left and right, the hallway curved into the distance, encircling the arena. Straight ahead was a concrete ramp that led up to a metal staircase. She could see the staircase, but not the stage to which it led.

Madeline strode past Jenkins and up the ramp toward the staircase. Celina followed her, Jenkins a half step behind.

"You're making a mistake, Celina," Jenkins hissed into her ear. "Stratham is no fool. He'll have security waiting. Private security. Men with lots of experience, and very little morality. Next time you see him, your boyfriend will still be alive, but he'll wish he were dead. Unless you go back upstairs."

Celina kept walking, staring straight ahead at her mother's back. Images tried to force their way into her mind, images of Cam, broken and bleeding, begging for mercy. Or worse, refusing to beg, too proud to give an inch.

She forced those images aside and focused on her mother's figure on the ramp ahead of her.

She could feel the rage coming off of Jenkins like the blast of an oven when the door is opened.

Good. An angry man is a stupid man.

An angry Jenkins would only make their plan easier.

"Go. Back. Upstairs." Jenkins' voice rose in anger with each hard-bitten word. "Now!"

He grabbed Celina's arm hard, jerked her backward, and spun her around.

Instinct took over.

Celina didn't fight the motion. She moved with it, used the momentum to break Jenkins' grip at his wrist. She continued the spin, bringing Jenkins' arm over her head, turning his body, twisting his shoulder, until she had him in an armlock, his wrist pinned in his middle back, his shoulder painfully torqued. Celina pushed her knee between his legs and turned her body to the side for leverage, and to avoid Jenkins' feet if he tried to kick behind him.

It was the kind of simple self-defense move her father had taught her when she was only six years old. The same move she'd taught Cam at the very beginning of their training a few months ago.

Apparently, it wasn't part of Jenkins' lessons. He gasped and moaned in pain. Celina pushed his wrist higher on his back, toward his scapula, torquing his shoulder even more. Jenkins moaned louder.

Celina heard her mother's name being announced over the public address system in the arena, heard the crowd roar in response. She looked up the ramp and saw her mother standing at the base of the stairs, looking back at her.

Celina nodded once to her.

Madeline nodded in reply, then climbed the steps to the stage. A moment later, fanfare erupted over the speakers and the noise of the crowd swelled into mania. Madeline Kinkaid had arrived, and the people loved Madeline Kinkaid.

"I tell you what," said Celina, turning back down the ramp, steering Jenkins from behind. "Why don't you go back upstairs?"

She steered Jenkins down the ramp toward the elevator. The doors opened immediately when she pushed the button. Celina shoved him hard enough against the wall for him to grunt as he hit. Celina pushed the button for the top floor, gave Jenkins one last hard shove against the wall, then backed out of the elevator.

"Remember this moment, Celina," Jenkins said, rubbing his sore shoulder.

Celina had never seen such pure, unadulterated hatred on his face. All traces of William James Jenkins, the politician, were gone. Celina was looking at his true persona now.

"This is the moment your life ended," Jenkins said. "I'll kill you with my own hands."

A smile came across Celina's face, so broad and genuine that the rage in Jenkins' eyes faltered, just a little bit, replaced by fear.

He was a scary fucker, no doubt about it.

But Celina was a hundred times scarier.

"You can fucking try," she said, as the elevator doors slid shut between them.

51

Cam would have preferred to wait until Stratham was distracted, or at least until he flicked his gaze away from Cam. But the man was a machine. His stare never left Cam's eyes. The aim of his revolver never left Cam's chest.

Cam couldn't wait forever, so he just went for it, hoping that his speed was better than Stratham's reaction time. If he couldn't distract Stratham, at least he could use the element of surprise.

It worked, at first. Cam dove low, driving his shoulder into the front of Stratham's desk with all the force he could muster. The cheap desk slid across the thin, worn carpet, jammed into Stratham's belly, and pushed him and his chair back against the filing cabinets.

Cam had hoped that Stratham would drop the gun, that the desk would break some ribs or at least knock the breath out of Stratham.

It did none of those things.

Stratham's cheap swivel chair was on casters. The blow made the chair roll backwards, dampening some of the impact.

But it did pin Stratham against the cabinets. And in the instant when he instinctively put both hands against the desk to push it away, aiming the gun toward the ceiling, Cam was on him, across the desk, fist on bone.

Stratham was stronger than Cam expected, even after two hard punches to the face. His glasses askew, he smiled after Cam hit him the second time. Blood outlined his teeth. He seemed to be enjoying himself.

Cam thrust hard with his hips against the other side of the desk, jamming it into Stratham's gut again. This time, with the filing cabinets against Stratham's back, Cam knew he'd done some damage. Stratham whooshed air and groaned in pain.

Cam dove across the desk for the gun still in Stratham's hand. On his knees on the desktop, he grappled the gun with one hand, pounded at Stratham's wrist and forearm with the other, trying to break his grip. Stratham slammed his other fist into Cam's back and kidneys. Even pinned between a desk and a filing cabinet, the man could deliver a punch. Cam knew he'd be pissing blood for days when he got through this.

If he got through it.

Stratham stopped punching for a second, then something drove into Cam's back. Something sharp, spearing pain through his entire body.

He screamed, arched his back, saw red at the edges of his vision. The sharpness worsened when his back arched. Something was lodged in it. He reached behind him with one hand, but could not reach whatever Stratham had stuck into his back. A knife or a pen or something.

Cam didn't lose his grip on Stratham's gun hand, but it weakened. Stratham bent both their hands toward Cam and pulled the trigger. Cam felt another pain, on his arm, quick like a knife slash, then a burning that built to a searing. Hurt like a motherfucker, but just a graze, he hoped.

Wild now with pain, Cam flailed at Stratham's gun arm, drove his knee into Stratham's face.

He heard the shatter of Stratham's glasses.

Moans of pain, he didn't know who from, Stratham or himself.

Stratham twisted the sharp object in Cam's back. Pain flashed through his nerves like lightning.

Cam kept his grip on Stratham's wrist, pounding his forearm, trying to break his arm with his fist. He drove his knee into Stratham's jaw, his temple. His arm and his knee worked independently, like some kind of brutal workout routine.

Cam didn't know what he was doing. All the technique Celina had taught him was gone.

He was in pain. He was feral.

He was fighting for his life.

At last, Stratham's grip weakened.

Cam ripped the gun from Stratham's hand, rolled off the desk, landed in a broken heap on the floor. His body screamed in protest, but he ignored it.

The sharp thing fell from Cam's back as he stood. A pair of scissors on the floor, the blades coated with Cam's blood.

Adrenaline pushed him to his feet. He cocked the gun, pointed it at Stratham.

Cam couldn't see out of one eye. Something hot and wet clouded it.

With his other eye, he saw Stratham, pinned between the desk and the cabinet, sagging in his chair, listing to one side. His head was limp, lolled forward. A pool of blood widened on the desk below him.

One shot.

You're already a murderer.

All it would take.

A monster.

One simple shot.

What's one more body?

Self-defense.

No one will know.

Rid the world of a villain.

And make the world a better place.

Cam's finger slid down to the trigger.

52

CELINA STOOD BEHIND THE TALL, thick, deep-blue curtain that separated the front of the stage from the small platform behind it. The stairs led down to the ramp Celina had just climbed, from there to the elevator she'd shoved Jenkins into twenty minutes earlier.

Her mother's voice echoed around the arena from the elaborate stage on the other side of the curtain.

"...a new generation of leadership. I see it in the eyes of the young women..."

Celina looked up at the box seats in the balcony above her. Jenkins was there with other guests from the party, chatting with each other and watching Madeline's speech on the televisions in front of them.

Jenkins looked down at her. His face was composed and natural, but his eyes still boiled with rage. Celina could feel it from forty feet away. She wondered if the guests seated beside Jenkins could feel it, too.

"...we fight for them..."

And she wondered how much worse it was about to get.

"...we fight for equality..."

That thought made her smile.

"...we fight for justice..."

Jenkins saw her smile and scowled down at her, his composure broken.

That made Celina smile even more.

"...and we fight for truth."

She turned away from Jenkins, turned to face the curtain.

It was time to get her game face on.

"Which brings me to a truth of my own," she heard her mother say, "a truth I've only recently learned. The kind of truth that rocks a woman to her core."

Madeline paused, no doubt with a serious, somber look on her face. She waited, letting the room settle, bringing it down to match her energy.

Controlling the crowd.

Madeline Kinkaid really was a fucking badass.

"I've spent my political life crusading for the rights of women," she said, "for our right to control our own bodies. Because I want every woman to have what I couldn't have, a child of their own, born at the time and in the manner of their choosing. Not forced upon them by some white male bureaucracy, using laws that were decided not by democracy, but by demagoguery."

The crowd swelled with the steel in Madeline's voice, but she paused once more, reeling the crowd back in again. Her voice dropped low.

"I lost the ability to have children, lost that right to choose. Twenty-eight years ago, I lost my child. Complications. No one's fault. Just fate, cruel fate."

The crowd murmured their sympathy, but it was a superficial, well-worn feeling. They'd heard all this before.

"You all know this story," Madeline said. "I've told it

many times, both so you all could understand where I'm coming from, and so I could help bring women's issues to the forefront. Bring them into the social conversation, into the legal conversation, into the political conversation. And I'm proud of over two decades of tireless effort devoted to doing exactly that."

The crowd cheered madly.

"I'm proud of what we've been able to achieve,"—Madeline raised her voice, let it ride the rising tide of cheers —"fighting together to make a better America for all women."

The crowd erupted, air horns bleating, American flags on little sticks waving.

Madeline let them cheer for several seconds, then pulled them back down again.

"But," she said, waiting for the crowd to quiet, "there's something you all don't know." Her voice was a distracted whisper now, as if she were talking to herself. "Something I didn't know until just a few months ago."

Celina could imagine every member of the crowd, every viewer at home, leaning toward the stage, toward their televisions, riveted. She looked up at the box seats. All chatting had ceased. All eyes were focused on the screens. On her mother.

Except for Jenkins. The rage on his face had turned to shock. He stared down at Celina. She grinned back.

You lose, fucker.

"That child I lost twenty-eight years ago..."

Madeline waited.

Let the words hang in the air.

Twenty-four thousand people in the arena, silent as a falling leaf.

"That child didn't die."

The crowd gasped, en masse, like they'd simultaneously seen a huge twist in the plot of their favorite television show.

"*My daughter*," said Madeline, her voice breaking, "is alive."

The crowd was stunned silent, the only sound Madeline's ragged breath, faint in the microphone.

Celina wondered if she was faking the emotion, if she was that good of an actress, or if the emotion was real.

Soft murmurs ran through the crowd, punctuated by a smattering of astonished shouts.

Celina decided to believe it was sincere.

"She found me a few months ago," Madeline continued, regaining her composure. "Knocked right on my front door and asked to come in." She laughed lightly, as if she could hardly believe it herself. She delivered the lines like she was talking to an old friend over coffee, not speaking to an international audience of millions.

Spattered clapping.

"We've been talking ever since," said Madeline, "getting to know each other."

Not a lie. Not how Celina would have framed it, but not a lie.

The clapping spread, rose to soft cheers as the crowd processed the information. Not the kind of thing they were expecting to hear when they walked through the arena doors.

"You can't begin to imagine how astonished and grateful I am," Madeline said. "There are *a lot* of unanswered questions, but right now, I don't want to question anything. I'm just relishing this unbelievable opportunity to get to know my daughter."

The emotion in Madeline's voice was so raw, sounded

so real, it was incongruous with the banal pablum the crowd had been hearing for the past three days. It took time for the realness to sink in.

But it did.

Slowly, it did.

The clapping spread. The cheers rose. Even from behind the curtain, unable to see anyone in the crowd, Celina could feel that these cheers were different. These weren't political cheers. They were personal cheers. The people out there seemed genuinely happy for Madeline.

"And— I can hardly believe I'm saying this. Seems almost inappropriate, but— She asked to come on stage tonight to meet all of you in person."

The cheers doubled in volume.

"Kind of a bring-your-daughter-to-work thing, I guess," laughed Madeline.

The crowd laughed with her and cheered even more.

"And so, it is with astonishment, humility, and the deepest, deepest gratitude, that I introduce to you all, my daughter"—her voice broke on the words—"Celina Maxwell."

That was it. That was Celina's cue.

Showtime.

With one last check on her outfit, Celina turned and looked up at the box seats once more.

Everyone there was standing and clapping and talking and staring at the television, apparently unaware that they could look straight down to see the big reveal ahead of time.

Except for Jenkins.

He was staring down at her, his face stony, his eyes burning with hatred.

The only way to beat a blackmailer is to beat them to the truth.

Control your own message.

And take away their leverage.

Celina stared back at Jenkins, raised the middle fingers of both hands, and stabbed them high in the air toward him.

Then she stepped through the curtain to meet the world.

53

Celina didn't give a speech. She stood on the massive stage, arm in arm with Madeline, waving at the crowd, smiling until her cheek muscles were quivering. They were not used to being used for that long.

She felt like she was on that fucking stage forever, but it was probably ten minutes before they ducked behind the curtain again. Madeline had warned her that the show would not be over. She and Celina still needed to meet with the press and get their story into the world before Jenkins could try to interfere.

But there was nothing he could do now. He'd used Celina's existence to blackmail Madeline, and Madeline had turned the tables on him. If he tried to cast any kind of aspersions on either of them, he'd be hurting his own ticket for the election.

The press conference was interminable. Forty-five minutes of questions. How had Celina found out Madeline was her mother? How had Madeline been in the dark for so long? What made Celina seek Madeline out now?

After the first five questions, Celina was essentially

saying the same things in different ways over and over for each reporter. Mostly lies, of course, laced with enough truth to make them believable. Some intrepid reporter somewhere would try to make her name by uncovering the truth. The situation was too weird not to try. But the most they would find was an odd absence of documentation. Celina's father had long ago expunged all records of Celina's birth.

Throughout the press conference, Celina could think of nothing but Cam. Each idiot reporter who asked another version of the same question cost her time, time she could be spending getting back to him. He hadn't answered her calls or responded to her texts. She didn't know if he was dead or alive. She needed to get back to Washington.

Sensing her increasing agitation, Madeline mercifully brought the press conference to a close. Her security detail carved a path through the still-shouting press gaggle and outside to a waiting car. Fans were there, waiting in the hundreds. They cheered when Madeline and Celina emerged from the building. The adoration directed her way stunned Celina. She wasn't used to that kind of attention.

She and Madeline waved as they got into the car. It pulled slowly through the throng of fans and flashbulbs, but once it was clear, the driver hauled ass toward the airport.

"That went well," murmured Madeline.

Celina didn't respond. She was staring through the soundproof glass partition and out the front windshield, hugging her arms around her and bouncing one knee, willing the car to drive faster, even as it screamed past the other cars on the 280 expressway. At some point—Celina had no idea when, but the woman was a magician—Madeline had arranged for her plane to move to Midway, cutting by two-thirds the time it would have taken to get to the executive airport they'd come into north of Chicago.

Twenty minutes later, they were wheels up for the longest ninety minute plane ride of Celina's life. She stared out the window at darkness the entire flight, knee still bouncing.

"Anything?" she asked Madeline, at one point.

Madeline pressed her lips together, staring down at her phone. "There's a commotion at the DOJ building," she said softly, lifting her eyes to meet Celina's, "but my people haven't gotten any details yet."

Celina wedged her thumbnail lengthwise between her front teeth like a baby's binky, flexed it over and over, teetering on the point of pain, for the duration of the flight. Once they landed, she was out of her seat and standing impatiently by the door while they taxied. Once they stopped on the tarmac, she hovered behind Femi, the flight attendant, while he opened the door and lowered the stairs.

She didn't wait for Madeline. Celina had her own driver waiting. She got in the car and peeled away, Madeline watching from the top of the jetway.

Celina had to get to Cam. She'd already wasted too much time.

She had to know if the man she loved was alive or dead.

54

Cam had already lowered the revolver before the security guards arrived at Stratham's office with their guns drawn. Their eyes bugged wide when they saw the scene. Most of them were ex-cops, taking the job at the Department of Justice for an easy gig to supplement their pensions. They never saw scenes like this with the usual pencil pushers that came to work every day.

But their experience and training kicked in quickly, and they comported themselves with competence and professionalism. When they entered, Cam raised his hands high and squatted slowly to set the revolver on the floor. The guards secured the weapon, cuffed Cam with zip ties, and locked down the scene, immediately calling for backup and medical.

From there, it was a whirlwind. More cops arrived, then the paramedics. They wheeled Stratham out on a stretcher, barely conscious, but still alive.

Two police detectives in black suits, a reedy man and a squat woman, arrived and immediately cut Cam free from his zip ties, then sat him down in one of the cubicles outside Stratham's office. They'd reviewed the footage from the security camera in Stratham's office and had a pretty good idea of how things went down, but they wanted to hear Cam's version of events.

Cam was surprised Stratham even had security cameras in his office, but he probably kept them for appearances or to adhere to some government policy. He was sure Stratham had planned to erase or replace the footage after he was done with Cam.

The paramedics wanted to take Cam to the hospital for imaging, but the detectives asked if he would stay for a few questions, and Cam agreed. The disgruntled paramedics had no choice but to wait for him to finish.

The male detective took a brand new package of nicotine gum from his suit coat, unwrapped the plastic, and popped two chiclets in his mouth. While he chewed his gum, Cam walked them through the whole sordid affair, hiding nothing, holding nothing back. His cell phone had shattered at some point during the scuffle with Stratham, so he couldn't show them any proof, but he told them about the texts Stratham had sent, imitating his mother. He described waiting in Stratham's office. He described the video call and the physical confrontation.

He used Jenkins' name. Repeatedly. No more blackmail. No more secrets. The detectives asked him three times if he meant Attorney General William Jenkins, the same William Jenkins who was about to be officially nominated as the Democratic candidate for President of the United States. Each time, Cam confirmed it, just as he did when they asked him four more times at various points in their conversation. They were doing their jobs, trying to get things right.

That's what Cam wanted, too. For everything to finally be right.

The interview with the detectives went on for hours. The pair had a kind of Abbott and Costello interaction between themselves, making for a surreal, but entertaining, interrogation. While they spoke, the forensics team arrived to process Stratham's office. The man went through half the package of nicotine gum, periodically spitting what was in his mouth into a nearby wastebasket and immediately popping more chiclets in.

Cam's adrenaline had worn off long ago, and his injuries were starting to hurt. A lot. The paramedics made him as comfortable as possible—though no painkillers were allowed until the detectives were done with him—but Cam was starting to wonder if Stratham had done some real damage. His answers to the detectives were becoming shorter, his voice duller. He watched forensics personnel go in and out of Stratham's office through eyes that were growing wearier by the minute.

And then Celina walked in, and Cam forgot all about his pain.

She must have slipped in somehow, because the cops seemed shocked when she appeared. They raced toward her, hands on their holsters, shouting for her to halt until Cam was able to reassure the detectives of who she was. Mollified, the other cops went back to their work, but the two detectives blocked her from approaching Cam.

The female detective, Costello, squinted sideways at Celina. "Aren't you the lady from the convention?" she asked.

The other detective, Abbott, snapped his fingers and pointed at Celina. "Yeah, the daughter," he said. "You're that senator's long-lost daughter."

"Congresswoman," said Celina, with a curt smile, craning to look over them at Cam, "not senator."

"Crazy story," Costello said, shaking her head. "How did your mom not know about you? She's a freakin' senator, for chrissake."

"Congresswoman," Celina repeated. "Speaker of the House, actually."

"Her whole life," Abbott agreed, nodding, "and she never knew her daughter was alive."

"Crazy story," Costello repeated.

They were talking like they were standing around the coffee maker in the precinct, waiting for a fresh pot to brew. Cam could see Celina's irritation mounting, could see her fighting to hold her anger in check.

"Would you mind if I..." she said, nodding past them toward Cam.

The two detectives turned toward Cam as if they had forgotten he was there, then turned back as if Celina hadn't just asked them a question.

"What is your relationship to this, uh, gentleman, exactly?" asked Costello.

"He's my boyfriend."

"Boyfriend, huh?" said Abbott. "Does your mother know about that?"

He smacked his gum as he grinned at Costello. She grinned back and punched him on the arm.

"Listen," said Celina, her voice dropping low. Cam could tell from her voice that she was at the end of her rope. "I have come a very long way in a very short amount of time to see if that man is alright."

Abbott smacked his gum and stared at Celina like an animal in a zoo. Costello glanced at Cam, then back at Celina.

"He seems okay to me," she said.

The muscles in Celina's jaw flexed. "Do you mind," she said through gritted teeth, "if I see for myself?"

She tried to step past them, but they shifted together to block her way.

Abbott pulled a notebook and pencil from his suit coat, flipped to a fresh page.

"What's your relationship with this man?" he said, his pencil poised over the paper.

"You already asked me that."

Abbott shrugged. "I forgot what you said."

Celina huffed. "He's my boyfriend."

"Uh huh, uh huh," said Abbott, scribbling something in his notepad. "And, uh, how long you two been together?"

"How is that relevant?" said Celina, her voice rising in anger.

"Just establishing the facts, ma'am," Abbott replied. "If you'd prefer, we could, uh..." He glanced at his partner.

"Yeah," said Costello, "we could pick this up down at the station."

Cam saw Celina flex and unflex her fists, saw her jaw working, saw her shift into an attacking stance, one foot at an angle behind the other. She wanted to beat the shit out of those detectives. He knew it, and they probably knew it, too.

"You saw the convention tonight?" asked Celina.

The two detectives nodded.

"You saw me with my mother on stage? The congresswoman? I have some powerful friends."

Costello squinted at Abbott. "I thought she was a senator."

Abbott shrugged.

Celina ignored it.

"Cam told you about the phone call? The video call?"

"How do you know about that?" asked Abbott.

"I was on the other end of that fucking call," Celina said. "It ended when I heard the fucking gun go off." She balled her hands into fists, pulled herself to her full height. "I've come all the way from Chicago to make sure that man,"—she pointed at Cam—"the man I love, is alive. To make sure he's okay. And if you two don't get the fuck out of my way, it'll be *your* loved ones coming to see if *you're* okay."

Cam stood, ignoring the pain in his back and side, ignoring the pounding in his head.

"You love him?" asked Costello.

Cam was wondering the same thing.

Celina took her eyes from them and stared at Cam. The anger fell away, revealing only worry.

"Yes," she said, "I love him."

The detectives stared at each other for a moment. Abbott turned to Cam, gum smacking.

"You love her, too?" he asked.

Cam's throat felt like sandpaper. He nodded.

"More than anything in the world," he said.

The two detectives stared at each other for a long moment, then they each swung to one side, like saloon doors opening, to let Celina pass.

In two strides, she had a hand on each of Cam's cheeks, kissing him deeply. She broke the kiss and pulled him into a long, firm hug. The wound in his back burned. His ribs felt like they were broken, pain like lightning shooting through his body.

But he didn't care. He had Celina in his arms again, and that was all that mattered.

"That guy bagged the senator's daughter," said Costello to Abbott.

Cam looked over Celina's shoulder. The two detectives stood together, watching him and Celina.

"Crazy story," said Abbott, shaking his head. He spit his gum into the wastebasket and popped two more chiclets in his mouth. "Ain't love grand?"

PART IV

55

FOUR MONTHS LATER

It was the first Christmas Celina Maxwell had spent with her fiancé, Cameron Hauk.

Fiancé. That word still sent shivers up Celina's spine. Good shivers. Shivers of excitement.

She never imagined she'd be married before she even turned thirty. Hell, she never imagined she'd marry anyone at all, ever.

But Cameron Hauk was not just anyone. He was unique. His own species of man.

Homo Celina. A species made just for her.

And Cam was the only specimen in the world.

She carried two mugs of hot chocolate from the kitchen to the living room, giant globs of frozen whipped cream melting into creamy puddles of deliciousness on top of the steaming chocolate. Celina had even dusted the drinks with crushed starlight mints.

She was already going soft, getting all domestic and shit.

Not a problem. She and Cam could spend a couple of hours in the training room later. Celina would kick his ass there, then fuck the shit out of him in the bedroom. If they even made it as far as the bedroom.

Domesticity was a relative measure.

She set the mugs on coasters on the coffee table, then stood to examine Cam's progress.

They had a Christmas tree set up in one corner, next to the hearth. Outside, the morning was uncharacteristically clear. The typical San Francisco fog had burned off early, and the ocean was a sparkling, dazzling blue on the other side of Celina's deck.

The tree was brand new, a Nordic Fir complete with simulated pinecones dusted with simulated snow. Twelve feet tall, its top nearly touched the beams on the sloped ceiling. Celina had insisted on a fake tree. Easy to set up and take down. No messy pine needles. No risk of fire. Cam hadn't put up too much of a fight.

The tree came with pre-strung LED lights that could shift color with the touch of a remote control, but Cam still wanted to decorate it. They'd spent a whole day driving around San Francisco from shop to shop, buying garland and ornaments and tree toppers and a whole bunch of shit Celina didn't even know existed, like stems and picks and floral wire to hold everything in place.

Cam was shockingly well-versed in Christmas decorations, and surprisingly specific in what he wanted. Cam's family had decorated their tree together every year, so he knew all about it. He had a vision, he said. Celina played along.

Five minutes into the shopping, Celina told Cam she

was happy to drive around with him, but there was no way she was going to spend her time putting all that shit on the tree. By the end, though, she was surprised to find that she was getting into the process. She found a few ornaments that resonated with her, a few ribbons she liked. Maybe they reminded her of things her dad had on the tree when she was little.

She didn't really remember Christmas. Her dad hadn't made a big deal about it. A few modest gifts, a small tree somewhere in the house. They hadn't gone all-out like Cam's family did.

But Celina was warming to the idea. The lights on the tree, the Christmas music in the background, Cam whistling along as he chose an ornament, then climbed a ladder to place it. Watching his gorgeous ass under his joggers as he did.

Being with Cam was a big part of it. Celina felt like they were building a tradition of their own, one they might carry on with their own family someday.

Another shiver of excitement ran down her spine at that thought.

She watched Cam teeter on the ladder on his tiptoes, reaching to place an ornament near the top of the tree.

"Maybe we should have gotten a smaller tree," Celina said. "This isn't the fucking White House."

"It's better than the White House," Cam said, his voice strained as he stretched across, then finally reached the branch he was trying for and hung the ornament. "It's our house," he said, beaming down at Celina. He looked up at the ceiling, angling to a high peak fifteen feet overhead. "And it's a big house. Big house, big tree."

"Yeah, well, get your ass down from that big tree and drink some cocoa with me."

Cam grinned as he came down. Celina handed him a mug and clinked it with her own. They stood side by side, admiring the tree and enjoying the cocoa. The whipped cream was cool, tempering the scalding chocolate. The combination tasted creamy and sweet and fucking amazing as it slid over Celina's tongue and down her throat.

Cam murmured with appreciation as he took his first sip, then went straight back for another sip. He set the mug down and twisted his torso in a gentle stretch. Celina rubbed his back with one hand, more for a show of sympathy than to help loosen Cam's muscles.

Cam had escaped the tussle with Stratham in decent shape, all things considered. Stratham had stabbed him repeatedly in the back with a pair of scissors. Most of the wounds were glancing or superficial, but two of them had gone deeper. One of those came within a few millimeters of puncturing his kidney. The doctors said he'd been very lucky, in the end. No real damage beyond those two wounds and a couple broken ribs. That was four months ago. Cam was mostly healed now, but he still got stiff in the lower back from time to time.

"You planning to break your ribs every Christmas?" asked Celina with a smirk.

"God, I hope not," Cam said.

The doorbell rang. Celina set her mug down and checked her phone for the time.

"She's early."

She opened the front door to find a huge man in a black suit and tie and dark sunglasses standing on her porch. Two similarly large, similarly dressed men stood behind him, their backs toward Celina, scanning the grounds in front of the house. They looked like agents from Men In Black.

"Hello," said Celina. "Is there an alien invasion I should know about?"

"Good morning, ma'am," the man replied without smiling. "May we have your permission to search the premises?"

"Do you need my permission to search the premises?"

"We do need your permission to step inside your residence, ma'am."

"What if I refuse?"

"Then we will return to Washington with the President-elect."

Celina snorted. "If you think *the President-elect* would go along with that shit, you don't know my mother very well."

She gestured with one arm for the man to come in. The others followed immediately, without turning or being called, as if they all had some kind of mind meld going on.

Inside, she heard Cam welcome the men and offer them hot chocolate. Celina smiled to herself.

On the curb in the distance, three large black Cadillac SUVs waited in a line, engines running, a thin line of exhaust rising from each tailpipe in the still-cool morning air. Another MIB character stood in front of the middle SUV, hands clasped before her, waiting.

Security around Celina's mother had been tight when she was Speaker of the House, but now that she was President-Elect, it had gotten crazy. Might be something to do with being the first woman ever elected President of the United States. Might be something to do with the death threats and vitriol spewed by the Republican fringe ever since she'd risen to the top of the ticket.

And it might have something to do with the fury Bill Jenkins had unleashed toward her—first in private, then in public—as the evidence against him slowly mounted. It was the biggest Washington scandal since Watergate.

Bigger, since it all broke so quickly. In the digital age, there are no secrets. Once a copy of the footage from Stratham's office came out, conveniently and mysteriously appearing in the inboxes of several reporters one afternoon, he'd been a goner. Over the next few months, the noose had slowly tightened around Jenkins' neck.

Celina might have had something to do with that.

She smiled a bit more.

She might have been the one pulling the rope.

She'd released her evidence against Jenkins a week after she sent the footage from Stratham's office. Again, she did so with anonymous emails to specific reporters, reporters Celina knew had curious minds and the experience and the guts to chase a story, but whose reputations were iron clad. She did not want this scandal dismissed due to shoddy reportage. She chose three reporters at two newspapers, included them all on the same emails so they could work together, and watched with glee as they fell on the red meat like hungry lions after a hunt.

Jenkins and Celina's mother were on the campaign trail as the news broke, each story building on the last until it reached a deafening crescendo. Madeline played everything perfectly, just as she and Celina had planned.

The scandal quickly overshadowed any nagging questions about Celina and her birth, knocking that issue out of the news cycle. At first, when the story was focused on Stratham, Madeline defended Jenkins, as if on principle. Over time, as more and more of Celina's evidence emerged, she slowly modified her position. In the end, she came off looking like she'd been fooled just as much as the rest of the country by a masterful politician who turned out to be an evil genius.

The election was only a few weeks away when Jenkins

was indicted. With Madeline's stratospheric approval ratings, it was a no-brainer for the Democratic party to force Jenkins to step down and elevate Madeline as the nominee for president.

In November, she won in a landslide, like the bad-ass she was.

Inside Celina's house, the agents—who were not MIB, but Secret Service—finished their security sweep. The leader said something into his sleeve, and Celina watched the woman outside open the door of the Cadillac.

Celina's mother stepped out.

President-elect Madeline Kinkaid.

She was dressed casually, which for her meant a loose, flowing navy blue jacket and pants over an open, high-collared white blouse. She looked like the CEO of a fashion design firm in Paris. Anna Wintour meets Nancy Pelosi.

Madeline strode easily toward the house. She looked gorgeous. Confident. Powerful.

She looked like everything Celina was and wanted to be.

"Hello, sweetheart," Madeline said as she stepped onto the porch.

They looked at each other for a long moment.

Celina smiled, a full, genuine smile.

"Hi, Mom," she said, and pulled Madeline in for a warm hug.

56

CAM FINISHED TRIMMING the tree while Celina and Madeline sat on the couch watching and pointing out bare spots and gaps in the tree limbs. The smartest woman Cam had ever known sitting beside the President-elect of the United States, and they chattered to each other like schoolgirls, occasionally exploding in cackles of laughter.

Cam didn't mind doing the decorating on his own. It reminded him of his parents. Every Christmas when Cam was a kid, they'd decorate a tree. And they always did it on Christmas Eve, a tradition from his father's side way back to his ancestors in Europe. Sometimes it was a giant tree—usually real, not artificial—like the one before him, sometimes it was barely a branch. Just depended where they were and what they were doing. But no matter what was happening, they always decorated something on Christmas Eve, and they always did it together.

Together was a loose term, though. Cam's mom tended to sit on the couch, just like Celina. Supervising, she called it. Cam and his father would stand the tree up and string the lights and the tinsel and the popcorn garland. They'd hang the ornaments, if they had them. And every year, when it was done, they'd all sit on the couch with a mug of cocoa for a few minutes, admiring their handiwork.

Celina and Madeline had added some Bailey's Irish Cream to their mugs, even though it wasn't even noon yet. Cam put the last few ornaments on the tree, then climbed down and set the ladder to the side to check the tree over.

"Beautiful, Cameron," said Madeline from the couch. "Truly. You could decorate the White House for me next year, if you want."

"You sure you want to be associated with a criminal like me?" Cam asked with a grin.

"If I refused to work with criminals, my dear, I would never get anything done in Washington." Madeline smiled. "Besides, you're a better person than anyone I know." She walked to Cam's side and handed him a mug of Bailey's-laced cocoa before giving him a one-armed side-hug. "I'm proud to call you my son."

She kissed him on the cheek, then lifted her mug. He lifted his own in return and they both drank.

Cam didn't know if it was the sentiment or the Bailey's, but he felt warm inside.

And why not? He had a lot to feel warm about.

Vernon Stratham was already in prison, awaiting sentencing. His trial had moved quickly, resulting in a verdict of guilty on all counts.

William Jenkins was out on a hefty bail awaiting the start of his own trial, but he was under house arrest with an ankle monitor and 24-hour surveillance, as the judge considered him a significant flight risk. The evidence against him was incontrovertible. Cam would never discount the possibility of a rich, white man escaping justice for his crimes, but with public sentiment as hostile as it was toward Jenkins, he felt cautiously optimistic that William Jenkins would be in prison for the rest of his life.

And Kat. Cam gulped hard on a swallow of cocoa and glanced at Celina, still sitting on the couch. She'd been understanding about Kat and the video. Cam had pulled it off the server at the DC house and showed it to her himself, not wanting to hide it. He loved Celina. He didn't want any secrets between them. No lies or cover-ups. He was ashamed of what happened with Kat, ashamed of his weakness.

Celina's face had gone white and stony when she watched the video. She watched it five times in a row, then sent a copy to herself. Cam saw her watching it later on her phone when she thought he wasn't looking. Cam deserved whatever punishment Celina gave him. If she broke up with him, at least he would know why he'd lost the best thing that ever happened to him.

But she didn't break up with him. She forgave him.

And she forgave Kat. Celina found out what Jenkins had done to get Kat to play his game. Not surprisingly, Jenkins had not paid up. Kat still didn't have control of her father's company. Last Cam heard, she was working on another startup, another product. Something that used technology to help women protect themselves from abusive men.

Celina asked Cam a lot of searching questions about how he felt during the video and afterward. He answered honestly, and Celina said she understood. She said she forgave him.

She said she loved him.

He didn't feel like he deserved her love. But as he looked at her on the couch, as the warmth of the cocoa and the Bailey's and the Christmas season filled him, he knew he would spend the rest of his life trying to deserve it.

"When is Paulie scheduled to arrive?" asked Madeline, shaking Cam from his thoughts.

Another thing to make Cam feel warm inside. His mother was free, after fifteen years in prison. And she'd spent the last eighteen months gallivanting around the globe with Simon.

But they'd promised to be home for Christmas this year.

Cam checked the time on his phone.

"I thought she'd be here by now," he said. He checked to see if he had any new texts from his mother.

"And so we are," came a voice from behind Cam.

He turned to see Simon strolling down the hall. But he wasn't coming from the front door.

"How the fuck did you get in?" asked Celina, running from the couch to give Simon a big hug.

"With all the suits out front, we decided to slip in the back way."

"You broke in?" said Madeline. "With my Secret Service detail guarding the house?"

Simon shrugged. "Old habits, I suppose."

He grinned at Madeline, that same panty-melting grin that Cam remembered from the first time he'd met Simon, when he feared it was Celina's panties that Simon was trying to melt.

"Hello, Madeline, my love," Simon said, kissing Madeline on both cheeks and wrapping her in a warm hug. "I suppose I should say President Madeline, now."

Madeline leaned back in the embrace and slapped Simon lightly on his chest. "If you start that kind of shit you can go back to bloody England, or wherever the hell you've been." She laughed, a light, easy sound that can only come after years of knowing someone, being totally at ease with them.

Their embrace had blocked Cam's view of Celina. When they separated, Cam saw Celina standing there, mouth agape.

"You two know each other?" Celina said.

Madeline tilted her head at Celina.

"Of course we do," she said. "Perry and I met Simon when we were first dating." She raised her eyebrows at Celina. "When you were conceived." She looked at Simon again, fondness and long friendship in her eyes. "We tried to get him to be your godfather."

"Two things that should never be associated with my name," said Simon.

"Two things?" asked Cam.

"God," Simon grinned again, "and father."

"That's a relief," said Paulie, entering from the same hallway as Simon. She patted her flat stomach. "This body is done having children."

Simon pulled her tight beside to him. "Still worth trying," he said, smacking her on the cheek.

"Hell yes to that," laughed Paulie before kissing Simon on the lips.

"Ew," said Celina.

Simon scowled at her. "After all the times we had to listen to you lot shagging like rabbits in DC?" he said, pointing between Celina and Cam. He looked at Madeline, eyes wide. "Two floors up and the fucking glasses were rattling on the table."

Celina grinned at Cam. "Fair point."

Simon released Paulie, and Cam bent to envelop her in a long hug. He breathed deep. She still smelled the same as he remembered as a kid, a mix of mint and spring rain that must have been part of her body chemistry somehow. He'd missed it. After fifteen years in prison, he'd only had a few months with her before she and Simon left for their adventure. Now she was finally back again.

They didn't say anything to each other. They didn't have to. She put a hand on each of his cheeks, searched his eyes for a long moment. In her gaze, Cam felt the same unconditional love he'd always felt with his mother. No judgment. Just love and support.

Paulie smiled and nodded to herself. She patted Cam's cheek softly, then stepped to Celina and pulled her into a long hug, too.

"I'm so happy," Paulie said. "For both of you." She gestured to Cam and Celina. "And for you." She gestured to Madeline, then slipped her arm through Simon's and squeezed it tight. "For all of us."

Madeline made hot chocolate and Bailey's for Paulie and Simon. That quickly graduated to cinnamon hot toddies made by Simon, then warm rum and eggnog with fresh-ground nutmeg prepared by Paulie, like she did when Cam was a kid (minus the rum for him, back then). Then came dinner, cooked by Cam and Celina.

And wine. Lots and lots of hot spiced wine.

By the end of the evening, Cam was fully sated with food and drink and love and friendship. The twelve-foot tree glowed, filling the room with soft white light. The fire roared in the hearth beside it, banishing completely the chill of the San Francisco night. They didn't exchange gifts. They didn't need to. Being together was all the gifts any of them wanted.

After they cleaned the dishes, the dishwasher humming contentedly in the background, Cam stood beside his mother in the kitchen, looking in at Madeline, Simon, and

Celina on the couches before the fire, a card game in-progress on the coffee table before them, Celina and Simon arguing good-naturedly about something or other and laughing uproariously while Madeline shook her head and smiled at them. Cam recorded the image in his mind and made a mental note to sketch it later.

"Your father would have loved this," said Paulie softly. She turned to Cam. "And he would have absolutely adored Celina."

Cam was already feeling warm from the drink and the fire and the love in the room, but that thought sent another wave of warmth washing over him. Tears pricked his eyes.

"I wish he could have met her."

Paulie didn't respond, just sighed and wrapped one arm around Cam.

"You and Simon?" said Cam. "You... good?"

Paulie looked up at him, her face completely open, completely at ease. She stared into his eyes in that piercing, searching way she had, seeing straight into Cam's soul.

"No one will ever replace your father," she said.

Cam's mouth went dry. "I know that," he rasped, his eyes pricking again. He nodded and swallowed hard. "But it's been a long time, Mom," he said. "You deserve to be happy."

Paulie kept her gaze on Cam for a moment longer, then looked at Simon. She pulled Cam tight.

"I am happy," she whispered. "Like I never thought I would be again."

Cam wrapped one arm around his mother, hugged her hard, and kissed the top of her head.

"Good," he said.

And he meant it.

"Good," he repeated, kissing her head once more. "I'm glad."

From the couch, Celina turned her head and saw them. She stood and walked over.

"You're missing it," she said, grinning. "Simon's being an arrogant prick again."

Paulie laughed. "Believe me, I've seen enough of that not to miss it this time."

Celina's eyes sparked, and Cam didn't think it was from the reflection of the fire.

"Yeah, but this time I'm about to take his ass down," she said. "Hard."

"Oooh," said Paulie. "That I do want to see."

She broke from Cam's embrace and stepped into Celina's. As they walked back to the couch, Celina glanced back at Cam. She smiled her sly smile, her dark hair draped over one shoulder, her green eyes dazzling in the soft Christmas lights. Just watching her move, watching her gorgeous face, watching that devious light in her eyes made Cam want to take her upstairs, downstairs, anywhere and everywhere.

Celina arched one eyebrow at him, as if she could read his dirty mind.

Her sly smile grew bigger.

God, Cam loved that woman.

Celina tilted her head for Cam to follow. He did, joining his new family by the fire.

ACKNOWLEDGMENTS

As always, my love and thanks to Holly. Without your support, my love, none of this would be possible.

ARTIFICIAL INTELLIGENCE USAGE DECLARATION

In the creation of this novel, I, the author, used artificial intelligence in the following ways:

- For suggestion of spelling and grammar corrections, with all final decisions made by the author
- For minor edits on cover images to remove background elements, using generative AI tools in Adobe Photoshop

ABOUT THE AUTHOR

Kevin Robert Aldrich lives in California and is the author of several mystery and romance novels:

If you love a twisting, pulse-pounding mystery, you'll love the Cameron Hauk series: Eyes in the Dark, Key Witness, Scale of Justice, Tête-a-Tête, and Burden of Proof.

If you love heart-pounding romantic suspense, you'll love Bare Trap and Flames of Freedom.

If you like vampires, witches, and forbidden love, get a copy of Spellbound now.

And if you love powerful contemporary romance, try Racing Hearts and Ollie & Alli today.

NEWSLETTER SIGN-UP

To learn more about Kevin Robert Aldrich and stay up-to-date with all of his stories and novels, please visit his website:

www.kevinrobertaldrich.com

To be automatically notified of every new release, sign up for the Kevin Robert Aldrich newsletter at the website above.

www.ingramcontent.com/pod-product-compliance
Lightning Source LLC
Chambersburg PA
CBHW062116290726

48975CB00001B/243